I0645064

Two murders of people I knew. What was going on?

I woke up Sunday morning with sore leg muscles. Stretching seemed in order if I didn't want to hobble around all day, so I turned on the TV news to have a distraction while I bent one knee and stretched my other leg behind me.

The anchorman's announcement toppled me to the floor: "The lifeless body of DC builder Evan Lancet's wife was discovered outside her Georgetown home this morning."

I stared up at the screen. A camera panned the front yard of the Lancet house.

An on-the-scene reporter filled in some details: "Ariel Lancet's body was discovered by family members this morning in the backyard of her home. According to the police, she was killed sometime last night, and foul play is suspected. This is the second murder of a young woman in less than three weeks to take place in what are thought of as safe neighborhoods in Northwest DC."

Foul play.

Murder.

First Penny, now Ariel. Two young women killed nearby, both in my sphere of contact.

A dark winter night. Sophie Myerson is a staff psychologist at an out-patient mental health clinic in Washington, DC. Her workday is over, but Sophie stays late to finish writing a psychological test report. Thoughts of her upcoming wedding distract her, and she is delighted when her fiancé calls to say he wants to stop by. He looks awful. She's concerned. And then he tells her their engagement is off. There will be no wedding. No marriage. The future she envisioned is gone. She lashes out, too shocked and distraught to listen, and flees down the clinic steps to the sidewalk and onto the grounds of the recreation center. Her foot hits something. She stumbles. A dead woman is staring up with vacant eyes—she's been strangled with her own scarf. A female patient at the clinic is soon murdered the same way. Sophie's life is in a tailspin. Her friends and colleagues are suspects. She misses her ex-fiancé. She doesn't know who to trust anymore. Scariest of all, if the murders are connected, she fears a serial killer is lurking in her neighborhood, hunting prey.

KUDOS for *Impulse to Murder*

In *Impulse to Murder* by Laura Munder, Sophie Myerson is a psychologist in Washington, DC. She is engaged to an attorney who suddenly calls off the wedding. Shocked and distraught, Sophie flees out onto the street and nearly stumbles over the body of a young woman, someone she knows. As the bodies begin to pile up, Sophie is determined to find the killer before anyone else dies. But Sophie doesn't realize she is putting a bulls-eye target on her own back and that, even if she finds out who the killer is, she may not live long enough to tell anyone what she knows. Munder's character development is superb, and Sophie is absolutely enchanting. Well written and fast paced, this is one that mystery fans are sure to enjoy. ~ *Taylor Jones, The Review Team of Taylor Jones & Regan Murphy*

Impulse to Murder by Laura Munder is the story of a psychologist in Washington, DC, who has a really bad day. First, Sophie Myerson's fiancé, a local attorney, tells her their engagement is off. Then when she flees from him in shock and dismay, she trips over a body in the park. A young woman is dead, and what is worse, the main suspect is a friend of Sophie's. When another young woman, this time a patient at the clinic where Sophie works, is murdered, Sophie wonders just who among her friends and associates she can trust. Since her ex-fiancé is also a prosecutor in Washington, DC, Sophie is determined to make him help her find the killer before the reputation of the clinic, and everyone who works there, is damaged beyond repair. But can she even trust her ex-fiancé? Or her coworkers, most of whom knew both victims? Written in first person for the main character, and third person for another, *Impulse to Murder* is intriguing, well written, and fast paced. The characters are charming and the author's voice refreshing—a really good read. ~ *Regan Murphy, The Review Team of Taylor Jones & Regan Murphy*

ACKNOWLEDGMENTS

Thank you to family and friends who offered help and support for my on-again, off-again efforts in writing this novel. I'm deeply grateful to all of you.

Thank you, Caroline Tolley, for critiquing, and the staff at Black Opal Books for editing.

IMPULSE TO MURDER

LAURA MUNDER

A Black Opal Books Publication

GENRE: MYSTERY-DETECTIVE/WOMEN SLEUTHS

This is a work of fiction. Names, places, characters and incidents are either the product of the author's imagination or are used fictitiously, and any resemblance to any actual persons, living or dead, businesses, organizations, events or locales is entirely coincidental. All trademarks, service marks, registered trademarks, and registered service marks are the property of their respective owners and are used herein for identification purposes only. The publisher does not have any control over or assume any responsibility for author or third-party websites or their contents.

DEDICATION

*To Charlie, who has proven the benefits
of marrying a man who loves to cook.*

CHAPTER 1

Sophie

Carrie stopped by my office at the end of the work day. Most of the staff at the Hartley Mental Health Out-Patient Clinic left around six—including me—but our hours were flexible to accommodate patients. Tonight, I needed to stay late and finish writing a psychological test report. My phone rang, and Barney's name showed in caller ID. Dr. Barnard Hisselman was my boss, the director of Adult Services at the clinic where Carrie and I were staff psychologists. He wanted me in his office.

"I bet he got wind of your wedding plans," Carrie said. She was bundled up in a winter coat, hat, and scarf. She pulled on her gloves. "Are you going to invite him, Sophie?"

"I can't see any way not to."

Barney hated to be excluded, and his sulking would have driven me nuts.

"If you hedge about the date, he might book a cruise and be unable to attend."

We waved goodbye in the hallway, and she headed

toward the parking lot while I went to Barney's office.

"Come in, Sophie. Sit down."

The room had a strong confectionary aroma. Barney had attended a conference that morning on Borderline Personality Disorder, which would have included caveats about suicide and litigation, which would have panicked him into checking patient charts for documentation of suicidal risk, which would have bored Barney and awakened his craving for sugar. The evidence was arrayed before me—an empty bakery box poked out of his wastebasket, patient charts were scattered on his desk, cookie crumbs coated his shirt, and his stomach rested on his legs like a blown-up beach ball.

"What's up, Barney?"

"Your hair looks different, Sophie."

He was stating the obvious. My thirtieth birthday was around the corner and, in a misguided attempt to stop looking like a teenager with big wiry hair, I'd worn it up that day. Instead of adding gravitas, I looked like I had an electrocuted animal in a state of rigor mortis on top of my head.

"Is that why you wanted me to stop by, Barney, to talk about my hair?"

It was not out of the question. Barney had spent a portion of my last employee evaluation discussing his nose hair. The nose hair discourse raised a perennial stumper: how in God's name had Barney Hisselman ended up running Adult Services? The only plausible explanation was that, upon completion of his psychiatric residency, Barney's supervisors, in a frantic attempt to steer him away from direct patient care, found him an administrative job. They must have figured it was more prudent to have him drive his staff crazy than to torment people whose mental health was already seriously impaired.

"What do you think about those low-carb diets everyone's going on?" Barney could no more stay on a diet than I could give up caffeine. And his food intake was something I never wanted to get embroiled in again. I knew more about his digestive tract than I knew about my own.

"I have no opinion on any diets, Barney."

"So, Sophie—" His high ears and long face meant that, when Barney's expression turned sheepish, he actually resembled a sheep. "—is it true you and Jeremy set a wedding date? You're getting married?"

I broke into a smile. I really couldn't believe my luck. Jeremy was sweet, reliable, funny, and, although raised in South Carolina, the Republican vestiges of his upbringing had disappeared, leaving behind a honeyed accent that melted my bones. "Yes, it'll probably be sometime in June. Carrie and Alan offered to hold the ceremony and reception at their house, which takes the pressure off. We haven't locked down the details yet, but you and Gayle are on the guest list."

"Who else are you inviting from the clinic?"

"Just Steve and Carrie." They were my two closest friends.

"I don't understand, Sophie, what about Jack Cassidy and Delores? And you're not going to invite your interns?" He seemed to be itching to expand my guest list.

"We want to keep it under fifty people." I stood and moved backward toward the door. "See you tomorrow, Barney."

I was on my way back to my office with wedding thoughts on my mind, nodding goodbye to staff members leaving for the day, when Jeremy's ringtone played on my cellphone. "Jeremy," I whispered into the phone, "I was just thinking about you."

"I'm on my way over, Sophie."

"Over where? I'm still at the clinic." Normally I'd be

on my way home, and Jeremy would still be at work. The pace of his job as an Assistant United States Attorney for the District of Columbia, ranged from busy to ridiculously busy, and he was in a ridiculously busy phase. "I'm staying late to write a test report."

"Oh."

"Aren't you in the middle of a trial, Jeremy?"

Ned Olmason, a psychology intern I supervised, walked by zipping up his coat. I smiled, and he raised a hand in a wave.

"Yes, I'm in for a long night, but I wanted to see you. I'll come to the clinic."

A man's voice carried from the waiting room: "Fuck you and fuck the horse you rode in on, fuck all the fucking horses."

"Hold on, Jeremy." I lowered the phone and hurried to see what the problem was. Two women sat in the room with tense expressions, avoiding the ranting man. I made eye contact with him.

"I'm Dr. Myerson. Are you here to see Dr. Cassidy?"

Jack Cassidy, our psychiatrist, worked late on Thursday nights doing medication checks, and this man clearly needed to have his medication checked.

He handed me a crumpled paper. "I have an appointment."

"Good. I'll let Dr. Cassidy know you're here."

"I can see you now, Tim." Jack came up behind me and motioned to the man.

I flashed Jack a thankful smile and brought the phone back to my ear.

"Sorry, Jeremy."

"I'll be there soon."

"Wait, you're coming to the clinic?"

He'd already hung up. I entered my office, feeling perplexed. Jeremy either came to my apartment after work, I went to his, or we met at a restaurant. He never came to the clinic. Something was off. He'd seemed tense lately, which had given me a flutter of anxiety, but then again, he was in the middle of prosecuting a rash of gang murders. Maybe the oddity was me working late. If Jeremy had already driven across town from the Department of Justice, detouring to the clinic instead of driving to my apartment was no big deal. I had broken our routine.

I stared at the test data on my desk. The idea popped into my mind that Jeremy had bought an engagement ring as a surprise. I'd told him the expense was unnecessary. We were saving money for a house, but maybe—

I put the test data in a folder and locked it in a drawer. My concentration was shot. I waited at the clinic entrance for him. Soon, he ran up the steps, lithe and agile. I let him in quickly with a blast of cold air.

"Come see my home away from home," I said when he arrived.

I scurried ahead to lead the way, eager to show him my office. Inside, I closed the door, turned to face him, and was stunned by his appearance. He looked like a zombie with dark circles under his blood-shot eyes. Prosecuting gang members who murdered potential witnesses created enormous stress.

I moved to kiss him, and he held me back. He had never rejected a kiss before.

"Jeremy, my love, what is it?"

"I can't do this, Sophie. I'm so sorry."

"What can't you do?"

"I can't marry you, Sophie. I'm so sorry."

He had proposed. I had accepted. "Jeremy, please, everything will be okay. We'll get through this. Tell me what's wrong. What happened?"

"I'm so sorry."

"Stop *saying* that." My head was spinning. Everything was a blur. "Whatever's bothering you, tell me. We can figure it out together."

"Not this, Sophie."

How could our relationship be fine one day and over the next? I'd been with Jeremy for two years. We knew each other. We *loved* each other. He didn't have a history of depression. There was no mental illness in his family, but something was way off kilter. Had he had a biopsy he hadn't told me about? Had he been given terrifying medical news? I touched his face. "Are you sick, Jeremy?"

"No."

His eyes filled with tears. I'd never seen him cry before. Nothing made sense. I wanted to tell him about the caterer I found. I made an appointment for us to sample their food over the weekend. And tomorrow night we were taking Carrie and Alan out to thank them for offering to host our reception.

I began to pace, grief and rage closing in on me. Jeremy had worked almost non-stop the past few weeks. He'd been too tired to make love, but that had happened once before when he was prosecuting a big case. What cues had I missed? His hand reached out to me as I passed by. I smacked it back and kept moving. He had no right to touch me.

Was he being threatened? I knew how tense his office was. Had the defendants' fellow gang members threatened the prosecutors' families? Was Jeremy calling off our wedding to protect me from harm?

"Sophie?" His voice seemed to come from far away. "Say something, Sophie, please."

"Is it the trial? Is that why you're doing this? You don't want the gang coming after me."

"The trial?" He looked confused. "No, Sophie."

He wasn't trying to protect me. This had nothing to do with keeping me safe. I didn't matter. My face was coated with tears. I grabbed tissues from the box on my desk and blew my nose. "Were you pretending to love me?"

"I wasn't pretending. You don't deserve this, Sophie. I am so sorry."

I sat down and stared at my hands. I couldn't look at him. "Why, Jeremy? I don't understand."

"I'm fucked up. It's completely my fault. This isn't about you. I never should have put you in this position." His phone rang. He put it on silence. "My life got turned upside down. I'm not sure where to begin." His phone vibrated again. The thought crossed my mind he had a girlfriend trying to get in touch. I grabbed the phone, furious, ready to throw it in his face, but he was getting a text message from his boss, typed in caps, demanding an immediate response. Gang murder trials were a high priority. They didn't want to screw this one up. I tossed him the phone. Rage burst out of me like a fireball.

"Go deal with your fucking emergency. I can't stand the sight of you." I ran to the door.

"Sophie, wait. I'll get back to him in a minute."

"Really, if I wait, I'll get *one minute* of your time? One fucking minute to understand why everything I've been looking forward to is never going to happen. This is the worst moment of my life."

"Mine too."

"You don't get to say that, Jeremy. That's like a murderer who shoots someone asking to be pitied because he doesn't like watching people die. Fuck you, Jeremy, and fuck the horse you rode in on."

I stormed out of the office. He might as well have thrown acid on my brain because all the memories that used to bring joy were rapidly corroding. I ran down the clinic steps to the street and raced along the sidewalk trying to numb my pain through movement.

"Sophie, *wait*." Jeremy was calling to me, but I kept going.

He was a runner. I wasn't. He caught up and handed me my coat. "You must be freezing."

I put the coat on, and he handed me my purse. Knowing Jeremy, he'd stopped to turn off the lights in my office and close the door behind him.

He put his arm around me. "Let me take you home, Sophie. I shouldn't have told you at the clinic."

I wanted to bite his hand. I shoved him away. Tears streamed down my face. "Leave me alone. Go live your stupid life."

There were other people on the sidewalk, an elderly man walking a dog, a couple of teenagers giggling as they approached. I ran onto the grounds of the neighborhood recreation center so I wouldn't be seen. The building was set back from the street at the end of a long driveway. Much of the area was dark, offering space to lose myself among the trees without trespassing on private property. Jeremy followed, which made him harder to hate, but not by any significant amount.

"Let me drive you home, Sophie. You can't wander around out here."

"Yes, I can." I kept moving. He kept pace with me. I could hear him in the underbrush. "Go away," I called over my shoulder. "Leave me alone."

My foot hit a tree root. I stumbled. Jeremy grabbed my arm as I pitched forward. I had a childish impulse to kick at the root, but I didn't want to stub my toe. Then, as my eyes adjusted to the dark, I realized the root was a young woman. She was lying on the ground, motionless. Her unblinking eyes were wide open in the cold night air.

CHAPTER 2

My vision tunneled into blankness. When I opened my eyes, my head was in Jeremy's lap. "You fainted, Sophie. I called nine-one-one. The police are on their way. We need to wait for them."

I swiveled my neck and found myself eye level with the dead woman, caught in that stupid game of seeing who would blink first, but I was no match for a corpse. A wave of nausea rose in my throat. Hers was the first dead body I'd ever seen. Being eye to eye with her was freaking me out. "I have to get up."

"Okay, but slowly, Sophie."

Jeremy held me steady, and we both stood. I couldn't stop shaking. I needed the warmth, so I let him put his arm around me. With the police due any second, I didn't want to start a discussion of why he no longer wanted to marry me. Meanwhile, the dead woman looked familiar.

"I've seen her before."

"I know, Sophie. She was at that party Carrie and Alan had in August for Alan's law firm. She was a summer intern. Penny something. I don't know her last name."

I remembered the party. Carrie had coaxed Jeremy

and me into attending so she wouldn't be marooned in a sea of corporate lawyers. Penny had looked beautiful in a summer dress that showed off her slender limbs. In fact, I'd seen Jeremy having an animated discussion with her. I hadn't asked him about it at the time—I never worried about him and other women.

"What were you and Penny talking about at the party?"

"I was extolling the virtues of being a public servant, and she was having none of it. She hoped to be hired by Alan's firm when she graduated. We only spoke for a few minutes."

I pictured them conversing. Penny had been rubbing her hands up and down her sleek arms, almost as if she were stroking herself. "What was your impression of her?"

"She seemed like a smart, young, law student, competitive and ambitious."

"Not flirtatious?"

"Not with me."

I peered down at her. Years of watching *Law and Order SVU* had taught me to look for signs of violence. Penny had no obvious injuries—although red spots showed in the whites of her eyes—and no external signs of sexual trauma. She was wearing wool pants, shoes, a buttoned winter coat, a scarf wrapped around her neck and gloves. Her handbag lay beside her on the ground, the strap slung over her shoulder. Combining those observations with the fact that our clinic was located in a safe DC neighborhood with little street crime, I concluded that her death was due to natural causes. "Do you think she had an aneurysm?" I asked Jeremy.

"I told the nine-one-one dispatcher we had a possible homicide."

"Why?"

Sirens almost drowned out my question. Two squad cars pulled up to the curb. Jeremy held up his lit cellphone to signal our location.

"Look at her eyes. The red spots are petechial hemorrhaging, which can be a sign of strangulation, plus we found her in a dark secluded area, and her scarf could have been used to strangle her." Jeremy pointed to a barrel-chested African-American man getting out of a car. "That's Reginald White." A woman emerged from the passenger seat. "She must be his new partner. I don't know her."

Detective White strode over to us while his partner knelt beside the body.

"Jeremy, my man, what's going on?" He and Jeremy shook hands. His partner lifted the scarf on Penny's neck. Then she lowered the scarf and opened Penny's handbag.

"Sophie literally stumbled on the body. We haven't touched anything. This is Sophie Myerson."

The detective and I nodded hello.

"What were you doing here in the dark?"

"I was running away from Jeremy."

The detective's jaw tightened. "Why, was he threatening you?" He shot a warning look at Jeremy.

I couldn't help myself. The words spilled out. "He broke off our engagement without any warning. Everything seemed fine between us. We were supposed to meet with a caterer tomorrow."

Reginald White's face was impassive. I needed to stop babbling.

"I ran off the sidewalk to be alone and stumbled over the body. We recognized the dead woman from a party we went to last summer. She's in law school. She interned at a friend's law firm. I can write down the name of our friend and the firm."

"Do it." He handed me a notebook and pen. I jotted

down the information and handed it back. "What have you got?" he asked his partner as she joined us.

Behind them, police officers from the squad car were putting up crime scene tape.

His partner held Penny's wallet open for him to look inside, and I took a peek, too. So did Jeremy. Credit cards and receipts were crammed into a pocket, but the billfold was empty. She saw us looking and motioned with her arms for us to move back. "I need you to step out of the way."

Detective White walked with us to the sidewalk.

"Is there anything else you need?" Jeremy asked him. "If I don't get back to the office, I'll be the next body you see in the morgue."

"Go. If you think of anything, give me a call." He handed me his card.

"Do you want me to drive you home?" Jeremy asked as we walked back to the clinic.

"You don't have time."

"I know, but it's the least I can do."

"Walk me to my car. And put your fricking arm around me, Jeremy. I'm shivering out of my skin." I was shaking so hard I felt ready to spin apart. I couldn't believe the evening, two horrible events. Jeremy had ruined my future, but Penny's future was gone forever. She was younger than me and dead, robbed of her *life*. I put my hand under my scarf against my throat. "Do you really think Penny was strangled?"

"Yes. I'm betting Reggie's partner saw something when she looked under the scarf. And there were no bills in Penny's wallet. Someone took her cash. Most wallets aren't completely empty."

Fear rose in my stomach. I didn't like the robbery aspect. Random violence scared me the most. Someone connected to Penny's life could be captured and punished. A stranger would kill again. "Do you think Penny knew the person who killed her?"

"I don't know, Sophie. The killer got close, so maybe. It doesn't look like she put up a struggle. On the other hand, if this was a street robbery, the killer could have pulled a gun, made her walk to a secluded spot, and told her not to turn around while he twisted her scarf."

We reached the clinic. The building looked the same as when I'd arrived in the morning, but now I was unloved and alone. Jeremy and I weren't getting married. We wouldn't have children together. Poor Penny would never marry or have a family of her own. She would never be the lawyer she wanted to be. She had been alive and vibrant in the summer. I couldn't believe she was dead. Her sightless eyes haunted me.

"I'm parked in back."

We walked through the dimly lit parking lot to my car. I wanted to ask Jeremy why he was dumping me, but my lips froze—the words wouldn't come out. I'd reached my limit for upsetting news. I didn't want to hear about a woman he'd been rubbing up against at work. The concrete pavement looked inviting. I wanted to lie down and rock myself to oblivion. Instead, I clicked the car door open.

"I'm so sorry, Sophie," Jeremy repeated for the umpteenth time as I got in.

I put the car in reverse and backed out, being careful not to run him over—in my state of mind, accidents did happen.

❧❦❧

When I was home, I called Carrie and blubbered into the phone. She sped to my apartment. We sat on opposite ends of my couch, facing each other. My mind was reeling. I couldn't stop talking about Penny. She and Alan had already gotten a call from Detective White.

"Alan is in total shock. He's meeting with the detective tomorrow." Carrie passed me the wastebasket to dump my tissues.

"Jeremy thinks Penny was robbed and murdered." Saying Jeremy's name brought a fresh wave of desolation. "How can he do this to me, Carrie?" My body felt cleaved in two.

"I don't know, Sophie. Did he say *why*?"

"Only that he's fucked up and everything is his fault, which tells me nothing."

"Do you think he decided he doesn't want kids?"

"Jeremy loves children, and he's great around them. He would have told me if he changed his mind."

Carrie nodded. "You're right. Do you think he's gay?"

"Jeremy?"

He'd always been eagerly heterosexual and, yet, it was an obvious question. Others might jump to that conclusion and assume I was too sexually inept to notice that the man I loved preferred men.

I let out a moan. I wasn't ready to face the social ramifications of being dumped by my fiancé.

"Did the two of you have a fight?"

"No."

"It's not like the wedding was going to be an extravaganza he couldn't face. Why would he bail? You guys seemed happy together. He didn't give you *any* explanation?"

"He kept going on about how sorry he was. He feels bad about hurting me, but if he didn't want to marry me, why did he propose? I can't believe this is happening."

"At the very least, he owes you an explanation."

"Was he forcing himself to make love to me while fantasizing about men?"

"I don't think he's gay, Sophie. I shouldn't have said anything."

"Jeremy works all the time when he's not with me. If he met another woman, it has to be someone in his office."

"Those things happen. But maybe it's something as simple as him getting cold feet."

Getting cold feet was not a desirable trait in one's fiancé, but it was better than the alternatives. Jeremy hadn't said he didn't love me.

"Or," Carrie continued, "maybe, like those noble, pig-headed people you read about in nineteenth-century literature, he has a rare illness he doesn't want handed down to your children, or he has a degenerative disease and doesn't want you burdened with his care."

Those explanations didn't fly. "Why break up with me when he's so pressed for time with the gang murder case? He's like the patients who tell you what's really bothering them on their way out the door."

"Except he's been on the gang case for months and maybe he saw tonight as a deadline because of our dinner tomorrow."

"What do you mean?"

"You and Jeremy were going to take Alan and me out for dinner to thank us. We would have spent all night discussing wedding plans. He couldn't sit through that and pretend."

"You're right."

"And he wanted to tell you at home, Sophie. That's where he thought you'd be. What did he mean that his world had turned upside down?"

"Something happened that had nothing to do with me. I was collateral damage."

I blew my nose and pictured Penny lying on her back with open eyes. She would never look into the faces of her loved ones again. A failed romance hurt like hell, but it wasn't the worst thing that could happen.

ʚৎʚৎ

After Carrie left, I considered calling my brother, but he was in his second year of medical school and stressed out studying for the boards. I didn't want to throw him off his stride with a family crisis. I dreaded calling my parents. They would be heartsick and worried, but they needed to know Jeremy and I were no longer engaged, and I needed their support. I decided not to tell them about Penny. If they thought a murderer was on the loose near where I worked, I wouldn't have put it past my mom to pirate a copy of my resume and begin filling out applications to find me a job near their home in New Jersey—maybe even *in* their home in New Jersey: she could turn the den into an office and line up patients for me to see.

My parents were as distressed by the news as I imagined they'd be. We said sad goodbyes and I ate two bowls of pistachio ice cream for dinner. Then I crawled into bed and sobbed my eyes out because the world was a scary place where bad things happened, and because Jeremy would never climb into bed with me again. The man I imagined as my life partner would soon become a stranger.

ʚৎʚৎ

My eyes felt glued shut Friday morning. Prying the lids apart took time and effort. I drove to the clinic on automatic pilot, downed two cups of coffee, and reviewed my schedule. The day was packed. The psychological test report I'd left undone would have to wait for the weekend. But maybe being swamped with appointments was a good thing. If I could stay constantly engaged, I wouldn't have time to dwell on my personal life.

The psychology interns were due for supervision at nine o'clock, after which I had patients scheduled at ten, eleven, and noon. I had a half hour break for lunch at one and planned to shut my door and eat alone, because sympathy from Carrie and Steve would start me blubbering. After lunch, I had four appointments, two of whom were seriously depressed patients, which worried me. They spoke so slowly, my own thoughts were bound to intrude. I'd have to fight hard not to sink into despair with them.

The sound of my ringing phone made me jump. I was in a hyper-aroused state, but it was only Barney wanting to see me. His umpteen calls each day were disruptive and annoying, but harmless. He sat behind his desk using the scissors on his Swiss Army knife to snip corners off his morning newspaper.

"Sit down, Sophie." He folded the scissors into the knife and held it up like a proud parent. For Barney, the cracked red enamel was part of its charm. "Can you believe I got this knife as a bar mitzvah present? I've been carrying it around for forty years."

I already knew the knife was a bar mitzvah present from his Uncle Irving. He also had a signet ring acquired at the same event and several tie clips. "Why did you want to see me, Barney?" I needed to conserve what little emotional energy I had.

He handed me the Metro section from the morning's *Washington Post* and pointed to a headline: *Woman murdered in Palisades Section of Northwest DC.* "This happened within blocks of the clinic. I knew the girl, Sophie. She and my daughter carpooled to gymnastics together when they were kids."

Barney's daughter was now grown and living on the West Coast.

The headline sent a chill down my spine—the events of last night were real. Thankfully, Barney seemed unaware I found the body. I skimmed the article. Penny Harrison had been twenty-five years old, a third-year law student living with two girlfriends in a rental house. One of her roommates was out of town yesterday and the other had gone straight from work to a happy hour and dinner with friends. Penny had retrieved her car from a parking lot at four in the afternoon after a law school class and then driven home. Her car was found parked in her driveway. Later she walked to MacArthur Boulevard where she withdrew two hundred dollars from an ATM. The bank receipt in her purse was stamped at five-fifty p.m. The money was missing. Jeremy and I were identified as "two passersby" who discovered Penny's body at six-fifteen and called the police.

I released my breath, relieved I wouldn't have to tell Barney about my involvement. He would have peppered me with questions and then misquoted my answers to everyone he could get to listen. And then he'd have misquoted them back to me.

"Your fiancé works with the police, Sophie. Ask him if he knows anything about this, will you? I hope to hell they catch the bastard." Barney tapped his Swiss Army knife on his desk. "I need to send a condolence card to her parents. What the hell am I going to say to them?"

I didn't envy him the task. "I have to go, Barney. The psych interns need supervision."

Marnie Washington and Ned Olmason spent half their time on the main floor of the clinic, in Adult Services where I worked, and half their time upstairs in Family and Child Services. Steve supervised their psychological testing at Adult Services, and Carrie and I supervised their work with psychotherapy patients. Because of time constraints, Marnie and Ned came together for our supervision. I grouped three chairs for our meeting.

Marnie arrived first. She was a gay, African-American woman in her late twenties with flawless skin and nails that were acrylic works of art. She sat down and pulled a folder from her backpack. The motion set her cornrows clacking. I wanted to clack, too, but there was no way I could carry off cornrows. "Ned said to tell you he's going to be late, Sophie. He got waylaid upstairs."

"Ah." The Family and Child Service supervisors were more stringent than us, possibly because they didn't have Barney as their director. They had rigorous charting protocols and required the interns to videotape sessions for review. Barney had never followed through ordering videotaping equipment for us. "Who do you want to start with?"

Instead of answering, Marnie smiled. "I heard you were getting married to that dude you go with. Congrats, Sophie. That's big."

My composure faltered. "Thanks, Marnie. Why don't we start with Katie—how's she doing?" My hand shook as I picked up my notes from our last meeting.

Ned sauntered in and took a seat. "Yo, sorry I'm late."

"That's okay, you haven't missed anything. Go on, Marnie."

"Katie is a twenty-three-year-old African-American woman. If anyone asks her for a favor, she gives in. She feels like she can't say no, and then she's filled with resentment."

"Can you give an example?"

"Sure. She agreed to be a bridesmaid in a friend's destination wedding. Never mind that she has student loans and will miss an entire week of work. Add in the cost of her dress, the island resort, flight, and all the rest—she'll pay over two thousand dollars which she has to charge on a credit card."

"Is Katie's problem that she can't say no to her friend, or that she can't say no to herself?" I wanted to establish if Katie really couldn't set limits with other people or if she looked for excuses to be self-indulgent. "Does she often do things she can't afford, is that a pattern? Or would she be genuinely relieved and happy if she didn't have to go to the wedding?"

"She really doesn't want to go. She can't set limits."

Ned stepped in. "Speaking of weddings—Marnie told me your news. Congratulations, Sophie."

I mustered a weak smile.

Ned wasn't finished with the topic. "Do you want us to do a mental status exam on the groom before you make your final decision? We might uncover something."

That wasn't a bad idea. Ned might have saved me a lot of trouble. "I appreciate the offer, but let's get back to Katie."

Ned tilted his chin at Marnie. "I can cure your patient."

"You think so, dude? Tell me how."

"I'd take a practical approach. Have her hire a hit man to off the bride. They probably cost less than she'd spend going to the wedding. They can't be that hard to find."

I stepped in. "That's an elegant solution, Ned, but I'd really like to focus on why Katie has trouble saying no."

My entire day was like that. I drank four more cups of coffee to stay awake. When five-thirty arrived, I slumped with relief. I could go home, eat ice cream, and cry. And tomorrow was Saturday. I could sleep late.

Carrie stopped by my office as I was putting on my coat. "Alan and I still have a babysitter for tonight, Sophie. Come out to dinner with us. We'll pick you up and go somewhere low key."

I hesitated. "What if I start bawling in public?"

"I won't let you. I promise. We won't talk about Jeremy."

"Then I'll come." I believed Carrie. She was that kind of friend.

⁕⁕⁕

"Comfort food. I'm getting an egg salad sandwich and a vanilla shake," Carrie said when we were seated in a booth at a nearby diner. She sat beside me across from Alan, so I wouldn't feel like the odd man out. Alan was a sweet-tempered nerd of the successful legal variety who would have stood in front of a moving bus to make his wife happy. He looked at me with sad eyes.

The menu was heaven sent. I couldn't decide whether to have a chocolate milkshake with my meal or wait and order an ice cream sundae for dessert, but when the waitress tapped her pencil to her pad and repeated, "What about you, hon?" I stopped dithering and ordered the chocolate shake along with a hamburger, medium rare, and French fries.

Alan asked for a Reuben sandwich and Blue Moon.

As soon as the waitress left, Carrie whispered, "Penny Harrison was having an affair with Howard Barrow."

Our eyes locked. This was a shocker. I chomped on a pickle as Carrie continued, "It started when Penny was a summer intern, and they kept seeing each other after she returned to law school."

Howard Barrow was one of Alan's law partners and a close friend of theirs. He was also married, the father of a son, in his forties, and going gray. His wife, Fiona, had accompanied him to the summer party. Penny's air of suppressed sexuality suddenly made sense. Her lover had been in the vicinity yet out of reach.

"I never could abide Fiona," Carrie said. "When she was pregnant, she acted like she was incubating a genius. She played classical music around the clock and read Proust out loud. Seriously, she was preparing the baby to emerge from her womb ready to place out of Freshman English. She couldn't believe he wanted to be fed and changed like all the other babies." The waitress brought our milkshakes and threw a handful of straws on the table. Carrie picked one up and removed the wrapper. "But you know, now that Howard is the prime suspect in a murder, it's so horrible, I actually feel sorry for her."

"Howard is the prime suspect?" I asked. He was the last person I would have connected with having an affair, let alone killing anyone.

Alan's expression turned grim. "It's awful. He's out of his mind with grief, and he's not thinking clearly. Two detectives came to our offices yesterday. Howard spilled his guts. He said things that can and will be used against him. He wanted me with him for moral support, but he didn't want any legal advice. He refuses to hire a criminal attorney."

The waitress set our plates down in front of us. I slathered ketchup on my fries and squirted a blob on my hamburger under the bun. That was as much meal preparation as I liked to do whether eating out or at home. "Where did Penny and Howard go to be together?" I couldn't fathom the logistics of an affair. DC felt like a small town.

"They went to Penny's home. She lived in Palisades near where she was found. Her house overlooks the Potomac."

Jeremy and I had looked at houses near the clinic. They were much too expensive for us to buy and houses overlooking the Potomac were even more expensive. "How could a law student afford to live there?"

"The house belongs to the parents of one of her roommates. They're in the foreign service. They wanted their daughter to live in their home with friends. I doubt they charged her much."

"Didn't Howard worry about Penny's roommates knowing about them?" I bit into my hamburger, perfectly cooked. I tasted a fry and added salt.

Carrie reached for the salt when I was done. "When I was in grad school, I lived in a group house, and one of my roommates was having an affair with a married lobbyist. He came over all the time, and we never told a soul. He lived in a different world from us."

"Does Howard have an alibi for the night Penny was killed?"

Carrie grabbed a bunch of napkins from the dispenser and blotted the Reuben drippings on Alan's shirt sleeves. His dry-cleaning bills were legendary. "No, and it's worse than having no alibi. Tell Sophie what he told the police, Alan."

"Howard told them he lied to Fiona and said he was working late Thursday evening, but he actually left work early to meet Penny at her house at six. Her roommates were out, as Penny said they'd be. But no one answered the doorbell when he rang, and Howard didn't have a key. It was cold out, so he sat in his car and waited for her to return. Her car was in the driveway, but that didn't mean she was home, because Penny often ran errands on foot. Howard kept calling her cellphone and texting, but she didn't respond."

I washed down a mouthful of fries with my chocolate shake. Howard not only didn't have an alibi, but he was also close enough to the crime scene to have killed her. "If the calls were made within the same cell tower range, he could have been standing over Penny's dead body and calling her number."

Carrie gave me a skeptical look. "How do you know that, Sophie?"

I waved my hand. "*SVU, NCIS.*"

Alan finished the last of his beer. "The whole thing is unbelievable. Howard said he sat in his car, unsure if Penny was blowing him off or if something had detained her. She usually let him know if she was running late, so he had a bad feeling, but never in his wildest dreams did he imagine she'd been murdered."

"Did any witnesses see him waiting in the car outside her home?"

"No, the house has a private driveway. The neighbors wouldn't have seen him."

"When did he leave?"

"Around seven."

I pushed the last bit of hamburger in my mouth. "Howard doesn't have an alibi. He was in the vicinity." I stopped for a quick slurp of milkshake. "And it's easy to imagine a motive. Penny might have broken up with him or threatened to sue him for sexual harassment or threatened to tell Fiona about the affair."

"What about the missing money?" Carrie asked.

"Howard could have taken her cash to make it look like a robbery."

Alan shook his head. "What do you have against him, Sophie? I've known Howard for years. I can't imagine him killing anyone."

I had nothing against him. "I like Howard, but I'm hoping the killer is someone Penny knew who has no reason to hurt anyone else. I don't want the danger quotient in my life to go up."

Carrie reached for one of my fries. "I feel the same way, Sophie, but honestly, if I was Howard, I would have killed Fiona years ago, so, to me, the fact that Fiona is still alive demonstrates enormous restraint on Howard's part. He's not a murderer."

I moved my straw around my glass and vacuumed up the last remnants of my chocolate shake. Carrie's unassailable logic brought our conversation to a close, and I felt a tidal wave of grief welling up. "Thanks, guys. This was great." I grabbed the check before they could and paid, despite their protests. Jeremy and I had invited them out for a fancy dinner that night. It wasn't their fault we canceled.

"I can't believe that yesterday at ten minutes to six Penny was still alive, withdrawing money from an ATM, and I was talking to Jeremy on the phone, wondering if he was going to surprise me with an engagement ring," I said as we walked to their car. I got into the back seat like a little kid.

Carrie twisted around to face me. "What time did you find Penny's body?"

"Around six-fifteen."

"It would have taken Penny five to ten minutes to walk from the ATM to where you found her—she must have been killed between six and six ten."

I shuddered. Jeremy was arriving and Barney was leaving at around that time. Many staff members left at six. Any of them could have driven past the murderer unawares. They may even have seen Penny as she walked unknowingly to her death.

୧୬୧୬

There was a message on my machine when I returned home—Jeremy asking if he could stop by over the weekend to explain. I appreciated that he hadn't called my cellphone, since the sound of his voice made me cry.

At least he'd learned not to sandbag me in public.

I considered calling him back, but I was completely beat. My last ounce of energy went into taking off my clothes and flopping into bed.

Saturday morning, I slept late. Fortified by coffee, I opened my laptop and cancelled the appointment with the caterer. There was no reason to dress in street clothes since I wasn't going anywhere, and my blue bathrobe was perfect for moping around in. I tried to work on the psychological test report, but I couldn't focus. Instead, I made a bowl of microwave popcorn and streamed episodes of *The Good Wife* on my computer, weeping my eyes out. I thought about calling Jeremy, but the morning paper reported that the gangland murder trial had gone to the jury late Friday. He would be exhausted, if not actually asleep.

Late in the afternoon, he called. I started to reach for the phone, but froze. A chill of foreboding kept me from answering. Sometimes when things seemed like they couldn't get any worse, they actually did get worse. I was already traumatized. What if Jeremy told me something that would disturb my mind and haunt me forever? I pulled my hand away and let the machine pick up. "Sophie, please call me."

∽∾∽∾

On Sunday, I tackled the psychological test report, which had to be done. The results would impact a person's life.

Just as I'd immersed myself in the data and begun to concentrate on the task, Jeremy called. I didn't want to break my hard-earned stride.

"Please pick up, Sophie," he said into my machine, "I'm so sorry. I know what I'm doing is horrible. I want to explain. Won't you talk to me?" He sounded distraught. There was anguish in his voice.

I felt a twinge of satisfaction.

I finally completed the report and ordered a small pizza for dinner. I was digging in when my parents called to check on me. Minutes later, call waiting beeped. Jeremy was trying to reach me again, but I didn't want to hang up on my parents and then have to call them back and explain. Jeremy could wait. He didn't deserve any special courtesy. After my parents hung up, I listened to his message:

"Sophie, please get back to me, *please*." He sounded desperate. He might even have been crying.

I was in a quandary over what to do. On the one hand, I wanted to know why he left me—the question never stopped ricocheting in my brain. On the other hand, I was scared of the answer, and his distress gratified me. I liked knowing I was on his mind. Once Jeremy explained why he no longer wanted to marry me, everything would be over between us. Jeremy liked wrapping things up. Case closed.

I finished eating the pizza and selected a carton of mint chocolate chip ice cream to round off the meal. I was savoring my first spoonful when realization struck— until I listened to what Jeremy had to say, he would be unable to stop thinking about me. He'd remain tortured with remorse. Only after he explained his rejection would he feel free to move on. His pleading calls would end. No more wrenching apologies.

My path was clear. I wanted Jeremy to think about me often and live in a perpetual state of torment. I wanted him drowning in guilt, absolution denied. In a perfect world, that wouldn't amount to much, but in my world, it was all I had.

CHAPTER 3

Until I was in better control of my emotions, I needed the clinic to be a safe zone where I could compartmentalize and do my job. Carrie and Steve were the only people there who knew about my broken engagement.

Monday, I ate lunch at my desk with my door closed. In the afternoon, I was heading back to my office from the ladies room when Ned Olmason called for me to wait up.

Watching him approach was like viewing a nature movie. He moved with a panther's muscular grace. I experienced him as vibrating with sexual energy, and I wasn't the only one. Carrie and Steve had the same reaction. He created an erotic force field.

"I'm sorry, Sophie, but I have to miss supervision on Friday." Ned's eyes were icy blue, like an arctic glacier. A lock of blond hair flopped across his forehead. He pushed it back with his hand. "There's a conference on one of my child cases. I have to be there."

These conflicts occurred regularly. "Not a problem. Maybe we can switch our time to Thursday this week. I'll email you and Marnie."

"That'd be great. Thanks." He touched my arm and walked on.

I flew to my office, closed the door, and leaned back to steady myself. There'd been no reason for him to touch my arm, but that wasn't what was troubling me. I had wanted to press my body up against his. It wasn't an idle musing or passing sexual fantasy. I had experienced an urgent physical desire to make love to a student under my supervision in the middle of the hallway during clinic hours.

This was not good.

My mind flooded with infamous political figures undone by sexual misdeeds, people I had previously scorned as narcissists living in a bubble, unheeding of others. But what if some of them were thoughtful people struggling through a dark time, like me, and their pent-up emotions made them vulnerable to sexual acting out?

To top off the day, Barney left me a message to stop by his office on my way out. "Sit down, Sophie. An interesting referral came in." He pawed at the clutter on his desk. "Here it is. Ariel Lancet, twenty-eight years old. She called me directly, didn't go through the normal intake process." He handed me the paper. "That's her phone number. Keep in mind there are privacy issues in a high-profile family like hers." He paused so I could take in that she was a member of a *high-profile family.* I outpaused him. I had no idea who she was. "She's Evan Lancet's wife, Sophie."

"Who's Evan Lancet?" The name meant nothing.

"Don't you ever get out? Lancet Developers? You must have seen all the new construction downtown. His signs are everywhere."

So they were. Barney was right. Lancet was putting up big office buildings on K Street and farther east where entire neighborhoods were being renovated. "Should I do the intake and staff it with you instead of at the meeting?"

"No. Have an intern do the intake and start seeing her in therapy right away. Ariel wants to come three times a week."

"Three times a week?" We had a waiting list of people wanting to come once a week. Ned was out of the question: his schedule was full. "Marnie is down one patient, but she doesn't have that kind of time."

"Tell Marnie she can skip our staff meetings. This is a priority. Ariel will go somewhere else if we don't accommodate her, and she's a full fee client. Her three sessions each week will help us see other patients for less. Anyway, it's a good training case, Sophie, so consider it a gift."

CHAPTER 4

The yard outside my apartment window was blanketed in snow when I awoke Thursday morning. Trees, robed in white, swayed like ancient priests performing a mystical rite. Snow exhilarated me. And I had a parking space in the building garage, so I didn't have to shovel a walkway or dig out my car.

My apartment was on Connecticut Avenue NW, a few blocks north of the Van Ness/UDC Metro station. From Connecticut Avenue, I took Nebraska Avenue to Arizona Avenue, all of which were plowed, but once I crossed MacArthur Boulevard, the streets hadn't yet been cleared. I skidded into the clinic parking lot, relieved to turn off the ignition and get out of the car. Bundled up in my ski parka, hat, scarf, gloves, and waterproof boots, I tromped to the rear door, stomped the snow off my boots, and stepped inside.

We were open for business. A few other hardy souls wandered the halls. I shed my outerwear and headed to the kitchen for coffee. I always drank a wake-up mug at home and a stay-awake mug when I arrived at work. It was my version of a fitness program. Marnie was in the kitchen making a cup of tea. She was twice as intrepid as

I'd ever be—every day she drove an unreliable car in from Northeast DC. "How was your drive?" I asked her.

"I didn't want to risk it. I got up early and took the bus, which was fine." Her cellphone vibrated. She glanced at the screen. "Dang, not again."

"What's the matter?"

She turned off her phone. "My friend Leila keeps calling. She stopped by a few weeks ago and met Ned and so, of course, they slept together, and now he won't return her calls, and she's upset, even though I told her straight up—Ned's into variety, not relationships. He was never going to see her more than one or two times. She knew going in."

My ears were hot. Ned was a cad. Carrie, Steve, and I had suspected as much. I was eager to fill them in on this tidbit. The interns knew each other better than we knew either of them.

Marnie and I walked to my office. Ned hadn't yet arrived, but staff members were straggling in late because of the snow. "We might as well get started. Tell me about Ariel."

Marnie unzipped her backpack and pulled out a folder. "I've seen her two times this week."

"What's she like?"

"The girl's a trip."

"You mean she's difficult?"

"No. Don't get me wrong—I like her."

"Yo."

We looked up. Ned tossed his backpack on the floor and dropped into a chair, his legs sprawled in the space between us. "Sorry I'm late."

"Marnie's presenting a new patient, Ariel Lancet, twenty-eight years old. They're meeting three times a week."

"Really? Why does she get special treatment?"

"Dr. Hisselman made the decision." I turned back to Marnie. "You were saying Ariel's a trip."

"The girl's got looks, money, you name it. Yet, she's telling me how lucky I am to have a profession, how lucky I am to know what I want to do with my life. Even—" Marnie turned to Ned. "—you'll like this: she thinks I'm lucky I can wear cornrows because they look funny on white people."

"She's right," he agreed, dashing the hope I had of trying them in my post-Jeremy life.

"She talks like she wants to be me, for real," Marnie continued. "I'm not the first person most people pick as their role model."

"Maybe she tells you your hair looks sweet so you'll say her hair looks sweet," Ned said.

"Could be, she has long, silky blonde hair."

"Whoa." Ned kicked back in his chair. "Ariel was the babe in the waiting room Wednesday morning? She had on a Patagonia jacket and hiking boots?"

Marnie frowned. "You better not go messing with my patient. I'm not playing, Ned."

"Chill, okay? I was just trying to picture who you're talking about."

"So now that you know who she is, do you think she was dissing my hair?"

"No, I think she was sucking up to you. That's how she gets along, telling people how great they are."

I decided to weigh in. "People must envy Ariel her looks and money. That can be awkward for her. She might have been trying to say that she values what you have. Let's assume she's sincere. She doesn't know what she wants to do with her life?"

"She spent years trying to decide between going to grad school and becoming a model. She couldn't make up her mind."

"Was she a model?" Ned asked.

"No, and she never went to grad school either. She worked as a cocktail waitress and moonlighted for a caterer, which is how she met her husband, Evan. She was working a catered party he threw. After they married, she quit work. She spent the past two years renovating and redecorating Evan's home in Georgetown. Now that it's done, she's started thinking about a career."

"What brought her in for treatment?" Most people didn't come three times a week for career issues, although most people didn't have as much time or money as Ariel. "Was there a precipitating event?"

"There was a big one. Evan is twice her age. He's in his fifties, and he has a grown daughter. His first wife died when the daughter was fourteen. She's now in her thirties and, until recently, she and Evan were estranged. When Ariel married Evan, she thought she and Evan belonged to each other, that it was just the two of them, that they were each other's family."

Ned locked his hands behind his head, looking amused. "And then what happened?"

"You know how it goes—she once was lost, but now she's found. Evan's daughter came back. She and her nine-year-old daughter moved in with them."

"What had led to their estrangement?"

"Evan didn't like the man his daughter married. He didn't trust her husband, and he warned her she was making a huge mistake. He cut them off, wouldn't give them a cent. But Patricia recently left her husband. She came back singing the blues, and Evan did a one-eighty turn. He wants to buy her a place in Georgetown near his home. He's setting up trust funds and taking Patricia and his granddaughter out to meet his friends."

The family system was being turned on its head. "No wonder Ariel's in a crisis," I mused.

"She feels erased—that's how she described it. All the attention, everything she thought was hers is going to them, and she's supposed to put on a smiley face."

"She should hire a lawyer and clean him out. Start fresh with a big bank account. She won't have any trouble finding a replacement."

"Thank you, Ned." My disapproving tone only made him smile.

Marnie got us back on track. "Ariel doesn't want to leave Evan. She loves him. She wants things to go back to the way they used to be. She cries a lot and wakes up in the middle of the night, feeling like she can't breathe."

"How would you diagnose her?"

"Her symptoms started a month ago when Evan's daughter moved back, so I'd say Axis One is an adjustment disorder with mixed anxiety and depression, acute, since it's been under six months. I don't know about Axis Two yet. She could have characterological problems, but I don't know."

I nodded. "Axis Two can take a while to assess, but an adjustment disorder sounds right for now. Are you going to refer her to Jack Cassidy for a medication consult?"

"I'd like to. I thought I should check with you first."

"Go ahead and see what Jack has to say. Do you know what Ariel wants from treatment? What she's looking for?"

"She wants someone to listen who can understand why she's so upset. She feels unheard at home and completely alone. It doesn't help that she's got an attitude, which could be characterological stuff. She stomps out of rooms, slams doors, and stays in the bedroom, sulking, refusing to eat with the rest of the family."

"She sounds like a sullen teenager."

"She thinks they're all against her, and now she's

scared that Evan's losing patience—if he ever had any to begin with, which I don't know."

"I wonder if we can get him to come in."

Marnie got a panicky look. "You mean see them as a couple?"

"Yes, but not you. Ariel already feels displaced at home. She shouldn't have to share you with Evan. If he'll come for couple's work, we'll refer them to someone on permanent staff." At four full-fee sessions per week, they'd practically be funding the clinic, but it made clinical sense.

Ned dropped his hands from behind his head. "So Marnie's forming a bond with Ariel, and Ariel is being heard. What else should Marnie do to move things along?" His legs were directly in my line of sight, muscular and lean.

"I can teach her anxiety reduction techniques," Marnie said. "I learned relaxation training in my last placement. We did deep breathing and guided imagery."

"That's a wonderful idea. You could also use a cognitive behavioral approach to help Ariel challenge the distortions in her thinking. Find out what it means to her when Evan pays attention to his daughter and granddaughter. How does she interpret it?"

"She thinks she's no longer important to him. That she doesn't matter anymore. She feels replaced."

"Do you think that's accurate? Has he replaced her?"

"I don't know. But there are people who can only get close to one person at a time. On the real: someone else comes along and bam, they're in, and you're out. That's how they roll. It's happened to me."

"But is Evan like that?"

"I don't know."

"He may be insensitive to how she feels, but that doesn't mean she's unimportant to him or that she's been replaced. He could be handling the situation in a hurtful way because he's at a loss how to integrate his family. In the meantime, her behavior's driving him away, which fuels her feeling neglected. You can help her challenge the belief that she's been replaced, help her check it out."

"Check it out how?"

"She could ask him where she fits in. How he wants the family to be reconfigured. If she's slamming doors and hiding in her room, there's no way to know what it means when he ignores her. He might be fed up."

"I think he is."

"If she wants more time alone with him, like she used to have, she could tell him that directly, instead of throwing a hissy fit. Tell him she misses him."

"I don't think she's done that."

"If you can help her find ways to be civil to his family—she doesn't have to smile all the time and go overboard—and if she can ask for what she wants in a more direct way, she'll be better able to assess his commitment to her. If she's been replaced, nothing will have an impact. But he might become more attentive."

"How about role playing?" Ned was offering a helpful suggestion.

I nodded approval. "Good idea. Role playing can help Ariel clarify her own thoughts and feelings and help her articulate them to Evan. It should cut down her reactivity."

"There's one other thing I need to bring up," Marnie said. "Ariel's freaked about the murder near here. We have appointments scheduled for Mondays and Wednesdays in the morning, but we have to meet late on Thursdays. She's nervous about walking to her car in the dark. There are so many rules about therapeutic boundaries, I don't know if I'm allowed to walk with her to the parking lot when we're done."

"What time? Maybe I can escort her," Ned offered. "I just switched someone to six on Thursdays."

"You're not coming on to my patient, dude. I'm not leaving her alone with you. Anyway, our appointment is six-thirty to seven-thirty."

"I don't see any harm in you walking outside with her, Marnie," I said. "Just be clear the session's over."

"They should do something about the lighting," Ned offered. "Anyone could hide between the cars."

He was right. The parking lot was an unlit stretch of asphalt behind the building. The staff didn't leave as a group because our work hours were flexible. I nodded. "I'll bug Barney about it."

Barney did, on rare occasion, get things done. He'd managed to finagle a reserved parking space for himself close to the clinic door.

"How about giving us a quick sketch of your cases, Ned," I continued, "and we'll start with them next time."

"Okay. Tom's a thirty-two-year-old depressed white guy who personalizes everything. We're doing cognitive behavioral therapy. He carries around a little notebook to jot down negative self-thoughts and changes in mood. He's doing well. When he stops buckling his belt under his armpits, my work will be done."

"What about your other case?" I asked.

"Ashley is thirty-six. She has social anxiety disorder."

"Right, we talked about her a few weeks ago."

He nodded. "You thought she had an Axis Two diagnosis of dependent personality, but Dr. Cassidy put her on Paxil, and she became more confident, less clingy, and not nearly as cautious."

"So the problem was chemical, not characterological, but she probably hasn't developed many social skills if she spent years avoiding social contact."

"We're working on it," he agreed. "She's putting herself in situations she used to avoid, and we're role-playing how to behave."

Despite his cavalier attitude, Ned seemed to be doing good work. I glanced at the clock. "Looks like our time is up," I said. "I'll see you next week."

CHAPTER 5

Saturday morning was cold and gray, a perfect day to stay indoors in my bathrobe and watch TV. I answered the phone when I saw Carrie's name in caller ID.

"You won't believe this, Sophie." Her words were slurred. She almost sounded drunk.

"Why, what happened?"

"We were driving to the Kennedy Center last night, and a car sideswiped us. We didn't get home from the ER till two in the morning."

"Are you okay?"

"Not really. I fractured my pelvic bone. It's a minor fracture, so I don't need surgery, but it'll take eight to twelve weeks to heal. I can't walk, I'm on heavy duty pain medications, and I'll be on crutches for weeks. I won't even be able to drive."

"I'm so sorry, Carrie. Is Alan okay?"

"Yes, if you don't count the fact that he's an emotional mess because of my injury and, also, he's completely obsessed with Howard Barrow's situation—Howard and Fiona are separating, by the way. Howard's still the prime suspect in Penny's murder, only the police don't have enough evidence to arrest him. And Alan is convinced he's innocent. He thinks Penny was killed by a stranger. Can you come keep me company? Alan took Ian to a gymnastics party in Rockville, and Ella's at a friend's house." Carrie paused to take a breath. The pain killers weren't just making her woozy. Her speech was pressured. They were making her high.

"I'll be right over."

I let myself in with a spare key to their house, so Carrie didn't have to hobble to the door. Neither she nor Alan drank coffee. They kept an ancient jar of instant on hand. As a result, their guests opted for tea. I made us each a mug and added sugar and milk to mine. Coffee required no such frills. Then I set out a plate of cookies and carried them on a tray to the living room where Carrie was waiting, propped up with pillows on the couch.

"Have you talked to Jeremy?" she asked, reaching for a cookie.

"Not yet."

"*Sophie*. You have to find out what happened."

"I know." I had reached the same conclusion. Jeremy's calls were becoming less frequent, and he no longer sounded as wracked by guilt. Silence was yielding diminishing returns.

Carrie tossed me her cellphone. Mine was in my purse on the kitchen counter. "Call him, Sophie."

"What am I supposed to say?"

"Jeremy, this is your former fiancée Sophie Myerson. I'd like to know why we are no longer engaged."

I stared at the phone. "Okay, this is Sophie Myerson your former fiancée." Carrie gave me an encouraging nod. I punched in his cellphone number. "Jeremy?"

"Sophie? I thought it was Carrie. How are you doing?" His voice was soft.

"I'm okay. How are you?"

"I'm okay."

Carrie was rotating her hand, motioning me to get to the point. "Actually, Carrie is right here. I'm at her house. She was in a car accident and broke her pelvis. I'll put her on to say hello." I thrust the phone at Carrie and reached for a wad of tissues. I was weeping and didn't want to blow my nose into the phone.

"I'm giving you back to Sophie," Carrie said after filling him in on her medical condition. "She has a question she wants to ask."

Why aren't we engaged anymore was front and center in my mind, but instead I heard myself say: "Any news on Penny Harrison's murder?" I winced at Carrie.

Jeremy ignored the question. "Can we get together to talk, Sophie? I feel terrible about the way I broke things off."

My heart pounded. "Terrible about *how* you broke up with me, or terrible *that* you broke up with me?" I lowered my head to my knees and curled in a ball, awaiting his answer.

"I feel terrible about what I'm doing, Sophie. I know how hurtful it is. I honestly don't know if I'm making a mistake or not."

I straightened up. He didn't know if he was making a mistake? "If you're not sure, let's talk about it."

"That's not what I mean. I've made a decision."

"You should have talked to me before making your fucking decision, Jeremy. It affects my life too. How could you leave me out of the discussion?"

"I know, Sophie, I know."

"It was a really shitty thing to do."

"I know. I'm so sorry. I didn't think it was fair to ask you to wait while I figured things out."

"And *this* is fair? Not giving me any say at all is fair?"

"None of this is fair to you, Sophie—I know that."

My head was exploding. "Is that what you called to tell me, that life is unfair, in case I didn't already know? You proposed to me, Jeremy, then you dumped me, and now you're calling to say life is fucking unfair!"

"You called me, Sophie."

So I had. I'd lost my thread. "What about all the times you called me?"

"I owe you an explanation. Can we figure out a time to talk in person?"

Carrie was motioning to me. "Find out if he's gay."

I threw her an exasperated look. She stared back at me. Jeremy was going to think I was nuts—we'd always had a close physical relationship. "Are you gay?"

"What?"

"I asked if you were gay."

"*No.*"

"That's what I thought. Carrie wants to know. She's high on pain meds."

He laughed. "Oh, God, Sophie."

I was seized with hysterical laughter and doubled over, tears spurting from my eyes, unable to speak. I switched off the phone and dropped it on the couch. It rang again. Carrie answered. I regained control and reached for her to hand it to me.

"Alan, what's up?" She listened, nodding. "Sophie's here. I'll ask her and call you back." She hung up.

I felt calmer. "Ask me what?"

"To pick Ella up at her friend's house. Alan's freaking out because of the weather. It's supposed to get slippery this afternoon. He's hyper alert about keeping everyone safe because of the accident."

"Of course, I'll pick her up." I looked out the window. Sleet was coming down.

"He wants you to go right away. Do you mind, Sophie? He was up all night with me, so I want to do things his way."

I understood. Alan was stressed, worried, and sleep deprived. Carrie needed to keep things simple. "No problem. I'm on my way."

"Ella's in Georgetown. Her friend's name is Mallory and Mallory's mother is Tricia. I'll let her know you're coming. And I'm emailing you their address right now. Okay, done. It's in your phone."

☙❧

The roads weren't too bad, and traffic was sparse. Ella's friend lived in a large red brick Georgian house with a graceful front portico. I wiped my feet on the mat and rang the doorbell. The woman who answered appeared to be in her mid-thirties with short sandy hair. She looked perplexed to see me on her doorstep. Carrie must have forgotten to call ahead. I smiled. "I'm here to pick up Ella."

"Oh. Come in. I'll get her. I didn't realize Ella had an older sister."

That was what I meant about not looking my age. She probably thought I was a teen who'd just gotten my license. "I'm a close friend of the family. Sophie Myerson." I held out my hand.

"I'm Tricia." A timer sounded inside the house. "Shoot." She raced off, calling back over her shoulder, "Leave your boots by the door. Come to the kitchen."

What a bossy pants. I didn't want to leave my boots by the door. All she had to do was call Ella to get ready while I waited. On the other hand, she hadn't expected Ella to be picked up so early. Also, and more importantly, the house was filled with a baking aroma and the heavenly scent of coffee.

I took off my boots and followed my nose.

"I'm sorry." Tricia looked flustered. "The timer makes so much noise. I had to turn it off and take the muffins out of the oven. Do you have time for a cup of coffee? Ella said her mom was in a car accident."

"I'd love a cup."

A few minutes more or less wouldn't matter. I hadn't had any trouble on the road, and the muffins had perfectly crusted tops with pieces of walnut poking out. Tricia set them on a table built into a curved breakfast nook. The nook was in front of a bay window that faced an enclosed garden.

She handed me a plate and a napkin. "Help yourself to a muffin. What do you take in your coffee?"

I sat at the table. "Black is fine."

"How is Ella's mom doing?"

"She broke her pelvic bone. It'll be two to three months before she's driving again. That's why she sent me to get Ella."

"Let me know if I can help in any way. I mean it. Ella can come here whenever she wants, and I'm happy to pick her up from school if need be. From our point of view, she's been a godsend. We just moved here."

"I'll tell Carrie." My cellphone rang. I fished it from my handbag. At the sight of Jeremy's name, I dropped it back in my bag. I wasn't going to talk to him in Tricia's kitchen. "Where did you move from?"

"We'd been living in Cleveland, but I'm originally from DC. This is the house I grew up in. My dad's letting us live with him while I get my life together. I'm in the middle of a nasty divorce."

The muffin was outstanding. So was the coffee. "You're lucky to have your dad."

"I know, although a lot has changed since I left. I now have a twenty-eight-year-old stepmother."

Holy shit—DC was a small town. I had landed in Ariel's house.

Tricia looked at me expecting a response, but I stuffed the rest of the muffin in my mouth and pointed to my bulging cheeks to indicate that I couldn't speak. The tactic worked. By the time my mouth was empty, Ella and Mallory had burst into the room.

Ella stopped short at the sight of me. "Sophie? Are you here to pick me up?"

"Your parents are worried about the weather. They want you home before it gets too slippery."

"Can Mallory sleep over?"

Mallory shot her mom a pleading look. Tricia gave me a nod—it was okay with her. I got out my phone and called Carrie, who said yes.

Ella shrieked with delight. Mallory joined in. Tricia yelled for them to quiet down, a harsh reaction, I thought. Suddenly, an ear-shattering blast of rap music shook the house.

"Run up and pack an overnight bag," Tricia yelled above the din. The girls scampered away. She pointed to the ceiling. "Mallory's twenty-eight-year-old grandmother resents when we make any noise. That's how she retaliates. I don't know how my father can stand it. She'll blast music for hours now to drive me out of my mind or out of the house. My father's at the gym. He only comes home when he has to."

There was nothing I could say. Ariel's therapy was confidential and completely off limits. In addition, if I became Tricia's confidante, I'd be unable to supervise Marnie's work with Ariel.

"I'll tell Carrie about your offer to help." I had to shout to be heard. "She'll be very grateful."

❧❧

After dropping the girls off, I called Jeremy. "I'm sorry I hung up before."

"That's okay. I called back, and Carrie told me you'd gone to pick up Ella."

"We might as well find a time for you to explain yourself." Why fight the inevitable? I already knew he didn't want to marry me. "Are you free tonight?"

Silence.

"Jeremy? Are you there? Do you fricking exist?"

"I'm sorry, Sophie, tonight won't work. I'm out of town. How about Monday or Tuesday night?"

What did he mean he was out of town? Jeremy didn't go away weekends. "Is your mother sick?"

"No."

"Then where are you?"

He hesitated. "I'm in Philadelphia."

"What's in Philadelphia?"

"The liberty bell for one thing."

"You went to Philly to view the liberty bell?"

"No. I'm visiting a friend."

"Someone I know?"

"No."

"Someone you just met?"

"No."

I felt like I was staring up at an approaching avalanche, about to be buried alive. "A woman?"

"Yes. I thought we could talk about this—"

The snow was cascading down. "You broke up with me for a woman in Philadelphia?"

"Sophie—"

I disconnected, the breath knocked out of me. He'd sworn he'd never cheat.

He'd given his word.

享

I woke up in the middle of the night shaking with rage. I wanted to kick free of the covers and stomp Jeremy into a soupy pulp. He was seeing another woman, a woman he'd known, someone he wanted more than he wanted me.

Why had he proposed? Why did he raise the stakes so high before bailing out?

CHAPTER 6

There was no point in meeting with Jeremy. His conscience might be eased by explaining he hadn't meant to fall in love with another woman, but I wasn't up to hearing the details of his betrayal. When did he meet her? How? What was she like? The questions whirled in my mind, but I didn't want images of him with another woman lodged in my brain. Losing him and the future we planned was hard enough.

I wanted him to have never existed in my life.

Seeing patients was a relief. Work took me out of myself, but Carrie's empty office gnawed like an unmet craving. I pattered back and forth to the kitchen for coffee refills. Soon I started buying cookies to keep in my office so I could reward myself with little treats throughout the day.

Friday morning, I sat waiting for the interns. The minutes ticked by. Jeremy had apparently started a trend, now even people who were required to meet with me blew me off. Soon the mailman would stop delivering my mail. I snuck a Mallomar. The combination of chocolate crunch and marshmallow softness helped me feel better.

I had decided not to tell the interns I'd been to Ariel's home. I hadn't actually met Ariel, and I didn't want to disrupt Marnie's treatment focus with extraneous information. With Carrie unable to drive, I expected to see more of Tricia and Mallory, and I needed to keep a boundary between my personal contact with them and my professional work. The important thing, for me, was to steer clear of the conflict between Tricia and Ariel.

"Sorry we're late. Our meeting in Child Services went overtime."

The interns dropped their backpacks and sat down. Ned had gotten his hair trimmed, making the blueness of his eyes even more pronounced. My own eyes were puffy from an early morning bout of tears, and my hair filled the room. I'd stopped trying to control it. Maybe my hair had scared Jeremy off, and our relationship frizzed out instead of fizzling out.

Ned slouched in his chair, his legs stretched out in the space between us so my line of sight traveled up his body to his face. He could have been a male model.

He looked at Marnie. "Tell Sophie who walked Ariel to her car after your session last night."

"I don't see why it matters." Marnie turned to me. "Ned thinks it's a big deal that Dr. Hisselman walked with Ariel."

Ned snorted. "He's not supposed to be hitting on clinic patients. You're always riding my ass, Marnie. What about him?"

Marnie gave Ned an exasperated look. "He was *talking* to Ariel—that's all we saw. The four of us left the clinic at the same time, and Dr. Hisselman walked ahead with Ariel. There's no reason to think he was hitting on her. Ned was no closer to them than I was."

"Barney didn't leave the clinic until seven thirty?" I was surprised. He rarely stayed that late.

"I walked by his office on my way out at seven,"

Ned answered, "and he noticed my *Simpsons* lunchbox."

Ah, yes. Barney loved *The Simpsons*. He was forever quoting old episodes. He must have called Ned into his office to ask where he got the lunchbox and talk of lunch boxes would have inevitably reminded Barney of lunch, which would have led to a discussion of what they ate each day. I could only imagine how bored Ned had been. But I was getting sidetracked. "Let's start with your patients, Ned. I'll save time to hear about Ariel when you're done."

☙☙

Despite my efforts to evade Barney, he nabbed me on my way out Friday evening as I was walking to the parking lot. "Gayle wants to invite you and Jeremy to dinner to celebrate your engagement. She'll be in touch when she gets back in town."

Gayle was Barney's wife. I dodged the topic with a deft subject change. "Where did Gayle go?"

"Where she always goes, Sophie, to visit her mother in Connecticut."

We reached his car. Despite having no need to rush home with Gayle away, Barney made no move to escort me to my car as he'd done with Ariel. On the other hand, Ariel was tall, blonde, and beautiful.

I called Carrie from my car. "If Alan is working late, do you want company? I can pick up dinner."

"Alan's here, but he's busy with a brief. I'd love company. We already ate pizza with the kids. There's plenty left for you."

I zipped over. Alan greeted me with a hug and the children wanted to see me, so I spent a few minutes looking at Ella's artwork and Ian's action figures. They were four years apart, Ella nine and Ian five.

I put the leftover pizza on a plate and sat on the couch next to Carrie. "How are you feeling?"

"Better. I cut back on the pain meds. They made me hyper and groggy at the same time. Tell me what's going on at work?"

"Supervision was interesting. Ned thought Barney was hitting on one of Marnie's patients—the young and beautiful one—but Marnie saw everything Ned saw, and she disagreed. Do you think Barney would do that?"

Carrie had known Barney when his first marriage was breaking up, before I came to the clinic. "I can't imagine him crossing that line. On the other hand, he cheated on his first wife. And after they separated, he had an affair with a psychology intern."

This was news—an intern? When I started working at the clinic, Barney was already married to Gayle. He'd always seemed like an avuncular dolt who loved his wife. "Talk to me, Carrie." To be fed not just food, but gossip, boosted my spirits.

"Barney and the intern used to disappear in the middle of the day. They never left or returned together, but the more astute among us noticed significant overlap in the time they were out. But that was long ago, and Barney seems happy with Gayle. I don't think he'd risk their marriage by fooling around, and he wouldn't risk his career."

"That's what I hoped you would say. I'm relieved."

"Barney likes to schmooze. Ned is the one who sexualizes everything."

Carrie was right—Ned did sexualize everything. And, around Ned, everything felt sexual. "Barney wants to invite Jeremy and me over for dinner." I knew what Carrie was going to say. I scrunched my face in anticipation. My cowardice was embarrassing.

"You haven't told him, Sophie?"

I lowered my chin to my chest. "As soon as I tell Barney, everyone at the clinic will know Jeremy dumped me. I can't face it."

"Okay, sweetie, we need to think of a way to spin the news."

℘℘℘

Saturday morning, I was in full slug mode, wearing my bathrobe, drinking coffee, munching a chocolate chip cookie, and reading the newspaper. When Carrie called to ask if I would take Ella out for the afternoon, of course, I said yes, but I had to overcome a serious amount of inertia.

"I should warn you, Sophie, Ella's not at her most lovable at the moment."

"That's okay. Neither am I."

By the time I dried off from a shower and dressed, I had come up with an inspirational idea. The previous night I'd watched Fred Astaire and Ginger Rogers glide around a frozen pond. They made ice skating look easy and fun. I'd always wanted to try.

"I only want to go if I can bring a friend," Ella said in response to my suggestion. "No offense, but it's more fun with someone my age."

"That's fine."

Ella looked at her mother.

Carrie let out a sigh. "Okay, you can try Mallory again. But you already left one message. I don't want you being a pest." Ella disappeared with the phone. "She's having a difficult day," Carrie said. "She's been calling friends all morning. Everyone already has plans or they don't call back."

Ella leapt into the room waving the phone. "See Mommy-Dommy, I told you Mallory would want to come. There's a mean lady at her house who never tells her when I call. Mallory didn't even know I left a message. She wants to come. And so does her mom. Can we pick them both up?"

CHAPTER 7

Ariel

Finally, Ariel could breathe. Tricia and Mallory were out of the house. She blasted her music, the kind she listened to with *her* friends. Megan, Chris, and the others were being really cool about letting her hang out again after the way she blew them off when she got married. But what was she supposed to do—mixing them with Evan didn't compute. Evan thought they were worthless dopers, even though they were no different from the way she'd been when she was single. Marrying Evan put her in a different category. He'd wanted to lift her out of her life. All the crap he fed her, how much she meant to him, that she was all the family he needed—he had actually said *'You're all the family I need.'* What a big, fat lie.

She missed having fun with her old group. What was so bad about smoking up and listening to music? They used to laugh till their sides ached, even if they could never remember what they'd been laughing at. She was young. She was supposed to have fun, not be cooped up in her room because some stuffy relatives had taken over the house, her house—hers as much as Evan's. He put her name on the title. He needed to watch how far he pushed her. If she wanted to hang out at Megan's and see the old gang, she would. There was nothing wrong with partying with people her own age.

You got to give it, give it, give it up, girl. She shimmied up and down, shaking her ass. She'd done what Marnie suggested. She told Evan she missed him and she felt left out of his life, and he promised to spend Saturday afternoon with her, just the two of them. They could actually be alone in their home together. Evan had to be getting horny—they hadn't made love in ages.

She heard him come in and raced downstairs. "Quick, Evan, follow me." She grabbed his gym bag out of his hand and started back up the stairs.

He ran after her. "Why? Where are the others?"

"They're out for the day—hurry."

He caught up with her in the bedroom. His face was tight with worry. "What's wrong? What happened?"

"Take off your clothes and see if you can figure it out." She smiled as she pulled off her top. She hadn't been wearing a bra.

His face relaxed.

"See? You're a pretty smart guy."

❧❧❧

Ariel couldn't believe what she was hearing. After a wonderful afternoon in bed together, just when she finally felt close to Evan again, he sprang the news—he was putting Tricia in charge of their charitable foundation.

"I should be heading the foundation, Evan, not Tricia. I'm your *wife*."

"Yes, you're my beautiful, sexy wife, and I love you, Ariel. But the foundation was Tricia's idea."

She stuck out her lower lip. "The money is half mine and half yours, not Tricia's. Why should she be in charge? It's not fair."

"As a matter of fact, I'm funding the foundation with money to which you have no claim, Ariel. These monies—" He was using his lecture voice. "—bladdy, bladdy, blah…"

She wanted to scream in his face. He was still blabbing on. "I'd planned on calling it the Lancet Family Foundation, but if you persist in fighting me, I'll call it the Evan Lancet Foundation."

Tricia ruined everything. "But I want you to use *our* money. I'm all about giving money to good causes—you know that. Why does Tricia get to hand out the money? *I* want to do it."

"Tricia needs to earn a living, you don't. The position is salaried."

"I don't care. That's not the point."

"Do you want me supporting her forever?"

"*No.* I want her out of the house and living on her own."

"Then be reasonable."

"I *am* being reasonable. Let her find a job. You don't have to employ her in addition to buying her a house, giving her a trust fund, and paying for Mallory's private school. Christ almighty—isn't that enough?"

"Tricia majored in business. She'll do a good job."

"Hooray for her. I don't give a flying fuck. We can hire people to deal with the technical stuff. The job is perfect for me. You know it is, Evan, you *know* it." She kissed his shoulder with pouty lips and nibbled his skin. Just when everything was going right again, he had to ruin it. "I could visit charities and help decide which ones to fund. We could present the money together."

"There's more to it than cutting checks."

Tears stung her eyes. "I'm not a stupid bimbo. Why did you marry me if that's what you think?"

"That's not what I think. Come on, Arie, you're acting like a child."

"Because I know exactly what's going to happen. You'll be talking to Tricia about funding this and funding that, and I'll be left out. I thought you wanted to share your life with *me*?"

"Yes, and I want you to share my life, Ariel, but not by fighting me on this. Tricia came up with the idea. This is her baby, not mine, and the foundation gives me national name recognition, tax benefits, something meaningful to hand down to Mallory. It gives my daughter a paying job, and I damn well want her in charge of it."

"Stop yelling. I get all that! I'm not stupid." Ariel reached for the ringing phone. She wasn't going to let Evan interrupt their discussion with one of his endless calls. "Hello."

"Hi. Ariel? It's Tricia."

"What do you want?"

"I wanted to let you know Mallory and I will be out late."

"Good. And I want you to know the foundation is not a done deal." She slammed down the phone.

"How dare you? Call back and apologize." Evan handed Ariel the phone.

She slammed it down again. "How dare *you* dream up these things behind my back? Do you ever stop and think how it makes me feel?"

Evan threw off the covers. "I didn't do anything behind your back." He sat on the side of the bed and pulled on his boxer shorts. "What was Tricia calling about?"

"She and Mallory are staying out late." Which meant she and Evan had the house to themselves for the evening. They could make up. Her mood lifted. She stroked his back. "Let's stay in tonight, please, Evan. Cancel the dinner with your stupid business buddy." She remembered what Marnie said about asking directly for what she needed. "I need more time alone with you."

His face softened. He reached out his hand. "I can't, Arie. He's flying back to Denver tomorrow."

"Why do you have to conduct business on a Saturday night? Can't you fly out to Denver on Monday? Or talk to him on the fucking phone? *Please*. We could order in Indian food and watch videos. We'll have fun." She pulled him down on top of her. "I wouldn't need to be in charge of your stupid foundation if you made time for me."

CHAPTER 8

Sophie

I skidded along near the outer rim of the skating rink so I could ram the wall if I needed to stop. Tricia had taken the girls into the center to teach them to skate backward. When the session ended, I wobbled to the nearest bench and waved the others over. The girls were rosy cheeked. Tricia looked radiant. I unlaced my skates and massaged my ankles.

"I used to skate all the time when I was young," Tricia said. "My mother took me for lessons early in the morning before school, but I had to stop when she got sick. I'm so glad you suggested it."

"I don't want to go back to Grandpa's house. Can we go out for dinner?" Mallory asked.

Ella turned to me. "Can we? Please? My parents won't care. Mommy has to rest all the time, and Ian keeps Daddy busy."

"And then can we go to a movie?" Mallory added. The girls clasped hopeful hands. Tricia handed Mallory a ten-dollar bill.

"Take Ella with you. You can get hot chocolate at

the refreshment stand. I need to talk to Sophie."

"Dinner and a movie sound good to me. I have no plans." I called Carrie, who gave permission for Ella to stay out.

Tricia took out her phone. "I should let my dad know. Ariel, hi, it's Tricia. I wanted to let you know Mallory and I will be out late." Her face tightened. She threw her phone back in her purse. "How my dad puts up with her is beyond me."

We went to a Mexican restaurant in Bethesda, early enough to beat the crowds. Tricia looked tense. When she wasn't chewing chips or fajitas, she was chewing on her lip. The girls carried the conversation. Fourth grade was a tangle of social activity. Ella and Mallory ranked all the girls in their grade—who they liked most, who they liked least and who was most popular. Then they started on the boys.

The movie we saw afterward was okay, nothing I'd recommend. I dropped Ella off at her home and then headed to Tricia's father's house in Georgetown. Mallory fell asleep in the back seat.

"Ice skating brought back memories of my mother," Tricia said. "If she hadn't died when I was young, I never would have married Brad. My life would have been so different. My mom helped me think clearly. She knew how to soothe me and help me calm down when I was upset. Dad was always too intense." Tricia glanced over her shoulder. Mallory was still sleeping. "Brad's attitude was: fuck the world. Here I'd spent my entire life worrying about my father's reaction to everything I did, funneling all my decisions through his eyes, and Brad didn't give a shit what anyone thought, least of all my father. It was so liberating. That's why I fell in love with him. Can you imagine a worse reason?"

I pulled up in front of their house. A porch light was

on, but the house was dark inside. "We might actually make our way upstairs and into bed without being glared at. Wouldn't that be nice?" She shook Mallory's shoulder. "Wake up, sweetie. We're at Grandpa's house. Thanks, Sophie. Let's do this again."

Ariel

Ariel loved the soft plush carpet beneath her feet as she padded around in her closet. Dressing up was fun. Too bad going out was such a bore. She hated making conversation with people she barely knew. The men ogled her, and the women ignored her. She never should have agreed to go with Evan tonight. If she wasn't such a wimp, she'd call Chris, score some weed, smoke up, and goof on the dinner. But Evan would hit the roof. He'd kill her.

Of course, they had reservations at a fancy restaurant. They never left home without them. The new hostess didn't recognize Evan. He had to point out his name—Lancet, table for four. The restaurant was filled with middle-aged cheek-peckers. Ugh. Evan's guests were already sousing it up at the bar. They carried their drinks to the table.

"An apple martini, thanks," Ariel told the waiter, ignoring the frowning tilt of Evan's eyebrows.

Phooey on him. The others were drinking, why shouldn't she? If she couldn't get high one way, she'd get high another. He was lucky she had no tolerance for alcohol. She was a cheap date. She'd only have one or two martinis, instead of three or four. Martini glasses were so cool. She loved holding the stem between her long fingers and raising the glass to her lips, watching the diamond sparkle on her finger.

The Denver business magnate was the biggest fucking bore in the universe. He had a blubbery face that hovered above the table like a big pink balloon. All she needed was a pin and whoosh—hot air would gush out, and he'd deflate into a lump of rubber. She doubted his wife would object, not with her medicated smile. She looked as glazed as a politician's wife sitting through one campaign stop too many.

Ariel ordered a second martini. Evan was listening to Balloon-Man go on about financing and debt risk, blah-blah-blah. The waiter came again to try to take their orders, but they waved him away, not ready. None of them had ever spent time waiting on tables. That was clear. Hold the phone—what was happening? She could barely believe her ears. They were actually ready to discuss hors d'oeuvres and wine, not make up their minds—no such luck for the waiter—but discuss. At the pace they were going, they'd be ordering dessert in the early hours of Sunday morning. She had bought her car in less time.

"I'm going to the lady's room," she whispered to Evan.

Standing up was harder than she expected. The martinis were strong. The place was packed, the tables closer together than they appeared. She swayed as she walked and almost landed in an old man's lap. He pushed her up with a steadying hand on her ass. She glanced around. Evan wasn't watching. Thank God, he hadn't seen. Good Christ, she needed to pee. If she didn't find the lady's room soon—there was the door. Relief was on the way.

She sighed at the joys of empty bladder-hood. But she didn't want to go back to the table. She took out her cellphone. Now that she was in touch with her old friends, she wanted to know what they were doing. Five of them lived in a rental house together. They knew how to have fun, and they ate when they were hungry instead of spending the entire fucking night deciding what to eat. "You're not going to believe this," she said to Megan. "I'm wasted on martinis hiding out in the bathroom of a restaurant too fucking cool to list their prices on the menu."

"Wait. I'm putting you on speakerphone. We're all here: Chris, John, the gang."

Ariel giggled. She felt like a spy calling headquarters, reporting in from outer space. "Hi, everyone."

"Hi, Ariel," they chorused back, like classroom kids greeting a teacher, giggling.

"God, I wish I could beam myself over there. What are you guys doing? I'm eating dinner with a balloon-man."

"No shit? You've got a man at your table hawking balloons?"

The idea made her laugh, the thought of Evan eating dinner with an actual balloon man. "No. He's not selling them. His head is shaped like one. It floats above the table."

"What a great idea for a sci-fi film, balloon men hovering in the air keeping an eye on everyone."

"You should do it," Megan said. She was talking to John. He'd been working on a movie script for years now.

Two older women came into the restroom eyeing Ariel as they entered the stalls. They might know Evan. Everyone knew Evan. "I better go," she whispered into the phone. "See you."

Evan held her arm when she returned to the table and slid in beside him. "What took you so long?"

"I felt queasy." She hated them all staring at her like she'd done something wrong. Fuck it. She made a sickly face. "Actually, I'm still not feeling well," she told the guests. "Would you excuse me? We live nearby. I can get myself home. I need to lie down." She pushed back from the table and started to walk away.

Evan followed after her, grabbing her arm. At the front of the restaurant, he retrieved their coats. "I'm walking you home, but I need to go tell them first. Wait for me," he warned.

"I'll be outside." She craved fresh air. God, it felt good to be out where she could breathe. The sidewalk was clogged with foot traffic, Georgetown bustle on a Saturday night. She wandered to the shoe store next door and stared at the shiny red thigh-high boots on display.

Evan took her arm. "You had too much to drink."

"No more than Balloon-Man."

"You're not making sense. You can't handle alcohol."

"Don't be such a stuffy old wet broomstick. I had to do *something*, for Christ's sake. I couldn't just sit there."

"Yes, you could just sit there, dammit." She hated when his lips got thin. He hissed his words at her. "You agreed to come as a favor to me, remember? I expected you to behave yourself."

"Yes, Daddy."

"You know what, Ariel? That's not funny. If I sound like your daddy, it's because you're acting like a bratty child. This dinner is important and not just to me, it's important to us. Wally has one-point-five-billion dollars at his command. That's one-point-five *billion*."

"Okay, I get the picture. Now, will you let go of my arm?"

He released his grip. "I don't ask a lot of you. You don't work. You do whatever the hell you want. But once in a great while, I need you to sit through a boring meal and behave like a grown-up. That's not too much to ask. I expect you to do it, damn you."

"Okay. I'm sorry. You want me to go back?"

"No. That'll only make things worse. I'll tell him you're sick, like you said. Otherwise, he'll think I dragged you back under protest. Wally's touchy. If he thinks he's being disrespected, he'll cut me off. You may have cost me the biggest deal of my life."

They were in front of their house. Evan had won, as always. She felt horrible. She couldn't do anything right. Everything she did ended up hurting him in some way. He was always trying to guilt trip her. And now he would use this as further proof why Tricia should be in charge of the foundation, which was totally unfair. One thing had nothing to do with the other.

She jutted out her chin. "It's not my fault I don't feel well."

He brought his face close to hers. "Cut the crap, Ariel. I'm sick to death of your bullshit."

She swallowed. She'd pushed him too hard. She should have kept her stupid mouth shut.

CHAPTER 10

Sophie

I woke up Sunday morning with sore leg muscles. Stretching seemed in order if I didn't want to hobble around all day, so I turned on the TV news to have a distraction while I bent one knee and stretched my other leg behind me.

The anchorman's announcement toppled me to the floor: "The lifeless body of DC builder Evan Lancet's wife was discovered outside her Georgetown home this morning."

I stared up at the screen. A camera panned the front yard of the Lancet house.

An on-the-scene reporter filled in some details: "Ariel Lancet's body was discovered by family members this morning in the backyard of her home. According to the police, she was killed sometime last night, and foul play is suspected. This is the second murder of a young woman in less than three weeks to take place in what are thought of as safe neighborhoods in Northwest DC."

Foul play.

Murder.

First Penny, now Ariel. Two young women killed nearby, both in my sphere of contact. Instinctively, I reached for the phone to call Jeremy, but he was out of the question. I tried Carrie instead. Alan answered and said she'd been too active the previous day and was knocked out. I needed to tell Marnie about Ariel, but my job was to help Marnie deal with patient crises, not call her when I was in a panic. I needed to calm down first. I tried Steve and got voice mail.

What to do? Craving something soft, green, and nutty, I opened the freezer and took out a carton of pistachio ice cream. Ten seconds in the microwave made it pliant. I dug in with a spoon and thought about calling my parents, but their protective instincts were overly developed. They would want me to move back into my childhood room where they could keep me safe. Other local friends were out of the question. I couldn't let them know I knew anything about Ariel other than what was being reported on TV. The fact of her being a patient at the clinic was confidential, which was another reason not to call Jeremy, although being in the DA's office, he'd find out soon enough.

By the time my spoon scraped the bottom of the ice cream container, the creamy sweetness and tasty bits of nuts had soothed me enough to think clearly. I had spent Saturday evening with Tricia. The police might want to talk to me. I found Reginald White's card and called. He answered. "Detective White."

"This is Sophie Myerson. I found Penny Harrison's body with Jeremy."

"I remember you."

"I saw on the news that Ariel Lancet was murdered. I was with Evan Lancet's daughter and granddaughter yesterday. I dropped them back at their house last night a little after ten."

"You're telling me you knew both victims?"

"Not really, I only saw Penny Harrison one time at a party last summer, and I never met Ariel Lancet, but I thought if you were checking out where the family members were last night…" I wasn't sure how to finish the sentence. I was beginning to feel foolish for having called.

"Where were they?"

"Tricia, Mallory, and I went ice skating in the afternoon and then had dinner and saw a movie in Bethesda."

"And you know Tricia Lancet how?"

I explained the Carrie/Ella/Mallory connection. I couldn't tell him Ariel Lancet was a patient at our clinic. That was confidential. He would find out, but not from me.

"When you dropped them off, were lights on in the Lancet house?"

"The porch light was on. The house looked dark inside. Tricia was relieved she wouldn't have to interact with Ariel."

"She said that?"

I could tell him what I'd learned from Tricia, but not disclose what Marnie told me in supervision. "Yes, she said words to that effect. Tricia thought Ariel resented her and her daughter moving in. She said Ariel found ways to retaliate against them, like blasting loud music when they made too much noise in the house. Tricia tried to stay out of Ariel's way. She was hoping to avoid seeing her last night. I'm sure she'll fill you in."

"Can you think of any way the two victims might have known each other?"

"No. I have no idea how either of them spent their free time."

"Okay. Well, look, thanks for calling and if anything comes up—let me know."

✐✐

Barney was in full crisis mode at the clinic Monday morning, barking orders like Patton in North Africa, demanding a supply of bakery goods be brought in immediately, and assigning a social work student to the task.

Then he instructed Delores to have fresh coffee available throughout the day, decaf and regular, and keep an urn filled with hot water for hot chocolate and tea. After issuing his demands, he summoned me to his office. I grabbed a cup of coffee on the way. He motioned for me to sit.

"What an awful thing, Sophie. We might have detectives stopping by. It hurts to think of such a beautiful woman dying so young." Barney caught my reaction. "Oh, for crying out loud, stop with the hairy eyeball. Losing *any* young woman is tragic, okay, Sophie? I know that."

I appreciated the correction. Ariel's beauty was not the issue. "I'm waiting for you to open the bakery box, Barney."

He had siphoned off one box for his personal use. My shift in topic dispelled the tension. Having a sweet tooth inspired Barney's trust. If I had written on my resume *I love chocolate chip cookies* when I applied for the job, I would have been hired without having to come in for an interview.

Barney felt around in his pants pockets and came up empty handed. He rummaged in his desk drawer. "Here, use your nails, Sophie. I can't find my pocketknife." He gave me the bakery box. I untied the string and helped myself to a black and white cookie. Barney sampled a petit four before speaking. "I called Evan Lancet to offer condolences and let him know we're available to him and his family. You and Marnie can handle whatever comes up. He'll call if he wants an appointment."

"There's a problem, Barney." Supervising Marnie's work with Ariel, whom I'd never met, was okay, but I couldn't work with Tricia's family when I knew her personally. Having a dual relationship with a patient went against ethical standards. "Evan's granddaughter and Carrie's daughter, Ella, are best friends. Ever since Carrie's accident, I've been driving Ella places, and I've hung out with Evan's granddaughter and his daughter, Tricia."

"Oh, boy, so you know the family. I didn't know that." Barney polished off the petit fours and picked up a chocolate leaf. He dunked the tip in his coffee. "Go ahead and assign Marnie a new patient off the waiting list. From here on in, I'll handle everything relating to the Lancet family."

"When you talked to Evan Lancet on the phone, did he say anything about Ariel's death?"

"He told me how they found her. His daughter was eating breakfast Sunday morning, and, when she looked out the kitchen window, she saw Ariel sitting on a bench in the garden." I knew the bench he meant. The garden was visible from the breakfast nook.

"What was Ariel doing out there?"

Barney gave me a withering look. "What she was doing out there was being dead, Sophie."

"I know she was dead, Barney." The newspaper account Monday morning headlined the fact that she'd been strangled with her own scarf just like Penny Harrison. I got a sick feeling in my stomach every time I thought about young women being targeted. "I meant, *why* was she in the garden on a bitterly cold night?"

Barney shrugged. "Your guess is as good as mine."

"Do you know when she died?"

"Some time Saturday night."

"The newspaper said she went to a restaurant with Evan and friends and left early because she felt ill. He walked her home but didn't go inside with her. She could have been out there all night. Assuming that she and Evan shared a bedroom, didn't he notice she wasn't in bed?"

"You're the one who supervises Marnie, Sophie, not me. What does she say about their marriage?"

"They were having problems. Ariel felt displaced by Evan's daughter and granddaughter. I have no idea what their evenings were like."

"What's your take on the daughter?"

"I like Tricia. She seems like a good mother. She and Ariel were at odds, but I can't imagine her hurting her physically. You'd think Evan would have noticed Ariel wasn't in bed with him."

"She could have gone to bed with him and then snuck out after he was asleep—ever think of that, Sophie? You would if you'd raised teenagers."

He had a point.

I returned to my office. The thought of a serial killer hunting for prey in two neighborhoods where I spent time was terrifying. I needed Jeremy. He'd always made me feel safe. My fear was strong enough to overcome my hurt. I picked up the phone and called. "It's me. What do you know about Ariel Lancet's murder?"

"Sophie." He sounded sad saying my name. "I don't know a whole lot. She was found in her backyard, been out there all night, strangled. Why?"

"I know Evan Lancet's daughter. She's the mother of one of Ella's friends. I've been at their house."

"The police are taking a hard look at the family, but the murder could be related to the killing near your clinic. You need to be extra careful when you're out."

"Thank you, Jeremy. I'll write that down so I don't

forget." I loved advice with no practical application. Was I supposed to run a zig-zag pattern every time I went to my car? I had already stopped wearing a scarf—that seemed more to the point. But even so, I felt better talking to Jeremy. He had broken my heart, but, in some ways, he was still the person I felt closest to.

"Can we talk about what happened with us, Sophie?"

I hesitated. I wanted to, and I didn't want to. "I'll let you know. I have a lot on my mind."

A serial killer on the loose was just what we needed in DC. I drove home from work in a state of heightened anxiety. I was on alert as I pulled into the underground garage attached to my building, but if someone snuck in behind me before the garage door closed, there'd be no way for me to stop him—I couldn't make the door go down any more quickly. Still, I watched through my rearview mirror to be sure no one scampered in on foot. Returning to the garage alone at night had always made me feel vulnerable and was one of the things I'd looked forward to leaving behind when Jeremy and I moved into a house together. Now there would be no house with Jeremy. All he had to give me was advice.

∽∾∾

The next day, I offered Marnie and Ned an extra meeting to talk about Ariel's death. "How are you doing?" I asked Marnie.

She looked as if she'd been crying. "Okay, I guess." She examined her nails as she spoke.

"Have you had contact with the family?"

"I sent Evan a condolence card, that's all. I'm having trouble believing Ariel's gone." She met my eyes. "I want to tell her to hang in there. In my mind, I'm telling her everything will be okay, things will work out. I know how cracked that is. Nothing worked out for her, nothing. Things can't be okay, not ever, not for her. But I keep playing these crazy scenes in my mind."

"Your instinct is to offer comfort. That's a good instinct, Marnie."

"I feel like I let her down. I didn't protect her."

"There was nothing you could do."

She shook her head. "Things like this go down all the time in my neighborhood. They're not supposed to happen to white chicks living in Georgetown."

Ned stepped in: "I met someone who saw Ariel at a party in Silver Spring a few weeks ago. She was hanging with a druggie crowd, getting high with everyone else."

Marnie frowned. "Why didn't you tell me?"

"That's what I'm doing—I am telling you. I only ran into him yesterday evening. We were talking about the murder, and he said he'd seen her, the victim, at a party that one time."

Marnie softened. "So, what'd he say about her?"

"She was smoking up, not hooking up. She didn't go off with anyone."

"So, Evan wasn't with her," I said.

Ned had a hint of a smile. "Not his crowd."

"How'd she know them?" Marnie asked.

"Look, I only know what this random guy told me. He said she used to hang with them back when she was single."

"She talked about a group of friends she got back in touch with after Evan's daughter moved in. She wanted someplace she could be herself." Marnie's tone was sorrowful.

Ned shrugged. "This dude said her friends think Evan whacked her. She was slipping out of his control—that's the theory."

Marnie's face went rigid. "I didn't sense a threat."

No, and I hadn't asked. Abuse hadn't seemed part of the picture. But if anyone was negligent, I was at fault, not Marnie. "Did Ariel ever say anything about being injured or threatened?"

"No, and I didn't see any injuries. No dark glasses. She never looked like she was covering anything up, although I could only see her hands and face. From what she said, I got the impression Evan was pretty controlled. He didn't even yell a lot. To me, Ariel felt neglected, like she was being replaced, not threatened physically in any way. There was nothing about any beatings."

"Was he restricting her life by cutting off outside relationships?" I should have asked the question before she was killed.

Marnie looked troubled. "He didn't approve of her friends."

"Did he object to her being in therapy?"

"No, he encouraged it."

"That's good. But the friend thing. Did she have any friends outside the marriage?"

"Other than her old friends? I'm not sure. But he didn't keep her confined to the house or anything like that."

"Did she say anything to indicate fear of her husband?" Had I missed something that put her at risk?

"No, nothing, she worshipped the man. His daughter Tricia was the one she resented. But she never sounded afraid of her. She just couldn't wait for her to leave."

"She may have been murdered by a serial killer," I offered, thinking about what Jeremy said.

"But this was in her backyard," Ned argued, "not some random street attack. Maybe Evan copycatted the other murder."

"I can't go there," Marnie said. "That's for the cops. Main thing for me—she's gone." She looked back down at her nails. "I didn't protect her. That's what I have to live with."

∾∾∾

"Sophie, come in, close the door." Barney's tone was urgent.

I prayed no one else had died. "What is it, Barney?"

He tilted back in his chair and rested his hands on his stomach. His posture was too relaxed for an emergency. Code red eased into yellow. "I had an interesting session with Evan Lancet. He and I will be meeting weekly for the time being. I'm diagnosing him as an adjustment disorder with depressive symptoms caused by the sudden loss of his wife, although, it's not clear-cut."

"Okay?" I had no idea where he was going with this.

"Anything I say about him is within HIPPA guidelines for clinic staff. I don't need to tell you it's confidential. Nothing can go outside of here, not to the police or anyone else."

The Health Insurance Portability and Accountability Act safeguarded release of patient information, but allowed considerable leeway within treatment agencies.

"Sophie, I'm telling you, Evan is wracked with guilt."

There was no new emergency—Barney wanted a hush-hush schmooze. The clinic was turning into a giant Clue board: Colonel Mustard in the ballroom with a candlestick or Evan Lancet in the garden with a scarf.

"You think he killed her?"

Barney opened his hands and shrugged. "Who knows? Evan says he left her in front of their house Saturday night and returned to dinner with a business contact and his wife, but Sophie, if you were out with Jeremy and you didn't feel well, would he drop you off at home and return to the restaurant?"

"No." I was going to have to fill Barney in on our break-up, soon.

"There's something strange going on. Evan kept saying he should have stayed with Ariel and seen her inside—but then, why didn't he? What man leaves a sick wife standing in the cold and goes back to a restaurant? Gayle would kill me. Okay, they'd been arguing. He was ticked off. Believe me, I've been there. And he was anxious to get back. He had a big business deal in the offing."

"What did he say about when he got home later?"

"The house was quiet. He thought his daughter and grandchild were in their rooms, asleep. Their doors were closed. The lights were all out. He went to his bedroom, and his wife wasn't there. So, what does he do?" Barney eyed me, waiting.

I hated rhetorical questions. "How the fricking hell do I know? You're the one he talked to, Barney."

"He goes to bed, Sophie. He goes to bed."

"He wasn't worried about her?"

"Pissed off, not worried. He figured she'd gone to stay with friends, friends she knew he couldn't stand. He thought she went there to spite him, so what does he do?"

"Spit it out for me, Barney."

"He goes to sleep."

"She must have had a cellphone. He didn't try to call?"

Barney wagged a finger at me. "He did, but she didn't answer. She didn't answer because she was dead, but he thought she'd turned her phone off for the night."

"Why is he so wracked with guilt?"

"That's the question. He said he felt terrible about leaving her alone. If he'd gone inside with her, she'd still be alive, but I don't know, Sophie. I get a weird vibe." Barney's phone rang. "Gayle," he mouthed her name to me before answering. "Honeybunch, I'm on my way." He stood up and reached for his coat.

My eyelid twitched. I needed to tell him the engagement was off. "By the way, Jeremy and I are putting things on hold for a while." That was the phrasing Carrie and I agreed on. I let out a nervous laugh. "I guess we won't be coming to dinner together anytime soon."

He looked at me. "Sophie, what happened? Did Jeremy get cold feet?"

I made my way to the door. "We decided to take a break, you know, back off from seeing each other for a while."

"You're talking to me, Barney. What really happened?"

Why couldn't I work with tech nerds or engineers? Barney was the tip of the iceberg. Therapists were overly interested in people's personal lives. My colleagues were going to assume Jeremy rejected me, and they'd feel compelled to dissect why, which meant speculating about what there was about me that made him flee the altar. That, in turn, would lead to in-depth discussions of my least desirable traits. Our sex life would be imagined and analyzed. It wasn't as if I never did those things with other people's lives—I always did. I understood the instinct.

What really happened is none of your fricking business, Barney was on the tip of my tongue, but saying it out loud wasn't a good career move. "Some other time, Barney, okay? I'm tired, and I have paperwork to do before I can go home." I didn't look forward to the word being spread, but I was relieved Barney knew. I could scratch that off my list of icky things to attend to.

I'd become less efficient since Jeremy's defection and didn't finish my paperwork until seven. A blast of cold air smacked me in the face as I walked out the clinic door. The night was moonless, the parking lot dark. I took out my car clicker. The few cars that remained in the lot were indistinguishable shapes in the dark.

Heavy steps sounded behind me. I glanced over my shoulder and saw a large figure in a bulky hooded coat. I couldn't remember where I'd parked that morning and clicked frantically until I heard a reassuring beep and car lights blinked back at me. I ran to my car, got in, and locked the doors. The hooded figure headed away. I was safe. Had I even been in danger? I couldn't tell. A car lit up as the owner got in. Marnie lowered her hood.

My nerves were getting the better of me.

CHAPTER 11

The Adult Service staff meetings took place on Friday afternoons. Our staff members included three psychologists, Carrie, who was still out on sick leave; Steve; and me. We had two psychology interns, Ned and Marnie; two psychiatrists, Jack Cassidy and a female psychiatrist. We also had two psychiatric residents; three social workers and three social work trainees; Delores, who was Barney's administrative assistant; and our fearless leader himself, Dr. Barnard Hisselman, at the helm.

I skidded into a seat next to Steve. I hadn't seen him all day.

"You look like shit," he whispered as Barney began to speak.

"I only got three hours of sleep last night," I whispered back.

Among other things making my brain whir in the middle of the night, my birthday was coming up. I was turning thirty on Sunday. The thought of celebrating depressed me.

Barney peered over his half glasses and addressed the assemblage. "Before we assign new intakes, I want to say a few words about the recent death of a patient. You're all aware that the young woman who was murdered outside her home Saturday night was on our rolls. Marnie Washington was working with her. In the aftermath of his wife's death, I've been treating Evan Lancet."

His chest puffed out like a mating bird on display minus the feathers. Steve poked me in the ribs. I poked him back, wishing Carrie were on my other side for a double poke.

Barney kept the three of us endlessly amused. "If any of you have information about Ariel Lancet that you've not yet told the police, I urge you to do so. You can come to me after the meeting, and I'll give you the detective's number."

The announcement was bogus, a star turn for Barney. Everyone who'd had contact with Ariel had long since been interviewed.

"Is anything being done about lighting the parking lot?" Ned asked.

"Good question," someone called out.

I nodded in agreement. I'd been scared out of my wits Thursday evening. I stole a glance at Marnie to reassure myself that Marnie was really Marnie and not a predator stalking the night.

"We're looking into it," Barney said. "A number of you have expressed concern. I asked Delores to send a memo to the director of the center. Now, is there any other business before we assign intakes?"

Delores flashed me a smile. I smiled back. We were buddies. But, suddenly, I realized her smile signified more than a simple *hello there*.

"I have an announcement," she said. "In honor of Sophie's very special birthday, we're having cake and coffee in the reception area at the end of the day. Everyone is invited."

❧

I gorged on cake and swilled it down with too much coffee. If alcohol had been served, I would have passed out on Delores's desk, snoring with my mouth open. I was trying to numb myself until I could flee home. As it was, I drove home with my stomach in an uproar, replaying the event over and over in my mind. I had announced my un-engagement to everyone who asked what Jeremy and I had planned for my birthday.

"So you're back on the market," Jack Cassidy had said, trying to sound upbeat about my change in status. He meant well.

Then Ned had come over, and Jack disappeared. Ned's voice still reverberated in my head, rippling through me like an arousing caress, which wasn't good. Not good at all.

"You're really thirty?" he had asked.

"I will be on Sunday. How old are you?" I was curious.

"Twenty-six."

"Oh, you're still a baby," I said it jokingly, laughing.

He had leaned close and whispered in my ear, "Not *such* a baby."

❧

I parked in the garage. No one had followed me in or appeared to be lurking. I rode the elevator up to my floor, skipping the lobby. My mail could wait. I was relieved to be home where I could get out of my clothes and into a hot bath then zone out on movies. That was my plan. Relax. Unwind. And get a grip on myself. Ned's words shimmered through me like an electric current. At least I'd had the presence of mind to stuff another piece of cake in my mouth and motion for Steve to join us. But cake and Steve weren't always going to be at hand.

I shed my coat and took off my shoes. In addition to being my supervisee and completely out of the question, Ned was a sexually provocative cad. My vulnerable state made me susceptible. I blamed Jeremy for putting me at risk of making a fool out of myself. Our standoff had gone on long enough. I wanted answers. Why he left. How he'd fallen in love with another woman. I speed dialed his number. "Are you going to Philly again this weekend?" I didn't bother to identify myself. He knew who it was.

"Yes, I'm on my way, on the train."

"What time are you getting back Sunday?"

"Not until eight. Do you want to talk then?"

"Yes, I want to talk then and could you please acknowledge that Sunday is my fricking birthday!" I wanted to rip my hair out and stuff it down his throat.

"I know it's your birthday, Sophie." His voice was so low I could barely hear him.

"How old am I going to be?"

"Thirty—fricking years."

I almost laughed, but tears spurted out instead. "I'll see you Sunday. And just so you know, I might not be sober."

Steve was taking me to a late lunch at a place he said, served wonderful white Russians.

"Sophie, you don't drink."

"That's right, Jeremy, and you don't cheat."

✑✑

I actually slept through the night and on into Saturday, ten hours of blissful sleep thanks to Jack Cassidy giving me a prescription for Ambien. One pill and my mind began swaying back and forth. The next thing I knew, it was daylight.

Carrie had arranged a birthday lunch for the two of us at her house. Alan picked up deli sandwiches, pickles, and coleslaw and set them out in the conservatory, her favorite room, so we could eat among the potted plants while looking out at the yard. Ian gave me a scribbled picture and Ella gave me a friendship bracelet she made. I thanked them both, touched by the gifts. Then Alan took the children out, and Carrie and I dug in.

A twinge of pain registered on her face. She looked worn.

"How are you doing?" I asked.

"My life is so boring these days I can barely stay awake to live it, let alone discuss it. I'll feel peppier after I start physical therapy. You talk."

"I'll tell you what I've been wondering about. Since we now know Jeremy has a Miss Philadelphia in his life, why couldn't he also have a Miss DC? What about Penny Harrison? They were chatting up a storm at the fundraiser you and Alan had until I came along. What if Jeremy was seeing Penny on the side?"

Carrie raised a dubious brow.

"Look, he had me completely fooled, and I'm not particularly gullible. That makes him an accomplished liar. He could have had a dozen women—how would I know? Maybe Penny was one. Maybe Miss Philadelphia doesn't even exist. When did Jeremy go to Philly? We spent every weekend together."

"Okay, Sophie, I'm confused. What are you saying?"

Actually, I had no idea what I was saying. I was confusing myself. It was the fact of Jeremy's betrayal—I no longer knew if *anything* he told me was true. "He could have made up the woman in Philadelphia to keep me from finding out who he's really seeing."

"Why would he do that? Once he's confessed to seeing someone, what's the difference where she lives?"

"The difference is I'll ferret out her identity if she lives around here. He knows I'm a snoop." I could feel the organizing energy of a mission taking form, a totally neurotic mission, but a mission nonetheless.

"So, you want to figure out who he's seeing?"

"It would be so much easier if we were still together. Then I could rifle through his things and log onto his computer." I felt a surge of resentment. I'd never even had the chance to root out his lies. Never had the righteous release of yelling *'J'accuse'* as I tossed a paper trail of incriminating receipts in his face.

"You could start by asking him, Sophie. He'll probably tell you."

My stomach did a cartwheel. Carrie was right. Now that he'd come clean, he would lay out all the excruciating details I could bear. But I didn't want to hear him talk about the woman he loved. "That would defeat the whole purpose."

"Do you want to know about her or not, Sophie?"

"It depends. I don't want to know if she has easy-to-manage hair she can swirl back and forth." My hair never swirled. It moved in a huge frizzy mass. "And I don't want to lie awake at night imagining her cuddled up with Jeremy in the house I wanted to live in with the children I wanted to have with him."

"Okay. So then, what exactly are you going to ferret out? I don't understand."

"These are good questions, Carrie."

"You've no idea what you want, do you?"

"Okay, I think what I'm after is more the process of ferreting than any actual result. I need an obsession to numb the pain. I want to stay up late poring over clues and fall asleep exhausted without having to take an Ambien. The clues wouldn't have to lead anywhere. In fact, I wouldn't *want* them to lead anywhere, just to absorb my energy and tire me out at night."

"I know exactly what you mean. I keep thinking about the murders. I hate to say it keeps me amused, because I don't mean it like that—I feel terrible for the victims. But puzzling over the killings takes me out of myself. We could scratch our brains together."

I liked that idea. "Does Alan still think a stranger killed Penny?"

"Yes, but he's willing to entertain my theory."

"I didn't know you had a theory."

"I do. I think Howard's wife Fiona did it. You know, Hell hath no fury—She's tall, physically powerful. And, frankly, I'd rather see her put away than Howard. There's only one snag."

"Which is?"

"She has an airtight alibi. Not only was she home with their son making dinner during the time in question, but a neighbor conveniently stopped by to drop something off."

"We're not making a lot of progress here."

"I know," Carrie said, giving me a smile. "But that's the point, isn't it?"

∞

Steve breezed into my apartment on Sunday, scarf tucked into his overcoat, holding a bouquet of long stemmed white roses. His close-cropped hair, beard, and moustache were neatly trimmed. As always, he looked elegant. "These are for you, happy birthday, darlin."

I put the flowers in a vase. They were beautiful.

"Now sit down and let me tame your hair. For starters, let's get rid of this old thing." He removed the barrette that clasped my hair at the nape of my neck. "Try this one." He handed me a gift box. Inside was a stunning cloisonné barrette.

"Wow. I love it. Thank you, Steve." I twisted around to give him a kiss.

"Sit still, Sophie darlin'." He clipped my hair back. "Much better, you look fabulous. Ready?"

"Where are we going for our White Russians?"

"Lunch, Sophie, we're going out for *lunch*, not to guzzle. The restaurant's in Adams Morgan. The menu's nothing special, but they have an extremely decorative waiter who makes the food worth eating."

"That sounds really special. Please tell me he's over twenty-one."

"He's over twenty-one. And he promised to give us very good service."

I smirked.

"Put on your coat, darlin'. We're stepping out."

❦❦

Snow was falling after lunch when Steve dropped me off in front of my building, big, wet flakes floating down from the sky. I was floating too. The sweet yummy White Russians had smoothed away the jagged edges of the world, and the waiter lived up to his advance billing. He fussed over our table, brought me birthday cake for dessert, and delighted Steve by standing seductively close to him while serving our dishes.

I glided through the lobby, nodding hello to anything that looked like a person and went up the elevator, third floor express, weaving down the hall into my apartment, where I flopped down on the couch and kicked off my shoes. My head was spinning. I grabbed a comforter and fell asleep.

When I awoke, it was dark outside. Luminous snow blanketed the terrace and yard behind the building and was still falling. Jeremy was on the train back from Philly, the new Jeremy who didn't love me anymore. The phone rang. Caller ID showed Jeremy's name and number.

"I'm snowed in, Sophie. The trains aren't running. They just made the announcement."

I felt myself sail out the window, floating down into the snow below. I hung up. He wasn't coming. A balloon seemed to expand inside of me, squeezing my heart. The phone rang again.

"Sophie? Sorry. We were disconnected."

"What do you want to do?" I carried the phone to my computer, logged onto the Internet, and typed in Amtrak.com.

"The week's going to be hectic. I'll be out of town taking depositions. Want to try for next weekend?"

I moved around the website. Okay, he was telling the truth about his train: it had been cancelled. "When next weekend?"

"Sunday night at six? I hope you're having an okay birthday, Sophie. I wish it was better."

"I'm sure you do. Let's plan on Sunday at six. We're about to be disconnected again." I hung up and called Carrie. "Was he even in Philadelphia, Carrie? That's the question. He could have been calling from next door."

"Sweetie, you're slipping into psychosis. Why would Jeremy stay in town and pretend to be in Philadelphia?"

"To avoid seeing me. I have a harder question. Why would he ask me to marry him when he's in love with someone else?"

CHAPTER 12

At supervision on Friday, Ned once again stretched his legs in my direction, his feet stopping shy of my chair.

I angled my eyes to avoid scanning his body. "So, let's hear about Tom, your depressed guy."

"He's not depressed anymore. Now he's anxious. He went on a date, and they're supposed to go out again. He spent our last session obsessing about whether to kiss her."

"I can't wait to hear your advice, only give me a minute." Marnie reached into her backpack for paper. "I want to be sure and write down your dating tips."

"I told him to go ahead and kiss the—" He glanced at me and smiled. "You know, kiss her. She can always say no, but she might say yes. Tom's a thirty-two-year-old virgin. I'd like to see him get laid."

"That's your therapeutic goal?" I asked.

"Ned wants everyone to get laid," Marnie said. "It's his world view. But look, dude, if your patients are doing okay, can I use the time? I have someone I'm seeing right after this, and I need help."

"Go for it," Ned said. "I can handle Tom on my own."

Marnie pulled a chart from her backpack: Teresa was a thirty-nine-year-old white woman, never married, who had recently stopped seeing the man she had hoped to marry and was in a panic about having children. She didn't want to adopt. She wanted to get pregnant. I knew how she felt. I'd wasted prime years of fertility with Jeremy, shedding eggs from a dwindling supply, when I could have been with a man who actually *wanted* to marry me, someone who would have shown up for our wedding.

"How did your session go?" I asked Marnie. They'd met together once already.

"Not great. All she could talk about was donor sperm and IVF. It's all about her genes and having a 'birth experience.' What about foster kids needing homes? Or special-needs babies?"

"Marnie, she's thirty-nine, and her boyfriend dumped her. Forget about the needy babies in the world. That's not why she came in. What is *she* dealing with emotionally?"

"She's dealing with loss, but they had a terrible relationship."

Where was Marnie's empathy? Without empathy, there'd be no therapeutic alliance and therapy would fail. "Look, we've all had our share of terrible relationships. The loss of the bad ones can be as heartbreaking as the loss of the good ones, because it's not just the actual person you lose, it's also your dream of the person, the fantasy as well as the reality. It sounds like Teresa was hoping to start a family with her boyfriend."

"She was."

"So, from her point of view, what's she struggling with? What are her internal conflicts?"

"She kept coming back to wanting a baby. Whether to go the anonymous sperm donor route or ask a gay friend to donate his sperm. She'd prefer her friend's sperm, but then he'd be the father, and down the road, he might want more of a say in the child's upbringing, and she wants full control. So, she was back and forth about what to do. And she's stressed about the risk of birth defects because of her age. She doesn't want to be saddled with a special-needs kid. Not *her*."

"Not most people, Marnie. What's going on? You're usually so good at connecting with patients, whatever their issues. What about Teresa is setting you off?"

"She's selfish."

"Because she doesn't want to take care of all the needy children in the world?"

"Because she's not thinking about the *child*. She'll be in her forties by the time she has a baby. What if she doesn't have the energy? Or gets sick? There's no backup. Her mother's dead, and her dad's an alcoholic who's not going to help. No siblings. Bottom line—she's got no one to turn to." Marnie's mouth twisted with emotion. I'd never seen her so intense. "If my aunt hadn't stepped in when I was coming up—"

Ned's foot was tapping against my chair. I wanted to tell him to stop, but I didn't want to distract Marnie from her thoughts.

"—my mom slammed me around. She's a great mom now. She's my heart. But she couldn't manage on her own."

"We're all affected by our own experience, Marnie. Recognizing that is enormously helpful, but you have to go beyond your experience and see Teresa for who she is, not as a version of your mother. She's dealing with loss. Your job is to help her."

Marnie's breathing slowed. "I guess I need to connect with her, offer comfort."

"Good. So she doesn't feel so alone in the world."

"She's pretty isolated. I can listen and help her through her grief, but that's not what she's talking about. For her, it's all about having a baby."

"Try asking questions about her boyfriend. What were her dreams? Did she gloss over disappointments to keep things going?"

"Do you think she might be open to other options if she faces up to her grief?"

"I don't know. After you've established a relationship, then you can ask about her reluctance to consider other options, and you can voice your concerns. But she might decide to go ahead with donor sperm and IVF. What would you do?"

Ned's tapping had escalated. He was kicking my chair, but I wanted to finish up with Marnie.

She looked confused. "What do you mean?"

"You could help her build a support network. Find out if there are any friends she can call on or functional relatives. Brainstorm how to find a nearby single mom's group and give her information on parenting classes." I couldn't ignore him any longer. "*Ned.* Would you *please* stop kicking my chair?"

He stopped.

"What's going on?" I asked.

"Sorry. I didn't realize." He pulled himself up. "I was thinking about something. I kind of have a crisis going on, a housing problem."

"Did your girlfriend kick you out?" Marnie asked.

"I don't have a 'girlfriend.' My landlady is getting divorced and putting her house on the market. I need a place to crash while I look around."

"No landlady is putting your white ass on the street."

"Yeah, well, that's what you think." He met my eyes. "I'm renting a basement apartment. It turns out that's against the zoning law, and my landlady can't show the house with me there because no one's supposed to know she has a tenant."

"Didn't you sign a lease?" Marnie asked.

"Not really, no. It's not your worry, okay, Marnie. I'm sorry I mentioned it."

For me to take him in was out of the question. Ditto for Carrie and Steve—he was our intern. I tried to think who I knew who might put him up for a few nights.

Marnie's eyes narrowed. "What happened to that woman, what's her name, short dark hair—I ran into the two of you together one time, remember? I got the impression you were living with her."

"You mean Gina?"

"Gina, right, she was talking like you were living 'to-ge-tha.'"

"Yeah, well, she lives next door. She thinks it's funny to pretend we're an old married couple, because she's embarrassed to be living with her parents. She moved back in with them after college, trying to save money."

"Oh."

"You thought I was living off her and messing around, didn't you, Marnie? Admit that's what you thought."

"Guys—you need to sort this out later. We're here to talk about your patients." I was having enough trouble keeping my personal concerns from leaking out at work. If I added theirs to mine, goop would start pouring out of my ears. My skull was too small to contain the chaos inside.

CHAPTER 13

Tricia invited me over Saturday afternoon, and I decided to go. There was no longer any boundary conflict with Ariel gone. The Lancet house was quiet. Tricia explained that Evan was out, and Mallory was asleep upstairs, sick with the flu. We sat in the breakfast nook, drinking coffee and nibbling low fat vanilla wafers. I asked if she had baked muffins recently, but no, she hadn't. The quiet was calming. Through the window, I could see the bare branched garden where Ariel had been found.

Tricia washed a bunch of purple grapes and set them out in a bowl. "Ariel didn't deserve to be killed, nobody does, but the truth is I'm relieved she's gone. I feel guilty saying this, but for the first time since moving back home I can breathe. Ariel gave me the same creepy feeling I used to have around Brad, like he was watching every move I made, always ready to pounce. The hard part for me now is seeing my dad suffer."

"Is he taking it hard?"

She popped a grape in her mouth. "He blames himself for not staying home with her that night. He thinks if he had put her ahead of his business concerns, she'd still be alive. The thought eats away at him. He keeps berating himself, but he couldn't have known she'd be killed. That's hindsight. What happened was horrible, but it wasn't his fault."

The low-fat wafers were tasteless and dry. I tried dunking one. Before I could catch it in my mouth, the sodden part plopped into my coffee and lay in the mug like untreated sludge. Tricia was still talking.

"The thing is, Sophie, I don't believe Dad really misses Ariel. He was sick with grief when my mother died. He wept his heart out. This is different. He's upset Ariel was murdered on his watch, but it's the fact of her murder that's driving him crazy, not losing her." Tricia cocked her head. "It's been quiet upstairs for a long time. I'm going to run up and look in on Mallory. I'll be right back."

She left the kitchen. The low-fat wafers weren't doing it for me. With Jeremy in love with another woman, I needed a cookie that tasted like a cookie, with sugar, butter and, God willing, chocolate. There was a large porcelain jar labeled *Cookies* on the counter. The label looked promising. I went over and removed the lid.

"What the hell are you doing?"

The lid flew from my hand as I spun around. A man advanced on me. His face was a mask of rage. I froze, wedged between him and the counter. Footsteps raced down the stairs.

"Dad, what are you doing? This is Sophie. I invited her over."

He backed away. I was shivering with fear. Tears spilled from my eyes. Tricia guided me to sit in the alcove.

Evan's face cleared. He began to look like a normal person. "Please forgive me. I'm very sorry. I thought you were someone else." He left the room.

I stared after him. "Who the hell did he think I was?" I wasn't used to being mistaken for other people. "Who would he treat like that?"

"Ariel had a group she sometimes hung with. He must have thought you were one of them."

"And that's how he behaved toward her friends?" I was outraged.

"He thinks they killed her, one or more of them."

"Why would her friends—"

Evan returned, looming in the doorway. My heart began to pound, but his voice was gentle. "Can I join you for a few minutes?"

He was looking at me, not Tricia. Our eyes met. I nodded permission, curious as to what he wanted to say. He slid onto the cushioned bench next to Tricia and faced me across the table. "I owe you more of an apology. I was completely out of line. What happened was that you startled me. I thought you were an intruder. I came in the service door to leave my gym bag in the utility room. I didn't remember Tricia mentioning having anyone over, and I reacted without thinking. I hope you can accept my apology. I've been on edge since my wife was killed."

"I told you Sophie was coming, Dad. You weren't paying attention."

"I'm sorry, Tricia. I must not have been listening. I've been in a fog."

My heart rate returned to normal. Sitting together talking, he seemed nice enough. "I don't understand. You actually thought I'd broken into your home?" I was amazed to be mistaken for a felon and, in an odd way, flattered. No one had ever thought I was that daring before.

"I know this sounds ridiculous, but the idea flashed through my mind that you were planting evidence. I'm aware that makes no sense. The police have been all over the place. Then I thought you were removing something you'd stashed, drugs maybe, the way you were poking around in the jar. That doesn't make sense either, because the police would have found anything in there. I wasn't thinking clearly. I haven't been sleeping."

That I believed. His eyes were bloodshot. I pointed to the plate of low fat wafers. "I wanted a cookie with real butter, so I went poking in the cookie jar. I think I broke the lid."

The porcelain top had chipped where it fell.

Evan's face softened into a smile. He pushed the plate of low fat wafers to the far side of the table. "I don't know why Tricia buys this stuff. What did you find in the cookie jar?" He brought the jar over and tilted it toward me. "Will you accept my apologies?"

I put my hand in the jar and pulled out an oatmeal raisin cookie. I hoped I wasn't allowing a murderer to mollify me with a cookie, especially one that didn't have any chocolate in it, but I nodded, accepting his apology. "Why would Ariel's friends want to harm her?" I asked.

"Could have been drug related," Evan answered. "I never understood her attraction to that bunch of losers. Ariel called them from the restaurant where we were having dinner the night she was killed. The police went over her cellphone records with me. She called from the restroom and talked for six minutes. Five of them live together, male and female, no rules, no boundaries. They live like pigs, even Ariel admitted as much. When she returned to the table after talking to them, she pretended to be ill and said she needed to go home and lie down. It seems obvious she arranged to meet up with them."

The drug angle was a relief. If Ariel's murder was drug related and if a lover or lover's wife killed Penny, then the world was no more dangerous than it used to be for me, since I, for one, didn't take drugs and didn't have a lover.

Evan was still talking. "I left Ariel on the sidewalk in front of the house. The police think she went around to the backyard without going inside. If she'd really felt ill, she would have gone straight up to bed, so she must have been meeting someone. My guess is she met her killer out there to smoke marijuana without getting the smell in the house. She must have been killed quickly, because there was no marijuana in her system. To me, that says her killing was planned. One or more of her so-called friends planned her death."

"Can the police tell how many people were out back?"

"No. Unfortunately, the ground was too hard."

I was caught up in his story. "Was anything left behind to suggest the others were smoking?"

"No, but they could have removed the stubs."

A call for "Mommy" drifted down from upstairs. Tricia gave me a questioning glance to make sure I was okay being left alone with Evan. I nodded yes.

"What kind of work do you do?" he asked when she left.

I had to tell him. There was a chance I'd bump into him at the clinic when he came to see Barney. "I'm a psychologist at the Hartley Clinic."

"Really? Ariel was seeing a therapist there. And I've started working with Dr. Hisselman. Barnard Hisselman. You must know him."

"Yes, he's my boss."

"So then, I don't understand. How did you and Tricia become friends?"

I explained about Carrie's car accident and ferrying Ella around, but I was beginning to feel grilled. I preferred talking about him. "Tricia told me how grief-stricken you were when your first wife died. It must be hard going through this again."

His eyes were suddenly moist. "I lost my first wife, Jeanine, to cancer. I've been thinking about her a lot lately. Ariel deserves to be mourned in her own right, but I can't get Jeanine out of my mind. They were so different."

"In what way?"

"Jeanine had an inner serenity, a reassuring presence. When she was around, nothing seemed impossible. Even with her cancer diagnosis, she plowed ahead and did whatever needed to be done. She was always hopeful. I never imagined she would die before me. I still can't believe she died at such a young age."

Tricia walked in. "Poor Mallory can barely lift her head off the pillow."

Evan eased out of his seat. "I'm glad to have met you, Sophie. I hope you can forgive the way I greeted you."

"I can. I have."

He turned to Tricia. "Is there anything I can bring up to Mallory?"

"No, she conked right back out again."

Evan looked back at me. "I'd like you to join us for dinner, Sophie, if you're free. We're ordering in from the new Japanese restaurant on Wisconsin Avenue, but we can get other food if you don't like Japanese."

❧❧❧

We dined in the kitchen nook—miso soup, tempura, sushi, and little cups of sake to drink. They actually ordered a bottle from the restaurant. I'd never had sake before and a few sips made me lightheaded. Outside, dusk gathered into darkness. There was a void beyond the window. The glass reflected us back at ourselves. We talked mostly about downtown DC and all the building going on. Evan knew every block of the city. We steered clear of Ariel's murder until Evan switched on the outdoor lights and illuminated the empty garden. I had a mental image of Ariel sitting on the bench in the cold night air—dead.

"Turn the lights off, please, Dad," Tricia said.

"I like having them on."

"I find it spooky." She switched the lights off without waiting for him to agree.

"I need to know what happened," he said. "Not knowing is tormenting me. I keep wondering if Ariel asked her friends for a drug buy and then didn't have money on hand to pay. But they wouldn't kill her for something so minor, and I would have known if she had a major drug problem. Maybe they wanted to rob the place, and she refused to let them in, threatened to call the police."

"Dad, this doesn't help. The police checked their alibis."

"Tricia dear, they covered for each other. We'll never know if they were home together or not."

"There was nothing in the garden for the police to go on?" I'd watched enough forensic shows to expect some trace evidence at the scene.

Evan shook his head. "The only thing the police found was an old Swiss Army knife in the grass by the bench. The enamel was chipped, but the knife wasn't rusty, so it couldn't have been outside long, which eliminates the lawn crew."

A worm of anxiety slithered through my intestines. "Were there fingerprints?"

Tricia shoved aside her miso soup. "They found fingerprints—and they weren't Dad's. You'd think the police would realize there's a murderer out there and leave Dad alone."

Evan turned to me. "The fingerprints don't match any prints in the criminal record database. And Ariel was choked to death with her scarf, not stabbed. The knife is a dead end. The police aren't letting me off the hook because of it."

"They aren't letting you off the hook because they're too stupid to see what's right in front of their faces, that you had nothing to do with Ariel's death."

"No, Tricia, they're not stupid. From their point of view, I could have murdered her and thrown down an old pocketknife one of the gardeners left in the mud room. I could have worn gloves to place it at the murder scene. If it belonged to a member of the lawn crew, there's a good chance his prints wouldn't be in a criminal database."

My brain spun away from the conversation. The day after Penny's murder, Barney was snipping the edges off a newspaper with his Swiss Army knife—chipped enamel, no rust. And yet after Ariel was killed, he felt in his pockets, and the knife was gone. "Did the police check the fingerprints against Ariel's friends?"

"The prints don't match," Evan answered, "although they only checked the five people living in the group house, the same five who gave each other alibis. I'm sure there are peripheral friends we don't know about." He rubbed his eyes. "My only hope is that one of the bastards in the group house comes forward, but I don't see that happening. I doubt we'll ever know who killed her. A lot of people will go to their graves believing I murdered my own wife."

His words led us into a conversational black hole, which was just as well, really, because I'd fallen into a black hole of my own. I couldn't shake the image of Barney showing off his bar mitzvah knife, which I'd seen him use many times. As far as I knew, the full extent of Barney's contact with Ariel was on the phone when she called for an initial appointment and then again in the parking lot when he walked her to her car. So how could his knife show up in her yard? And why, of all the therapists in the DC area, did Evan turn to Barney for help with his grief?

CHAPTER 14

Once again, I needed Ambien to sleep. I couldn't stop ruminating about Barney's Swiss Army knife. I'd seen him search for it the Monday after Ariel's body was found. Maybe Ned was right, and there had been something between them. But could Barney really be that duplicitous? My mind wouldn't stop spewing thoughts. I swallowed a pill and waited for relief.

When I awoke, it was a new day. I worked on the Sunday *Washington Post* crossword puzzle and tried not to think about Jeremy coming over in the evening. I wasn't sure I had the resilience to face what he was going to say.

I passed a few hours chatting on the phone with my parents and Carrie and several other friends. I'd just hung up with one when my phone rang again and caller ID showed an unfamiliar number. "Hey, Sophie, this is Ned, Ned Olmason. I hope you don't mind me calling over the weekend."

"What's going on?" I was available for an emergency consultation, if necessary. But his patients had seemed stable.

"Nothing much, I was wondering. Any chance I

could come over, and we could maybe take a walk?"

The question left me dumbfounded.

"Is that okay? We could get a cup of coffee or something."

Jeremy was due in two hours. There was time—but was it okay? I was happy to meet if there was something important he needed to go over before work on Monday, but hanging out as friends was a boundary I didn't want to cross. Then I remembered his housing problem. Other concerns had nudged it from my mind. "Do you have something you want to discuss?"

"Yeah, I do. And we don't have to walk. I just thought you might be more comfortable being outside with me."

More comfortable being outside when the weather was freezing—he didn't know me very well. But he meant sexual comfort. He could tell I was attracted to him and not comfortable about feeling that way. Cripes. I cringed with embarrassment. But if Ned had something specific to discuss, I didn't want to be rigid just because I was alone and horny. On the other hand, running into someone I knew would be awkward. "You can come over here, Ned. I'll make a pot of coffee. But I'm meeting someone at six, so sooner is better than later. Can you come now?"

"Yeah, great, thanks. Tell me where you live."

☙❧

I forbade myself to primp. No fussing with my hair. No tidying up the apartment. Ned was a junior colleague seeking guidance, period. I made coffee, nothing more.

At work, Ned was always clean-shaven. I'd never seen him bristly before, but it was Sunday, and he hadn't shaved. In his rumpled khakis, he looked like a model for chic men's wear. I let him in and suddenly felt shy having him in my apartment seeing where I lived. Other than Steve, the only man who hung out there was Jeremy.

Ned looked around. "Hey, cool couch. This is a nice place. You're lucky you have windows. I was getting sick of being in a basement. Can I see the rest?" He was peering down the hall where there were two doors, my bedroom and bathroom. The bedroom door was shut.

"My room's a mess. But there's the bathroom if you want to use it."

"No. That's okay. You've got a lot of space."

I poured us each a cup of coffee. "Tell me what's on your mind."

"I thought you might know someone with space to rent or maybe have some ideas about where I can look. I don't know the area. I moved here in July for the internship. I'm a hayseed from Kansas."

A hayseed? I knew little about his background. "How did you find your current place?"

"Through a friend of a friend. I also need a place to crash. My landlady has people looking this weekend and next week. I had to move all my stuff to a friend's house."

"And the friend doesn't have room for you?"

He shook his head no. I shouldn't have asked—if his friend had room, he'd obviously be there. I was stalling. I had a collapsible futon I could haul out. And company would be nice. If I hadn't been his supervisor, I would have invited him to stay while he looked for a place. "What about Marnie?"

"She didn't offer, and I didn't ask. Marnie doesn't go out of her way for me."

I was curious about their relationship, but they were both my students—I didn't want to invite gossip with one about the other. I busied myself setting out a plate of cookies, bananas and Clementine oranges.

"The internship stipend is really small," Ned continued. "I can't afford much rent, but I can fix stuff to make up the difference, or take out the garbage, whatever. Any ideas?"

"Have you tried Craigslist or the newspaper?"

"Yeah, but the places listed are either too expensive, in a horrible part of town, or there's a long commute. Usually, the best thing is if someone knows someone. I don't mind renting a room in a house."

Most of my friends were in relationships. As a favor, they might put up one of my out-of-town relatives or, perhaps, a shy, retiring friend, but I couldn't ask them to take in a sexually provocative stranger. Ned polished off a banana and reached for a Clementine.

What were his options? Homelessness happened to people. The interns were kept too busy to work a second job. My parents had supplemented my income during my internship year. Ned obviously didn't have that kind of help. He could end up on the street or in a homeless shelter. I had to think of something. "Do you want a sandwich?" I asked as he was peeling his second Clementine. "I can make peanut butter and jelly."

"Hey, that'd be great." He followed me to the kitchen and stood at my elbow while I worked. I couldn't imagine the humiliation and terror of having nowhere to go.

"I'm thinking," I said, as he devoured the sandwich.

Wracking my brains was more like it. He needed a place to stay, and he'd come to me for help. I couldn't send him away to wander the streets. I had to offer him something, at least for a few days to give him time to find a more permanent home.

"Any chance I could crash here for a day or two?" he asked.

I gave him a helpless look. "No, I'm sorry."

"I'm not hitting on you if that's what you're worried about. I need a place to stay."

"I know." Awkward as I felt, it had to be doubly awkward for him. I felt a deep stab of compassion for people with nowhere to go. No safety net. No parents like mine to provide financial cushioning when in need.

"You're uncomfortable around me, aren't you, Sophie? I can tell. What do you think I'm going to do?"

His question made me feel claustrophobic. I was finding it hard to breathe. "I don't think you're going to do anything, Ned. I'm trying to think of a place you can stay, and I have someone due over soon." The tension of finding him a place and Jeremy's imminent arrival was getting to me.

"I'll leave, don't worry."

"I don't want you to leave if you don't have a place to go. I'm trying to think of someone. Let me get my address book."

I needed something to jog my thinking. But then the answer came to me—I knew someone who lived alone and owed me big.

❧❧❧

Jeremy arrived right on time. I watched his eyebrows shoot up at the sight of Ned sprawled on the couch like a stud who'd been hanging around for casual sex. I gave Jeremy a moment to imagine us together. He glanced from Ned to his watch, as if the explanation for Ned's presence lay in Jeremy arriving too early, which he hadn't. I'd had my moment of fun. "This is Ned, an intern at the clinic." I turned to Ned. "Can you give Jeremy and me some time alone?" I hated to send him out in the cold, but we needed privacy.

"Sure, when should I come back?" Ned was pulling on his jacket and gloves.

"I don't know. Maybe in an hour. I'll call you. I have your number in my phone."

Jeremy watched him leave. "You're awfully chummy with your intern," he commented. We sat down on the couch.

"It's not what you think." I explained Ned's housing situation. "Can you put him up while he looks for another place? You're rarely home, anyway."

Jeremy had a pullout couch that wasn't particularly comfortable, but other guests had slept on it.

"Sure. I'm happy to."

He actually looked pleased, which was irritating. Relieved as I was that Ned would have a place to stay, I hadn't meant to provide Jeremy an easy salve to his conscience. "You can give him your set of keys to my place, Sophie." Another unintended consequence—Jeremy would get his fricking keys back without having to beg me for them. But it was interesting to know the keys still worked. He hadn't changed his locks. I could have let myself in anytime and snooped to my heart's content.

"You still have my keys, too, Jeremy."

"I know. I'll get them back to you. I feel terrible about what I've done, Sophie."

"You should." I thwacked him with one of the pillows on the couch. He didn't look surprised, so I thwacked him again. I liked the sound of the pillow hitting his chest. I was getting a rhythm going when he grabbed it away from me.

"That's enough, Sophie."

He was treating me like a child, which I found annoying on many levels particularly since he was the one who had behaved badly—why should he come off as mature while I was flailing? I held my hand out for him to give me the pillow back and he did.

Bad move. I thwacked him one last time for good

measure then put the pillow back where it belonged.

"I want to know why you betrayed me after swearing you would never cheat. Do you remember our promise to talk to each other if there was tension between us? Instead, you withdrew like a fricking coward and ran to someone else. How could you break your word like that? I didn't even know you were unhappy. I had no clue."

"I wasn't unhappy. And I didn't betray you, Sophie."

"What are you saying—there is no Miss Philadelphia?" Could I have misunderstood? Was I, in fact, delusional? *Had he even broken up with me?*

"There is someone, Sophie, but I didn't betray you. I didn't start up with her until after I told you I couldn't get married."

"Oh, come on. Give me a fucking break."

I reached for the pillow. He wanted me to believe he cancelled our marriage and *by coincidence* met someone in Philadelphia the very next week? A city he never visited? I walloped him hard.

He grabbed the pillow and put it behind his back. "I've known her my whole life. We grew up together. But I hadn't been seeing her behind your back. I swear to you."

This was an outrage—his hometown sweetie appearing on the eve of our marriage? I was literally trembling. My eyes felt like fireballs.

"I wasn't unhappy with you, Sophie. I love you. You know that, don't you? But not the way—not so that we should get married."

I couldn't hold out against the onslaught of grief welling up inside of me. Crying was bad enough, but hiccupping sobs convulsed my body. Jeremy moved closer and held me until I settled down.

"You know what, Jeremy? You might as well go ahead and tell me the whole story." I had nothing left to lose. I plucked a handful of tissues and blew my nose. "What's her name?"

"Heather."

"Go on."

"I've had a crush on her as far back as I can remember, but she always had one boyfriend after another."

"Really, one boyfriend after another? She sounds stable."

"We finally went out together the summer after college. We had both moved home for the summer, so we were living in our parents' homes."

"In other words, you had to find places to be alone together." That meant secret, intense sex and heightened romantic longing.

"Yes."

I gave my nose a big honking blow. If nothing else, I could at least elicit a startled response from Jeremy. He waited for me to finish blowing my nose.

"We might have gotten tired of each other in the normal course of events, but we broke up when she got a job teaching in South Carolina, and I moved to DC for law school." That was nine years ago.

"And then? What happened next?"

"After graduating from law school, I went to see her and visit my parents. I was thinking of moving back. If she'd been free, I probably would have. But she had a boyfriend, so I stayed in DC."

"And she waited until you were about to get married to make herself available? She left you on the shelf until just before your expiration date, but she couldn't quite bring herself to throw you away." Very apt—I was pleased with my analogy.

"That's not what happened, Sophie. Her marriage ended."

"Does she have children?" I was ready to hate her more if she did.

"No. They had fertility problems."

Good. I let out my breath. "When did her marriage end?"

"They separated two months ago. They're getting a divorce."

"*Two months*? She didn't waste any time."

"Things hadn't been good between them for a long time."

"I never thought of you as a complete asshole, Jeremy, but she comes to you with a sob story about her marriage, and you dump me *the next fricking week.*" I got off the couch. I needed to pace. "You know what? I'm glad we're not getting married. Anyone as stupid as you should be quarantined as unmarriageable. You need to keep your gene pool to yourself, because blind stupidity shouldn't be passed on to an innocent child." I picked up his jacket and threw it on the couch beside him. "Why don't you leave?"

"What about your friend?"

I'd forgotten about Ned. Remembering him threw me off stride. Anyway, I didn't want Jeremy to leave. I wanted him to have a brain transplant. "How did Heather pitch things to you?"

"It wasn't a pitch. She said she hadn't thrown herself into her marriage the way she should have because I was always in the back of her mind." He had the good grace to look embarrassed, which was lucky for him, because I was ready to climb on the back of the couch and jump on his head.

"How long did she remain miserable in her marriage and pining for you?"

"I don't know, but she said she had always carried around the idea of us being together. We both had the fantasy. We used to talk about ending up together—I don't mean recently, Sophie, I mean years ago, before I met you."

"Why did she accept her husband's proposal, if she was in love with you?"

"I'm not sure, but I was seeing Marcy at the time."

Marcy was his former girlfriend, whom he also dumped for reasons I had thought made sense, but in retrospect, maybe he started fantasizing about Heather, and poor old Marcy hadn't stood a chance.

"Heather called me before her wedding to kind of check out where I was."

I had a surge of kill venom. "And you did the same thing? You called her after proposing to me, so you could check out where she was? If you don't think that's a betrayal, Jeremy, I don't know what is. How come I never knew how fucked up you are?" He hated rhetorical questions as much as I did. "How come I never knew?"

"I didn't call her, Sophie. I wasn't thinking about her. I was thinking about you, about us. She called me. She didn't know I was involved with you when she called."

"And she lives in Philly now?"

"She and her husband moved there a few years ago, which I also found out. I didn't know. We hadn't been in touch. This fantasy we've carried around undermined her marriage, Sophie. I didn't want the same thing to happen to us. From what she said, she tried to make her marriage work, but she couldn't stop thinking about the possibility of being with me, because we'd never given it a try. I started to worry that if you and I got married, I'd have the same doubts, and I wouldn't be present the way I should. I started to think about those things. Five years down the road I wouldn't want to tell you I wasn't sure we belonged together."

"Did you have doubts *before* Heather contacted you?"

"No, but talking to her aroused old feelings. I wish they hadn't. I wish I didn't feel the way I do, but I've always had a thing for her. And knowing what happened to her marriage—"

I was ready to look up the number for NASA. See if I could join the space program and sign up to live on another planet. "Jeremy, this is a truckload of crap. You're behaving like a duckling imprinted at an early age—and now she's the only one you'll follow. I mean this is right out of the Manchurian Candidate. She activated you. You put away murderers, Jeremy. How can you fall for this?"

"Don't you think I know I could be making the mistake of my life? I'm terrified, Sophie. This is tearing me apart. But I feel like I have to spend time with Heather and see what there is between us, because if I don't, the possibility will always be there, and it could ruin our marriage. I can't commit my life to you until I work her out of my system, but I don't know if that's what will end up happening. I can't predict. There's so much uncertainty. The only thing I know for sure is how much I'm hurting you."

This was an entirely new turn of events. Jeremy's eyes were soft, almost pleading. He was holding out a lifeline for our relationship. The conditions sucked, but I felt a flutter of hope.

"What are you saying? You want me to wait on the sidelines while you and Heather have a fling, so you can decide which one of us you want the most?"

He actually smiled the old Jeremy smile, a tad rueful. "I can't ask that of you, Sophie. It would be outrageous."

"It *is* fucking outrageous, but that's what you want, isn't it?"

He had a crap load of nerve.

"Yes. But I know how unfair it is."

"You'd better know how unfair it is." I sat back down. "Okay, take me through what happened again after you heard from Heather. I want to understand." This was terrain I could navigate. "Start with 'I was happy with Sophie. We were planning to get married and start a family…'" Giving orders felt good.

"I was happy with Sophie. We were planning to get married and have children."

Out of habit I shifted position and rested my feet on his lap. He began massaging them in a way that went straight to my pleasure center. He was so well trained. The thought of starting from scratch with someone new was too depressing to contemplate.

"Then I got a call from Heather. She wanted to know how I was, what I was doing. I told her about our plans to get married. I asked what was going on with her and she said her marriage was ending, and she felt guilty because she never put herself into the marriage the way she should have. She felt she'd made a mistake not trying things out with me, because things either would have worked between us—in which case we'd be together—or they wouldn't have worked, and she would have been able to move on and commit to her husband in a different way."

"How did you go from telling her we planned to get married to breaking off with me?"

"She asked if I still had feelings for her and I said yes. I feel awful telling you this, Sophie. But hearing her voice, those feelings rushed back. She'd been in my mind since high school, elementary school if you want to know the truth. She said we owed it to each other—and to you, Sophie—to give things a try and find out if we were meant for each other or not. Get it out of our systems."

If getting a foot-rub hadn't lulled me into a stupor,

I'd have kicked him in the balls, hard. I mean *really*. The idea that she was doing me a favor by fooling around with my fiancé was an insult to my intelligence and to his. But Jeremy gave the best foot-rubs in the world. I mustered a disgusted "cripes" and waited for him to continue his tale of self-delusion.

"I was up all night. I didn't know what to do. All of a sudden, I went from a life that made sense to everything being a mess. I didn't think it was right to marry you feeling the way I did about her. She asked me to spend time with her, to come to Philly for the weekend."

"Holy crap. Don't you see a character issue here, Jeremy? She wanted to start an affair with you *after* you told her you were engaged. How can you trust her?"

He evaded the question. "I didn't go, Sophie. I told her I wasn't going to sneak around behind your back. I had to figure things out."

"And have you figured them out?"

"No. But I couldn't get her out of my mind. And I didn't see how I could get married to you when I was obsessed with another woman. But the last thing in the world I want to do is hurt you, Sophie."

"Did it ever occur to you to get professional help? Talk to a therapist? We do actually help people."

"I know. I started seeing someone. He thought I was getting in too deep by not saying anything to you. I was stuck. I kept putting Heather off and feeling uneasy around you. It was making me sick, literally. I decided, right or wrong, I had to make a decision and tell you. But I didn't get very far explaining because you took it so hard."

"You were in Philly seeing her last week. How did that go?"

"I don't know what's going to happen, Sophie."

"Here's the thing, Jeremy. I'm scared I won't find

anyone else who gives such good foot rubs." He did other things well, too, but I wasn't about to feed his ego. "And while you're right that it's outrageous to expect me to wait around while you and Heather are off together, I still love you, even knowing you have a blind spot for a sociopath who's manipulating the crap out of you."

"She's not like that, Sophie." His voice was soft. He wasn't arguing. He was stating a deeply held belief. Here he was, the love of my life, and I was ending up as a footnote to an infatuation that spanned decades. Still, I had a plan.

"Let's do this, Jeremy. Why don't we meet for dinner in three months and see where things stand. In the meantime, you can go off and screw around with Heather, and of course, I'll screw around with anyone and everyone I please. How does that sound?"

"That sounds wonderful. More than I deserve."

He wasn't taking the idea of my screwing around seriously. "We'll need to get tested for HIV if we get back together, but, of course, I'll be careful, and I trust you will too."

"That goes without saying, Sophie."

"Maybe we should make it two months, or, you know what, how about six weeks?" Waiting around for him was going to be nerve-wracking. Even six weeks was a stretch. "And don't smile, Jeremy. You have a crap load of nerve."

CHAPTER 15

With so much inner turmoil about Jeremy, I forgot about Barney's missing Swiss Army knife until Monday morning when Barney and I were both in the kitchenette waiting for the coffee to brew. "Can I use your pocketknife, Barney? I need the little scissors for a hangnail." My request was a ruse. I didn't have a hangnail.

"I can't find it, Sophie. Gayle keeps telling me it'll resurface like all the other stuff I misplace. I hope so—that knife was a bar mitzvah present."

The probability that Barney's knife was the one found near Ariel's body had just zoomed into the stratosphere. Added to that—Barney was alone the weekend Ariel was killed. Gayle had been visiting her mother. I doubted he had an alibi. I couldn't begin to process the implications. My brain was spazzing out. "How is Gayle's mother doing?"

"You really want to know, Sophie? Have a seat. We'll be here awhile." There were no actual chairs. The kitchenette had room for a coffeepot, sink, and mini-fridge. Barney leaned against the counter, and I did the same. "The woman is a world-class hypochondriac. The energy she puts into kvetching could power a small country. To hear her tell it, every system in her body is breaking down. But you know what? She'll outlive us all. You want some advice, Sophie?"

"Sure."

"Marry an orphan."

"No in-laws, that's your answer, Barney?" The coffee was done brewing, but I wanted to keep the conversation going.

He poured himself a cup. "Yup, that's the sum total of my wisdom."

"You must find it hard having Gayle away so much." Barney had no hobbies that I knew of. Basically, he liked to eat, and Gayle liked to cook. They socialized with friends. Other than that, he had favorite TV shows and went to lots of movies. "What do you do when Gayle's away? How do you spend your time?"

"Why? Do you want to get together? Gayle will be away again this coming weekend. We could grab a bite and take in a movie. I know you've been having a difficult time."

Cripes. I should have anticipated his response. On the other hand, hanging out with Barney away from the clinic would give me a chance to ferret out more information, which I needed to do, because nothing made sense. His being involved in Ariel's murder was unfathomable. "Let's do that."

"Good. We'll set something up."

Jack Cassidy stepped into the kitchenette as Barney left. "What are you two setting up?"

We all kept tabs on Barney as a defensive maneuver to thwart his attempts to launch us into dubious projects.

"Don't worry, it's not work related," I said. Jack never pried, so I considered leaving it at that, but being secretive wasn't a good idea when Barney and I might be seen out together. "We're both alone for the weekend. We're going to see a movie."

"Yeah? What are you going to see?"

That was what I loved about Jack. He didn't troll for gossip.

"We haven't decided." I took a sip of coffee. Jack was clinically astute. I wanted his opinion. "This is a serious question: do you think Barney has a dark side?"

"I don't think of Barney as having sides." Jack scanned the hallway to make sure we wouldn't be overheard. "He's a blob, Sophie."

There it was. Jack's view echoed my own. Barney was a blob. He might reach his fork into your dessert uninvited, but he wouldn't stick his fork into your throat. I couldn't conceive of him killing anyone. How could the lost pocketknife possibly be his? The idea didn't compute.

What to do? The police investigation was stalled. I couldn't withhold valuable information. I needed to tell Detective White about Barney's knife. On the other hand, I didn't want to expose Barney to police harassment or impair his therapeutic relationship with Evan if the knife didn't belong to him.

What to do?

I could tell Barney my dilemma. Ask if he'd been to Ariel's house. But he would deny being there. On the other hand, he might agree to be fingerprinted. The procedure wasn't a big deal. I was fingerprinted every four years to renew my psychology license. If Gayle had only been home the weekend that Ariel was killed, things would be so much simpler.

But Gayle was away and, knowing Barney, he'd spent that Saturday night home alone eating popcorn and binging on a TV series. I didn't want to taint Barney with suspicion, especially if Ariel's killer was never found.

Hanging out with him over the weekend would give me a chance to learn more. I also had plans to see Tricia. If anything broke in the case, she might know. Maybe there'd be news that made the Barney issue moot. If not, I would decide what to do when I knew more.

CHAPTER 16

Ned arrived a few minutes early for supervision on Friday. He dropped his backpack on the floor and sprawled in a chair. "Thanks for putting me in touch with Jeremy. The apartment's great. I appreciate what you did."

"I'm glad that's working out."

"Yeah, it's cool. I have the place to myself this weekend, so if you want to stop by—"

"I don't think so." I hoped he was joking.

"So, you and Jeremy, what's the deal? Is it totally over between the two of you?"

"We're here to talk about your patients, Ned, but do you have any leads for a more permanent place to live?"

"Not yet. I have to admit I'm not looking as hard as I was. Jeremy said I could stay a couple weeks. It's much nicer than anything I can afford. He's got cable, and there's a work-out room in the building."

"I'm glad you have a good deal, but please don't take advantage of him."

"Don't worry. I'm not in his way. Dude's never home. And I'm helping out. I'm going to clean the bathroom and kitchen this weekend."

Marnie arrived, and I clamped our boundaries back in place: I was the supervisor, they were the interns, and there was work to do.

❧❧❧

Saturday I headed over to Carrie's. The plan was for me to pick up Ella and go to the Lancet home where Ella would hang out with Mallory while I hung out with Tricia. But first I visited with Carrie and filled her in on my life. She had begun physical therapy and was starting to look healthy again. I handed her a cup of tea.

"Thanks, Sophie. I'm glad you and Jeremy are talking."

"You don't think I'm a fool to hold out hope and be willing to take him back?"

"No. Granted, if Jeremy ends up with Heather, you'll be a total mess—we both know that. And you'll be upset that you needlessly prolonged your suffering, and you'll feel like a complete idiot."

"And the upside?"

"You'll have given it your best shot. Having things work out with Jeremy is worth the emotional risk—at least I think so. Finding the right person isn't that easy, and you love him, Sophie. And Jeremy loves you. And you're good together. The reality of Heather could fall far short of the fantasy."

"Even if it does and he wants to get back together, how will I be able to trust him?"

"Because you know him, Sophie, and you know this isn't a pattern with Jeremy. My gut reaction is there's no reason for it to happen again."

I loaded Ella into the car and drove to Tricia's house, feeling lighter at heart. Ella scampered upstairs with Mallory and I joined Tricia in the sun-filled kitchen. The chaos in my head was soothed by hazelnut coffee and cranberry muffins. Tricia had started baking again.

"Did you learn any more about the pocketknife?" I asked.

Tricia's gaze wandered out the window to the bench where Ariel had been found. "No, the police are too incompetent to figure out who the knife belongs to, so they've decided not to worry about it. But the knife is the only piece of hard evidence they have. The pressure on my dad is unbelievable. Thank God, he's in therapy. At least he has someone he can talk to. I'm too reactive to help him. We set each other off."

Acid surged into my throat, a wave of nausea. Somehow, even though I knew Barney was Evan's therapist, I hadn't connected the dots. Evan was obsessed with his wife's murder. He must have told Barney an army knife was found at the scene. "Excuse me, I need—"

I ran to the bathroom. *Barney knew about the knife.* He had to know. But had he gone to the police? Were they investigating behind the scenes so as not to disturb his relationship with Evan? Or was he holding back?

I emptied my guts then sat on the bathroom floor, too limp to move. If the knife was Barney's, what did that mean? Sex? Had he gone to Ariel's place to proposition her and been turned down? I couldn't imagine Barney taking a risk like that. He wouldn't dare show up at Ariel's house unless Ariel invited him over when Evan was out. But according to Ariel's phone records, she called her group of friends from the restaurant and made no other calls that night. And why would a beautiful young woman agree to an assignation with Barney?

None of it made sense.

And yet when Barney and Ariel talked in the parking lot, Ned had reacted. Something had seemed off about Barney's behavior. Marnie hadn't thought so, but she had a deep desire to earn approval from those in authority. She looked up to Barney, trusted rules, liked having structure. Her early life had been chaotic and scary until her aunt stepped in and created a semblance of order. Ned was wary of authority. He wanted to make his own rules and was probably more attuned to that urge in others.

There was a tap on the bathroom door. "Are you okay?"

"I'll be right out." My stomach felt settled. I stood up and rinsed my mouth. A sexual relationship between Barney and Ariel was too far-fetched to imagine—that was probably Ned's projection, as Carrie thought. But Barney was a medical doctor. He could write prescriptions. Ariel might have talked him into prescribing painkillers for her or her friends, or maybe something to heighten focus like Ritalin, or benzodiazepines to take the edge off and help them unwind. There was a huge market for prescription drugs. Ariel could have traded sex for drugs, although I couldn't see Barney being that crass. It was more likely that she charmed him into doing her a favor.

Maybe she had a hiding place in the secluded garden where she asked him to leave prescriptions. That would account for Barney having been there and dropping the knife. But what had gone wrong? Had they quarreled? Ariel could have ruined his medical career. He'd have lost his livelihood. Gayle might not stick with a ruined man. Barney provided a comfortable income. Without his income, he was just Barney.

But I couldn't imagine Barney killing anyone. Maybe he'd left the prescriptions and inadvertently dropped his pocketknife—things were always spilling off of Barney as well as spilling onto Barney. Ariel's death might have happened later when her friends came by to pick up the prescriptions he left. That made the most sense. Killing no, but I could imagine Barney crossing an ethical line to please a beautiful young woman. I splashed water on my face and dried it with a towel from the stack provided for guests.

"I was getting worried," Tricia said when I returned to the kitchen.

"I'm sorry. This almost never happens to me. I can't remember the last time I was sick to my stomach."

"I hope you're not coming down with the flu."

"I don't feel achy. Something I ate must have been spoiled or contaminated." A more likely explanation was that stress had caused my bodily systems to go awry, but I kept that to myself. "I better go home in case I have another bout."

"That makes sense. I can drive Ella home later." Tricia was eyeing me like a potential germ carrier. She wanted me to leave.

"Thanks. I'll let Carrie know." I put on my coat. Outside the cold air felt bracing. I breathed deeply. It was time to get some answers.

❦❦❦

Barney's teeth pulverized a piece of scone for my viewing pleasure. We were having cappuccino and scones at a bookstore café before the movie Sunday afternoon. No one had taught him to chew with his mouth closed.

"You know, Sophie, for all of Evan's money, I feel sorry for the son-of-a-bitch. He's been put through the ringer."

Barney swilled the mush in his mouth down with a few gulps of cappuccino. I handed him a napkin and pointed to his upper lip. He dabbed the foam, put down the napkin, and brushed it to the floor with his arm. Foam transferred to his sleeve. Then he rested his arm on the table and crumbs from his scone adhered to the foam. And that was the problem with Barney being the killer. He wasn't just a blob—he was a slob. He would have left a lot more than a Swiss Army knife at the scene.

I couldn't think of an offhand way to segue our conversation to the knife, but I had a plan to get a set of Barney's fingerprints. Barney picked up another napkin, wiped the crumbs from his face, and stuffed the napkin inside his empty cappuccino cup. The cup was disposable cardboard. We had fifty minutes before the movie started, time for another round.

"If you get more scones, Barney, I'll clear this mess away, and we can pretend we just sat down." I flashed a smile.

He grinned back at me. "Now you're talking, and how about another round of cappuccino?"

"Sounds good." I handed him a ten-dollar bill to cover my costs. He walked to the counter. I pinched a clean napkin between my fingers and used it to pick up his coffee cup, which I dropped into the baggie I'd brought along. I put the baggie in my handbag, tossed the rest of our trash and waited expectantly for Barney to bring our second course.

❧❧❧

After the movie, Barney and I went our separate ways. I called Jeremy from my car to tell him what I'd done.

"Sophie, calm down. I can't understand a word you're saying. Where are you?"

"In Bethesda." I started the ignition.

"Did something happen?" I could hear the anxiety in his voice, a touching reminder that he cared.

"No. Where are you, Jeremy?"

"I'm home. I just got in."

"Can you meet me at my apartment? It's important."

He sounded nervous. "Can't we talk on the phone?"

"I have something I want to give to you." There was silence. "Is Heather with you?"

"No."

"Then why aren't you saying anything?"

"I need to know what you want to give me before I come over."

"Jeremy." I released a weary sigh. "I need to talk to someone I trust and, due to a congenital abnormality I was saddled with at birth, that person is you."

He hesitated but gave in. "Okay, I'll be there."

"Thank you." I put the car in reverse and backed out of my parking spot.

જ્જ

Jeremy was on my couch reading the sports section of the morning paper when I walked in. I should have asked him to pick up carryout, but I hadn't thought ahead. There wasn't much food to scrounge.

I grabbed a sheaf of carryout menus from a drawer near the fridge. "Are you hungry?"

Instead of answering, he took the menus from my hand and held them behind his back.

It did me good to be reminded of his more annoying traits. Jeremy didn't experience hunger like normal people.

"What are you so keyed up about, Sophie?"

I reached for the menus, but he was too agile. "First tell me why you were hesitant to come over."

He considered a moment. "I thought you had second thoughts about our discussion, and you were ready to kill me. I don't feel good about what I'm doing. Now tell me why I'm here."

"You really thought I'd try and kill you?"

"Not literally. Why am I here?"

"You're here to talk about Ariel's murder, but can we please order food first?" I reached for my cellphone. I had the local Indian restaurant on speed dial. "They're answering, Jeremy. Hand me the Indian menu."

A smile tugged the corner of his mouth. He felt superior indulging me, as if I'd never indulged his appetites when he was experiencing them with pressing intensity. I harrumphed, but only inwardly, and counted my blessings. Jeremy was there, and food was on the way.

∽✄∽

"Barney Hisselman?" Jeremy shook his head in disbelief.

We were sitting at the dining table eating tandoori chicken, curried chickpeas, spinach, and naan.

"I'm not saying Barney killed her, Jeremy, just that he might be involved."

"How?"

"The Swiss Army knife at the scene might be his. If it is, then he knows more than he's saying. I don't want to hurt him, Jeremy, but I don't want to protect him at the expense of Ariel's murder going unsolved."

Jeremy pointed to my handbag. "What evidence did you collect?"

I pulled out the baggie. "Barney's fingerprints are on the napkin and coffee cup. Will you deliver them to Detective White and explain what's going on."

He took the baggie. "Yes, good work, Sophie."

"If the knife belongs to Barney, what will happen?"

"The police will question him and check his alibi for the night Ariel was killed."

"Gayle was away. He was home alone."

"Then they'll also interview your interns about the interaction in the parking lot."

"Am I doing the right thing, Jeremy?"

"Absolutely. Two women are dead, and the investigation is stalled. I'll ask Reggie to keep you out of it. If the fingerprints match, he'll approach Barney without using your name."

We finished eating and moved to the couch.

"How are things working out with Ned?" I asked.

Jeremy began massaging my feet. I didn't stop him. Even if he ended up choosing Heather over me, I wasn't going to regret getting one last foot rub.

"Fine, I barely know he's there."

"He said he would clean your bathroom and kitchen while you were away. Did he?" I couldn't restrain myself from asking.

"The place looked clean," Jeremy said. "I didn't do an inspection."

"Ned might be getting a little too comfortable. If you want him to leave, you'll have to give him a departure date. He likes having cable TV and a fitness room."

"I'll give him two weeks to find a place. I don't mind extending the time if he has to wait to get in somewhere, but I don't want him staying indefinitely."

"That's generous."

"I'm doing it for you, Sophie, not for him."

"You're helping him out of guilt for loving another woman," I corrected. "Speaking of which, how was your weekend with Heather?" He stopped rubbing my feet. Maybe I shouldn't have asked.

"The weekend was good, but I feel like I'm living in a fog. How are you doing?"

I wriggled my feet for him to resume rubbing them. His answer told me one important thing: he was confused, which wasn't a bad place for him to be.

⌘

I avoided Barney at work Monday, hiding in my office between appointments. Jeremy called that evening. "You were right, Sophie. The knife is Barney's. His were the only fingerprints on it."

I collapsed on the couch. Now that there was proof, I couldn't believe it. My whole body was trembling. What in God's name was Barney Hisselman doing in Ariel Lancet's backyard on a Saturday night?

Jeremy was still talking: "Reggie dug up a set of Barney's fingerprints on file from some government program, so you don't have to worry. Barney will think his prints showed up in the system as a match."

My brain was whirring—*Barney knew Ariel*. He wasn't the person I thought he was. "There's something else, Jeremy. Barney knew Penny Harrison. She and his daughter were childhood friends."

"I'll pass that along."

I couldn't fathom the thought of Barney killing one young woman, let alone two. But the knife belonged to him.

⌘

Detective White came to the clinic early Tuesday morning. After he left, Barney's face was white with fear.

Jeremy called later and told me Barney not only had no alibi for the time of Ariel's murder, he had no alibi for Penny's murder either. Penny was killed a few blocks from the clinic shortly after Barney left work and neither he nor Gayle could pinpoint the exact time he arrived home.

Barney took sick leave the rest of the week. The clinic was rife with rumors. Everyone knew he was a suspect. The interns arrived for supervision wanting to talk about Barney's alleged involvement in Ariel's murder. I insisted we attend to their cases first to make sure everything was going well. Then we switched to what was most on their minds.

Ned gave my chair leg a gentle nudge. "We know you have an 'in' with the DA's office. Is Dr. Hisselman going to be arrested?"

"I have no idea."

Barney's lack of motive was holding up an arrest. The evidence against him was too circumstantial to build a case without motive, but that didn't mean one wouldn't be uncovered.

"He was up to something that night with Ariel in the parking lot. You weren't watching his face, Marnie. He had a weird expression."

Marnie shook her head. Her cornrows made a sad clanking sound. "I get what you're saying. I just didn't see it."

"What do you think, Sophie?" Ned's foot pushed gently on my chair. "Do you think he murdered her?"

"I honestly don't know what I think."

Marnie leaned forward. She looked on the verge of tears. "Clinically, do you think he has it in him to do something like that?"

"I don't have any answers, Marnie." I wasn't comfortable trying to diagnose the head of our clinic with the interns. Barney was still my boss.

Marnie sank back in her chair and turned toward Ned. "I wish I'd paid more attention to what you were saying. Ariel might still be alive if I had."

"Don't feel bad, Marnie. Few people are as astute as me."

Ned grinned, and Marnie smirked. He had brought us back to the land of the living.

CHAPTER 17

Carrie and Alan had a long-standing commitment to host a charity fundraiser at their home the upcoming Sunday evening. Arrangements were put in place long before Carrie broke her pelvic bone and Penny and Ariel were murdered. Many of us at the clinic had purchased tickets to the event, which benefitted the homeless, and Carrie had invited the interns to attend for free. Originally Jeremy had planned to come with me. He emailed Saturday morning and asked if I minded his coming. I emailed back that as long as he didn't bring Heather, he was free to do as he wished.

Unlike lawyers, bankers, and lobbyists, I typically wore corduroy pants and a sweater to work in the winter. We didn't have a formal dress code. I owned two dressy skirts and tops for more formal occasions but hadn't worn them in some time. On Thursday evening, it occurred to me to try on the skirts. Because of a recent anomaly—my underwear had begun riding up my ass—I started with the larger skirt. Also, my inner thighs now rubbed together when I walked, fraying the corduroy between my legs.

I took a deep breath and stepped in. I couldn't pull the skirt over my thighs and ass. A quick check confirmed the zipper was fully open. Sucking in my stomach was useless. The seams were straining. The skirt encased my legs up to where flesh drooped over it like a mushroom cap. Rats. I kicked free of the skirt and sat on the bed to sulk. My thighs looked like big blobs of sausage.

I let out a moan. Weight was one thing I never had to worry about before and now, without warning, I had gotten tubby. I went to my closet and eyeballed my other clothes. They'd been stretching to accommodate me and hiding the truth like well-intentioned friends. I called Steve. "It's Sophie."

"I know who it is."

"I have a question, and I want an honest answer." I paused, gathering courage. "Have I gotten pudgy?"

His silence was more telling than words.

"You heard me, Steve."

He was breathing into the phone, cornered, unable to devise a delicate way to speak the truth out loud.

"I'm *fat*," I wailed.

"You're not *fat*."

There it was: my trap had lured him into the open. Denying I was fat underscored the salient fact—*he hadn't denied I was pudgy.* "I have nothing to wear to Carrie's house Sunday night. This is a shopping emergency."

Steve was the best shopper I knew. He actually enjoyed going to stores.

"Hold on tight, darlin'. I'm on my way."

∽∾

There were advantages to shopping with Steve that went beyond his knowledge of clothes and aesthetics. Being male, he couldn't come into the dressing room with me, so I was spared humiliating stares while trying on clothes. He whizzed through the racks choosing and discarding. In the end, he discovered a watered silk navy blue suit that was classy, elegant, *and* fit my expanded body.

"Your hair is next, darlin'," he said as we seated ourselves in a little café to recover from shopping exhaustion.

I knew I needed a trim. I hadn't gotten around to it. My hair was too frizzy to wear short or layered, so I wore it long and chopped the ends off every few months. My default hairdo was to clasp it with a barrette at the back of my neck and let it fan out below like a hyperactive child heading off in twenty directions. Wearing it up wasn't worth looking like I'd poached game and was carrying the dead meat home on my head.

"I'll make an appointment."

"Darlin'?"

Steve fished the ends of my hair out of his coffee cup. He wiped the tips with a napkin and returned them to me. It was a mortifying moment.

I signaled the waiter to bring Steve another cup and held my hair to the far side of my head where it couldn't get into any further mischief. He fixed me a stern look and pulled his cellphone from his pocket. "Are you calling the hair police?"

"I'd like to avoid going that route. There's a place near Dupont Circle that does crisis intervention. You pay extra, but they'll see you on short notice." He keyed in a number and handed me his phone. "Tell them you need your hair thinned, trimmed, and you want them to condition the crap out of it. I'll give you the address."

e⁊e⁊

They agreed to fit me in after work on Friday. Leanne introduced herself as my stylist, worked a piece of gum in her mouth, and pointed me to a chair in front of a large window at ground level looking out on Connecticut Avenue where I could be seen by passing foot traffic. She tied a bib around me, wet my hair, and ran to answer a ringing phone. I closed my eyes and prayed no one I knew was walking by. When Leanne returned, she plopped my hair up and down with her hands as if weighing the heft of the job. "I got something really good that will calm it down."

"Pour it on."

A lilac scent filled the air. She massaged a creamy lotion on my hair and scalp then cut and thinned, rinsed, washed, rinsed, and conditioned again before blowing dry my locks. When she rotated me away from the window to face the mirror, I stared in amazement. I almost didn't recognize myself. I put my hand up. Soft, my hair felt *soft*. The conditioner was like Valium for hair, mellowing out my frazzled strands. I tilted my head to the side. My hair glided. It didn't swoosh like straight hair but glided, it definitely glided. I tilted to the other side and watched it glide in the other direction. I paid the bill, tipped Leanne twenty dollars, and bought every bottle of conditioner they had stocked on the shelf.

∾

Initially, I'd been uneasy about seeing Jeremy at the charity event, but having soft, manageable hair and a snazzy new outfit changed the equation.

Steve picked me up so we could go together. "Your hair looks fabulous, darlin'. I'm speechless." He darted proud glances at me during the short drive to Carrie and Alan's house.

The place was bursting with people. Caterers roamed the rooms offering hors d'oeuvres. A bar was set up in the living room. The dining room offered a dinner buffet. Carrie made her way to us slowly, using a walker. "Sophie, wow, your hair looks wonderful." She kissed Steve on the cheek.

"You look good, Carrie." She had dolled up for the event. "How are you feeling?"

"So, so. My plan is to sneak away and lie down if I get too tired." She squeezed my arm. "I have to mingle. Ned and Marnie are here somewhere. Barney came alone. He said Gayle was desperate to get him out of the house for a few hours." Carrie eased away.

"I'm going to say hi to Barney," I said.

"Good for you," Steve said. "I'm getting a drink. Want one?"

"Not yet."

Barney was sitting alone, eating hors d'oeuvres and looking glum. He greeted me warmly. "Boy, oh boy, it's good to see a friendly face."

"How are you doing?" I felt a twinge of guilt for ratting him out, even though I knew I'd done the right thing.

He blew out his breath with a heavy sigh. "You really want to know?"

I hedged. "More or less."

"I'm up four or five times a night, back and forth to the bathroom, and then I can't fall back asleep. Every system is out of whack. My digestion is acting up again—"

Whether he was a murderer or not Barney was still Barney. "Your GI tract is off limits. Don't go there with me."

"No? Okay. You want to hear the paranoid thoughts I've been having? That's what I was leading up to. That's what's troubling me."

Paranoid thoughts? I didn't like the sound of that. My newly softened hair stiffened on my scalp. "What thoughts are you having?" Our eyes locked. I had no idea if he'd figured out my role in his fingerprinting.

"Who would do this to me, Sophie? Who's out to get me?"

"What do you mean 'out to get you'?"

"What do you think I mean? Someone planted my pocketknife near Ariel Lancet's body. I've never been to Ariel's house in my life. I mean, come on, Sophie, you know me—what would I be doing over there? I don't even know where she lives." There was an odd glint in his eye. "I think you can guess where this is leading."

I had no idea. "I'm not sure what you're getting at."

"There's only one person with a personal stake in what happens to me."

"Who?"

"Who do you think? Gayle. Who else? That's where my thoughts lead, and it's dangerous territory. She could easily have taken my knife."

"You can't honestly think Gayle's behind this?"

"I know it sounds crazy, but you never know. Look at Jeremy over there."

Jeremy? My heart thumped. He must have just arrived. I scanned the crowd. He was walking over to Steve who was waiting in line for a drink. "Who would have thought Jeremy would be seeing someone on the side? You didn't know. Same with Gayle. I thought we were happy. I took her trips to see her mother at face value."

"You don't anymore?"

"My mother-in-law always had it in for me. I was too old for her daughter, I was too fat, and I was too…" He smoothed the strands of hair that lay across the top of his head. I could see he was having trouble saying the word.

"Bald?"

His ears flushed. "The point is, Gayle's mother would have no qualms lying for her."

"Lying about what?"

"What do you think, Sophie, about a man, what else? Gayle uses her cellphone when she visits her mother."

His reasoning was too far off base to ignore. "For cripes sake, Barney, even if Gayle were having an affair—which you don't know—she wouldn't murder an innocent woman to implicate you. That makes zero sense. You'd be easy enough to divorce. You don't even have children together. Get a grip. She didn't kill anyone to set you up."

His face cleared. "Yeah, you're right. I've been torturing myself with these crazy thoughts. I don't have anyone to talk to about this stuff."

"You're out in the ozone, Barney, and I need food."

"Come on, let's get something." He gave a wary glance around the room. "You okay being seen with me? I'm a pariah these days."

"Most of the people here don't know who you are and, frankly, I'm too hungry to care."

The buffet was sumptuous. I heaped my plate and waited for Barney who had more trouble making up his mind than me. We ate sitting on a couch watching the other guests, which included several local politicians and a celebrity who was on the board of the charity.

"I'll tell you what I'm not imagining, Sophie, Gayle is completely on edge around me. Ever since the police questioned her, she's been acting like I'm a deranged psychopath. She sneaks looks to see if I have a knife in my hand and a crazed look in my eye. The tension is unbelievable. We don't talk anymore. We watch TV during dinner. That's why I'm here tonight, if you want to know the truth. We needed a break from the tension."

"Everyone is spooked."

"Spooked? This is more than spooked, Sophie. Your former boyfriend over there—" Jeremy was still talking to Steve, but now they had drinks. "—he knows the shit they put people through. They questioned my friends like I was a depraved criminal. I'm embarrassed to show my face at the clinic. You know what it's like to have people stare and think I strangled a girl no older than my daughter?" He took out a handkerchief and wiped his forehead.

"Sophie?"

I looked up at the sound of my name. I didn't recognize Howard Barrow at first. His eyes used to sparkle with humor, but the luster was gone. He looked like a lost soul. The death of his lover, loss of his marriage, and stress of being a murder suspect had drained away his vitality. He and Barney had a lot in common.

"Mind if I join you?"

"Of course not." I made room on the couch and introduced the two men. "This is Barney Hisselman, my boss and also Carrie's boss, and this is Howard Barrow, a partner in Alan's law firm, and a close friend of Alan and Carrie's." My mother had taught me to introduce people by mentioning something they had in common as an icebreaker, but I wasn't convinced saying they were both under investigation for murder would ease the conversational flow.

"I guess you heard my wife and I split up," Howard said to me.

"Yes. I'm sorry. I'm sorry for your other loss, as well." Expressing condolences for the death of an illicit lover who may have died at his hands was tricky.

Curiosity lit Barney's eyes. He sniffed gossip. "You lost someone recently?"

Howard nodded. "A very dear friend was murdered." His lips quivered. "You might have read about her, Penny Harrison. She was a wonderful person."

For a hard-assed lawyer, he had lost all guile.

"Penny was a friend of my daughter's growing up."

Howard leaned across me to Barney. "Really, you knew her as a child? Tell me what she was like."

"Penny was a lovely girl. She was a good athlete, but fickle. My daughter never knew if they were going to be friends that day or not. There was great rejoicing in our household whenever Penny called. Tears when she didn't. You know what young girls are like."

"No, I only have a son," Howard said.

"I didn't realize your daughter and Penny were so close," I said to Barney. I wanted to hear more about her, too. Her fickleness was not irrelevant. If she was fickle, she might have been ditching Howard for someone else.

"I remember one year, maybe fifth or sixth grade, when Penny was all we heard about. If Penny sat next to her at lunch, my daughter had a good day at school. If Penny didn't sit next to her, the day sucked. The entire class was vying for Penny's attention. Our daughter would have sold us out in a heartbeat if Penny asked her to."

"Did Penny make difficult demands?" I asked, wanting to understand her character.

"Nah, normal kid stuff, but if Penny called, our family plans got scrapped. Penny didn't demand it, but that's what happened."

"What about boys?" I asked. "Did they worship her too?"

"I'm sure they did. She was very popular."

Howard had been hanging on Barney's every word. "I would have done anything for her, anything she asked."

"You didn't leave your wife." The words flew out of my mouth before I could stop them. I wasn't trying to be confrontational, but *really*, Howard was a married man who had gone home to Fiona every night. He hadn't exactly been giving his *all* to Penny.

He flushed, his eyes moist. "I wanted to get a divorce and marry Penny, but she wouldn't hear of it. She liked that I was married. I'm afraid it was part of my appeal. She didn't want a commitment."

"I'm sorry, Howard, I didn't mean to put you on the spot. This has to be so painful for you."

"You want to hear painful?" Barney was back in the conversation. He must have felt neglected. "I'll give you painful. You might not know this, Howard, but I'm a suspect in Ariel Lancet's murder. The police are railroading me. It's a hell of a thing to go through. Boy, oh boy. You wouldn't believe the pressure I'm under."

"Sophie." Alan motioned to me. I excused myself from between Howard and Barney.

"What's up? Is Carrie okay?"

He pointed to the entranceway where Tricia stood in jeans and a winter coat, tension radiating from her body. "She dropped Mallory off to play with Ella and asked me to bring you over. She didn't feel dressed up enough to come inside." The rigidity of Tricia's expression made me brace myself as I approached.

"Hi, Tricia."

"I saw you talking to Dr. Hisselman." No hello. She didn't even compliment my hair.

I glanced over my shoulder. Howard and Barney had closed the distance where I'd been sitting and were deep in conversation. "He's my boss, Tricia. Why wouldn't I talk to him?"

"You know why. He's implicated in Ariel's murder. He lured my dad into therapy so he could pump him for information about the investigation. The man is completely unethical."

"First of all, he hasn't been charged. And it's quite possible he's innocent, like your dad. How do you know who he is, Tricia? Have you met him before?"

"The police showed me his picture. They wanted to know if I'd seen him hanging around our house."

"Had you?"

"No. But that doesn't mean anything."

"I'm not going to apologize for keeping an open mind. I've done nothing to betray you or your dad. To the extent that I've been involved, I've been trying to uncover the truth. And Barney didn't *lure* your dad into therapy."

She had the beginning of a smile. "That's true. My dad has never been lured into anything. It's just weird to see Dr. Hisselman sitting there."

"I get that, but he has a right to be here."

"I know. I'm sorry, Sophie. I was out of line."

"It's okay. Everyone's jumpy. I understand."

"So, you're not angry at me? Do you want to do something next weekend? We can get the girls together."

"Sure. That sounds good. I'll call you."

She left, and I headed for the sunroom. I needed to clear my head, away from the crush of people. The din was getting oppressive. I scanned for Jeremy, but couldn't find him. Ned and Marnie had also retreated to the sunroom. They sat in matching wicker chairs, drinks in hand. Ella, Ian, and Mallory were on the floor eating pastries and chocolate treats from the dessert table. I greeted everyone and sat on the chaise. Ned pointed to Ian's head.

"Look, Sophie. Isn't that amazing?"

I leaned forward. "Isn't what amazing?" Ian looked up. The girls stopped eating. Ned raised his hand to Ian's ear.

"*This*." Ned opened his palm to reveal a shiny quarter. Ian's face flushed with pleasure. Ned handed him the quarter. "I found it in your ear. It belongs to you."

Ian quickly pocketed the coin. "Do the trick on Ella.

She's my sister." He pushed Ella in front of Ned. Ella's shoulders hunched around her ears. She was suddenly shy.

"I don't know the research, but I'm pretty sure ears that grow quarters are a family trait. They're often genetically linked. Your hair is in the way, Ella." Ned waited while she flicked her hair behind her ears with the expertise of someone whose hair was easily flicked. He examined her right ear like an ENT doc. "Nope." He turned to her left ear. "Ah, just as I thought." He put his hand up and came away with a quarter.

Ella plucked it from his palm, allowing herself a little smile.

"You did that. You put it there," Mallory insisted.

Ned gave her a puzzled look. "Why would I put a quarter in her ear?"

"So, this is where you vanished to." Steve and Jeremy appeared in the room. My heart lurched. Behind them, Ian was scrambling up Marnie's chair, stepping on her as if she were part of the furniture so he could use the chair as a perch to launch himself at Jeremy. Jeremy must have caught my panicked look, because he glanced over his shoulder in time to anticipate Ian's airborne arrival on his back. He absorbed the impact and anchored him in place piggyback style. From the first time Jeremy came over to Carrie and Alan's house with me, the children adored him.

Steve sat beside me on the chaise. "Your hair is a triumph, darlin'." He leaned closer and whispered, "Jeremy noticed."

"I owe you dinner, anytime, anywhere, with any waiter you want to ogle."

"Speaking of ogling, I must be off. I have another engagement tonight. Can you catch a ride home?"

"Yes, of course." I lived a five-minute drive away

and had plenty of options. "Run off and play."

Mallory had been waiting in front of Ned to have a quarter plucked from her ear, but Ella was tugging Jeremy's arm to drag him away while Ian clung to his back. Mallory abandoned Ned and joined the action.

"Help us take him to the dungeon," Ella said. "Push from behind."

Jeremy resisted just enough to make them struggle for their victory. They were taking him to their playroom in the basement.

Alan appeared in the doorway. "The speeches start in five minutes. Carrie wanted you to know in case you want to duck out before they begin."

Ned grinned. "That would be me."

"And me." Marnie stood up with him. They were gone in a flash.

Alan had hosting duties to attend to. I wandered down to the playroom. Jeremy was twirling Ian while Ella and Mallory practiced dance steps. I watched and applauded their moves. To be hanging out in Carrie's basement with Jeremy and the children felt so right, I let myself pretend that it was.

My sadness didn't settle in until Jeremy dropped me off in front of my building and said, "Goodnight, Sophie."

CHAPTER 18

A bright spot the following week was that Steve and I were scheduled to attend an all-day conference Friday that freed us from attending the staff meeting marking Barney's reentry into the clinic.

I took the Metro at Van Ness/UDC, rode two stops, and got off at Woodley Park. The hotel was within shouting distance. Steve met me in the lobby. We put on our identifying tags and set off in search of coffee before finding seats for the keynote address to be given by Dr. Jon Kabat-Zinn from the University of Massachusetts Medical Center. His topic was mindful awareness and the role of meditation and awareness in healing.

I settled back, fortified by coffee and croissant, and opened my mind to the speaker. I listened to my breathing, became centered in my body, and entered into the spirit of his talk. Steve was carried along, too, judging by the absence of elbow jabs. We were shown a videotape of two teams, the dark shirts and white shirts, each passing a ball, and were instructed to count how many times the ball was passed between the white shirted team.

I harnessed my concentration. The video had the quality of a home movie, a bunch of young adults in a small space running, weaving, and passing a ball. The amount of movement made focusing difficult. At one point, the number of people seemed to shift, but I wasn't sure. I was keeping my eye on the ball, counting the times the ball passed between white shirted hands, fifteen, I was pretty sure.

"Fourteen," Steve whispered to me. I nodded. He'd missed one, but we were being mindful, not competitive. The speaker asked for a show of hands. How many counted thirteen, fourteen, fifteen? Hands came up for each count making me wonder if I had counted an extra one. He didn't tell us which number was correct. Instead, he ran the video again to see if we noticed anything out of the ordinary while we counted.

This time, I was aware of a shadowy shift in the background. One of the dark shirted team appeared to disappear in the midst of the action. Again, we were asked if we noticed anything out of the ordinary and there were a few titters among the audience. I had no idea what the levity was about. Then Dr. Kabat-Zinn asked if any of us noticed a gorilla entering the play and crossing the screen.

Steve turned to me. We'd overlooked a *gorilla*?

Dr. Kabat-Zinn replayed the tape and holy crap— there it was. While I'd been watching the white shirts, a man in a gorilla suit had sauntered into the scene and taken a leisurely stroll through the ball-throwing action before exiting the other side. The tape was shadowy, but still—the gorilla was impossible to miss. There was no way I'd ever view the tape again and not notice. And yet, when focused on the light shirts, I'd seen only dark shifts in the background and had a vague sense of something happening just beyond my awareness.

I had a sudden frisson. The man in a gorilla suit posed no threat. But an evil being, lethal and real, lurked in the shadows of my life, a killer who blended in, trusted by his victims.

☙❧

Barney called Saturday morning and suggested we go to a movie that afternoon—Gayle was out of town again. I said yes. I had no plans for Saturday night and even with a gorilla in our midst, I found it difficult to be wary of Barney. For one thing, he wasn't going to murder *me*. We could barely handle the clinic workload with Carrie still out on sick leave. And I didn't fit the willowy profile of the two murdered women. If sausage-shaped women were being targeted, I'd have been on my guard.

Saturday was mild. Barney and I went to an afternoon movie at Mazza Gallery and afterwards strolled to The Cheesecake Factory for dinner. I ordered a salad entree and asked Barney how he felt being back at the clinic the previous day.

"How do you think I felt, Sophie? Everyone stared at the floor when they saw me. But it got easier. People warmed up. And I needed to go back." He patted his gut. "I had too much time to graze in the kitchen, and Gayle kept finding things for me to do. I'm telling you, Sophie, stay home, and you're a sitting duck."

I took a sip of water. "Is Gayle at her mother's again this weekend?"

A sad look crossed his face. "No. She's visiting a friend in Virginia and won't come home until after I leave for work on Monday. She's freaked out because I'm a murder suspect, but you know what, Sophie? I'm not exactly having the time of my life. *She* should try being the suspect and see how it feels."

"It must be awful."

"You're not kidding. Gayle blames me because our

friends were questioned by the police—like it was my fault."

I didn't like knowing Barney's wife thought him capable of murder. My stomach felt empty in a way a salad wouldn't fill, although a carbohydrate might. I reached for a piece of bread.

"I have no idea how my pocketknife ended up at the Lancet home. I didn't do anything wrong and, for once in my life, I'd like to have a wife who took my side. Gayle knows I could never kill anyone, but she thinks I must have been cheating or my knife wouldn't have been there. I swear to God, I haven't touched another woman since the day I married Gayle. You want to know my mistake? I was too honest with her. Never admit to past indiscretions, Sophie. Keep your mouth zipped. I told Gayle my whole history. I should have known better." His forehead was drenched in sweat. He wiped it dry with a napkin while I pieced together what he was saying: Gayle thought him innocent of murder but guilty of adultery.

"Did you cheat on your first wife? Is that what you told her?"

"Look, I made some mistakes. We all did—Clinton, me, Newt Gingrich. I could easily name a dozen more. The list is long. You didn't know my ex. She was on my case every waking hour. For all I know, she hammered away at me in my sleep. She couldn't let anything go."

"So, you had affairs?" I was finally getting the Barney Hisselman story.

"She put me through the ringer, Sophie. On top of everything else, she cut me off sexually. I had to plead with her just to get laid in my own home. *Just to get laid.* I'm not talking great sex. I'm talking very basic stuff. She acted like she was doing me such a big fucking favor. You can't imagine. So yeah, I cheated. Of course, I cheated. What the hell was I supposed to do? Who wouldn't cheat under those conditions?"

"Did you go together for marriage counseling?"

"We tried. The truth is we were a mismatch. We were both better off after the divorce."

"I heard a rumor that you had an affair with a psych intern before you married Gayle."

"Boy, oh boy, you heard that?" He wiped more sweat from his face. "Look, I did a lot of stupid things, although I'll tell you, Sophie, I don't regret the intern. Not for a minute." His mouth twitched. "She was a sexy woman, and don't go off on a feminist diatribe about our age difference and the power differential because having sex with me didn't do her any harm. Not one bit. She was a star fucker. You know what that is, Sophie? She slept with her drama teacher in high school, and she slept with her dean in college, her *dean*. She was into men in positions of power, and I headed the clinic, so she wanted to sleep with me. I didn't come onto her. She made her desire as plain as day. She wasn't looking for love. She wanted sex, pure and simple. Boy, oh boy, she was something."

I dipped back into the breadbasket. Knowing Barney had sex was like knowing Dick Cheney had sex—a really creepy thought. The glitter of desire in his eyes made me cringe.

I concentrated on selecting a piece of bread. The multigrain looked good. There were big nutty things on the crust. I spread on butter, hoping by the time I looked up Barney's remembrance of lust would have faded away.

I dared to raise my eyes. "What did the intern look like?"

"She's a practicing psychologist, Sophie." He was testy, which was a relief. "She's married now with kids.

Why do you want to know who she is? I haven't seen her in years."

"I don't want to know who she is." Not exactly true—I did want to know, of course, but that wasn't my primary purpose, and there was no need to get side-tracked. "I was wondering if the police might connect the way she looked with the victim's profiles, assuming they know about her."

"Oh, I see what you mean. She was five-six or so, slim and pretty, same as Ariel Lancet. I suppose she fits the overall description of Penny too, but as I told the police, I hadn't laid eyes on Penny Harrison since she was a kid. This whole thing is straight out of Kafka. Fuck it, Sophie. Enough already, let's talk about something else. How about dessert?"

The waiter removed my salad plate and handed me a dessert menu. The neurons in my diet control center were too weak and slow to be effective. By the time they fired, I had perused the menu and ordered a hot fudge sundae. Life was short. It might as well be sweet.

I staggered into my apartment after dinner, desperate to get out of my pants and release the pressure on my stomach. There was a message from Tricia on my land-line, confirming that she'd checked with Carrie, and I should bring Ella with me when I came over Sunday af-ternoon.

❧❧❧

The Lancet house was beginning to feel welcoming and familiar. Mallory led Ella up to her room and Tricia steered me to the kitchen for coffee and cookies.

I was going to tell her that I'd decided to ease off fat-tening foods, but Tricia had a bossy side, and I didn't want her to monitor my intake, so I reached for a cookie.

We were seated in the breakfast nook. "The weather is really mild," was all I could think to say. I nibbled the edge of my cookie to make it last longer. Conversation had always flowed easily between us, but suddenly it felt awkward. "I'm not trying to protect Barney," I finally blurted out.

"I was out of line, Sophie. I owe you an apology. It's just that Dr. Hisselman must have a connection to Ariel. For that reason alone, he had no business becoming my father's therapist."

"I agree, although he denies having any relationship with Ariel."

"Come on, *really*? His Swiss Army knife was at our house, and Ariel was into older men. She married my *father,* for Christ sake." Tricia got up from the table. She began rinsing dishes and banging them into the dishwasher. Her agitation filled the room. I reached for another cookie. She turned around from the dishwasher and faced me. "He had something to do with her death, Sophie."

"I'm not ruling it out."

My instincts weren't infallible—I had overlooked a fricking gorilla that was right in front of my eyes. The fact that I believed Barney didn't mean he was telling the truth. Barney was a high-maintenance spouse whose wife had been away a lot taking care of her mother. Also, he'd fooled around in the past with an intern who was into older men in positions of power. If that turned Ariel on as well, Barney wouldn't have needed to be handsome or charming. He only needed to be the man in charge. Seducing him may have been Ariel's way to regain a sense of control during a vulnerable time when she felt neglected by her husband.

Thoughts buzzed around in my mind. Maybe Barney had known Ariel from before she met Evan and before he married Gayle. Ariel would have been young, but past the age of consent. She had been a recreational drug user unsure of what to do with her life. Why not hook up with Barney? If they had been together prior to their marriages, it explained why Ariel called Barney's direct line, when she decided to come in for treatment, instead of calling the clinic number like most people did. People often turned to friends in the mental health field for guidance when they needed help. That would also explain why, when Barney ran into Ariel in the clinic parking lot, they had plenty to discuss. Not surprising if they knew each other.

Tricia came back to the table. "I was hoping we could get out for a walk."

"Sure." I carried my dishes to the sink. "A walk would be good."

"The girls are old enough to be left alone," Tricia said, reaching for a jacket from the hall closet. "We won't be out more than an hour."

"Your father isn't home?" I'd been wondering where Evan was.

"He had a business meeting. We'll be back before he is. Let me just run up and tell the girls."

Outside, we ambled down brick sidewalks past stately Georgian homes, then made our way to Wisconsin Avenue where we poked into shops and read menus posted in front of restaurants.

"My father's doing better," Tricia said as we strolled toward the canal. "Thank god, he's no longer the prime suspect. He's taking care of himself again. The truth is he's better off with Ariel gone, but he doesn't like to admit he made a mistake marrying her."

We stopped on a small bridge spanning the narrow waterway. The water was brackish and still.

Ariel wasn't just *gone*. She was murdered. I was taken aback by Tricia's dismissal of her, but Tricia was simply stating the truth as she saw it. And I was happy for Evan. "I'm glad things are easier for your dad."

"They are. We're moving ahead with the foundation, which is a great way to absorb our energies. How are you doing?" Tricia asked. "Are you finding life any easier on your own?"

I hadn't heard a word from Jeremy since he drove me home from Carrie's house. I assumed he was spending the weekend with Heather. "I don't know. Things are very up in the air."

Tricia spoke again as we headed back up Wisconsin Avenue. "There are definite benefits when your ex is a monster. Breaking free feels like liberation. Every day without him is a gift. There's no way I could possibly feel worse being on my own than being with Brad." We turned onto a residential street where the houses almost abutted the sidewalk. They had street level doors painted in glossy primary colors. Tricia pointed toward the direction of her home. "We should go back and check on the girls."

The front door flew open as we approached, and Mallory and Ella ran outside. "Can we go to the place where you paint our own pottery?"

Tricia and I gave our assent. "Do you want to walk or drive?" she asked me.

I was enjoying the novelty of moving parts of my body other than my mouth. "Let's walk."

"I know the way," Mallory announced.

"Turn left on Wisconsin and right onto M Street," Tricia said. "And don't get too far ahead of us. Make sure we're behind you."

"Don't worry," Mallory called over her shoulder.

She and Ella threaded their way through pedestrian traffic, and we followed, hastening our steps when a panhandler assailed us with a monologue. Farther along a wedding party exited a fancy restaurant just as we approached. We slowed down. The crowd thickened around us. In seconds, we lost sight of the girls. I had to trot to keep up with Tricia, who was scanning the throng of bodies with a panicked look.

"Boo!"

I jumped. Mallory and Ella flanked us on either side. They looked delighted with themselves, grinning ear to ear. They had purposely given us the slip and snuck around behind us.

Tricia's hand was pressed to her heart. "Don't do that again. I mean it, Mallory. Stay where I can see you."

"But I could see you the whole time," Mallory said.

"That's not the same thing. We're going home if you don't stay right in front of us."

"Okay."

The girls walked slowly, turning to throw giggling glances our way. Suddenly they stopped short and Tricia, and I bumped into them, a pedestrian fender bender.

Ned faced us, a young woman by his side. I saw him dip his hand into his jeans' pocket while we all greeted each other. He cocked his head with a quizzical look and peered down at Mallory. Her hair was pulled back in a ponytail.

"This is amazing." He put his hand to her ear and opened his palm to reveal a quarter.

The woman with him laughed. "Can you do that to me?"

He handed the quarter to Mallory as the woman steered him away. The girls were abuzz, whispering excitedly back and forth. If Carrie had been with me, I'd have been whispering to her like a stirred-up schoolgirl. I blamed Jeremy—he was responsible for me being so horny. First, he got me used to having really good sex then he flew off to feather his nest with Heather. I felt a spurt of empathy for Barney. In a visceral way, I understood how he could blame his ex-wife for his flings.

But being simpatico with Barney Hisselman was not the direction I wanted my life to take. I had already begun eating like him. Thinking like him was an alarming turn of events.

⌘

Tricia and I spent the afternoon painting pottery with the girls. I selected a coffee mug because I wanted a new one and painted it pale yellow inside and out. Sticking to one color without a distracting design made the most of my artistic ability. I was pleased with the result. The yellow reminded me of daffodils bursting forth in the spring. I decided to name my creation Daffodil Number 1. That was the great thing about abstract art.

When we were done, we voiced admiration for each other's efforts and left our pieces to be fired overnight. Tricia offered to pick them up the next day, deliver Ella's to her, and hold mine until my next visit. Then we set out on foot to meet Evan at a French bistro for an early dinner. He had called Tricia's cellphone earlier and made the plans.

Evan was there when we arrived, looking fit and handsome. He stood to greet us and kissed my cheek as I took the chair beside him. Needless to say, the smooch took me by surprise. I opened my linen napkin and rearranged my silverware to have something to do. Mallory told him how she and Ella had snuck up on Tricia and me in Georgetown and also that we'd run into the man they met last week at Ella's house, and he pulled a quarter out of her ear. She held the coin up for her grandfather to see.

"It was a magic trick," Ella interjected. "He had the

quarter all along. He did the trick with me and Ian at my home."

The wine steward appeared, and Evan ordered a pricey bottle of red wine. Few wines were sweet or bubbly enough for my discerning taste, but this wine was so smooth that being sweet and bubbly didn't matter. I drank it down easily. The atmosphere was friendly and relaxed. When we finished eating, the girls scooted to the restroom together. I leaned my elbows on the table for balance and propped my chin on my hands as I tried to follow Evan's story about a contractor he'd hired or that he fired—I wasn't sure. My addled brain had stopped decoding subtle distinctions. I liked watching Evan talk. He had great bone structure.

"The girls have been in there a long time," Tricia said. She glanced uneasily in the direction of the rest rooms. "I'll be right back."

She left, and I downed the last of my wine.

Evan faced me with a gentle smile. "Tricia said you were engaged and things didn't work out."

I twitched my shoulders. I didn't know how else to respond. For one thing, being dumped was embarrassing, but also, at the moment, I was fighting an urge to crawl onto Evan's lap. Some people should never drink.

"I'm sorry, Sophie. You deserve better."

I smiled. "That's what he said." Not really, but close enough.

"He was right."

The girls wiggle-walked back to the table and skidded into their seats ahead of Tricia. She signaled the waiter who handed the check to Evan. I considered making a token offer to chip in my share, but Evan very clearly intended to pay, so I thanked him instead.

We had walked to the restaurant. He had driven. The valet brought his car around, and I piled into the backseat with the girls. Tricia sat up front. The idea was to drop Ella and me at my car, but I was in no condition to drive.

"I'm afraid I'm not entirely sober." I made the humiliating announcement from the backseat. "Do you mind driving Ella and me home? I'll take a cab in the morning and pick up my car." I didn't want to drive impaired.

"Tell me where you parked," Evan said. "I'll drive you home in your car. Trish can drop Ella off and then swing by to pick me up." He was a man with a plan. No wonder he'd gotten ahead in life.

After finding my car, I gave Tricia directions to my place, and she drove away with the girls. Evan and I were alone on the street. I fumbled for my keys. He was taller than Jeremy, muscular and fit. He took the keys and held the passenger door open for me. I got in and leaned back against the headrest, imagining life with him in his Georgetown mansion drinking yummy tasting wine in front of the fireplace.

"Are Tricia and Mallory still planning to move into their own place?" I asked. They weren't part of my fantasy.

"Yes, I think it's the best thing. They'll live nearby, but we won't have three generations under one roof. The days of Lassie are over."

Lassie—I had no idea what he was talking about. Not that it mattered. I was glad we'd have the place to ourselves in my imaginary life. I closed my eyes content to keep moving and never arrive, but he stopped in front of my building.

"Where do you park?"

"The garage is around the corner." I directed him, and he maneuvered into my space. Soon we were back in the cool night air walking up the side street toward Connecticut Avenue. "I really appreciate your driving me home."

"It's my pleasure, Sophie. I'm glad you spoke up." He hesitated. "You know you've been a tremendous comfort to Tricia and me." His lips touched lightly on mine, a second smooch, this one on the lips. He straightened up and took my arm. "Tricia and Mallory will be waiting."

We rounded the corner, and there was his car, Tricia waving from the front seat, Mallory in back. I waved back toward the car.

Before I knew it, I was lying in my bed with no memory of getting there and Evan's kiss swirling through my befuddled brain.

I looked at the clock. I was unable to sleep. The time was way off. I got out of bed, wondering if there'd been a power outage. My watch said eight-forty-five, the same as the clock. No wonder I couldn't sleep. I never went to bed that early. I padded into the kitchen and drank a glass of water. Evan Lancet had kissed me.

My fridge was sparse, but the freezer was packed. Choosing between mint-chocolate-chip and pistachio ice cream wasn't easy, but the pistachio carton was already open, so I dug in with a spoon. How could this be happening? Evan's kiss held promise, but he was well into his fifties, and my dad was fifty-seven.

I called Jeremy on his cellphone. I couldn't remember if phone calls were allowed between us, but since I was the one making the rules, it didn't really matter. "Where are you?" I had to be sure he wasn't still in Philly. I didn't want to converse while he was lolling in bed with Heather.

"Could you try saying hello first," he answered.

"Hello, Jeremy. This is Sophie Myerson, your former fiancée. Where are you?"

"Hi, Sophie Myerson, I'm home. What's up?"

"I need to talk to you. Can you come over please?"

No response.

"Jeremy, I need to talk to you about the case."

"The *case*, Sophie?"

I had a mental image of his condescending smile, but he was no match for me. I'd condescended to my younger brother since his birth, honing my skills beyond anything Jeremy could hope to develop as the youngest of four boys. I sighed, a slow deep intake of breath followed by a loud resonate exhale. "Jeremy, when a homicidal maniac is on the loose, and I happen to know all the primary suspects—in fact, when one of the suspects has recently kissed me on the lips—I think I have a right to call it a case. So can you come over, please? Because while you were busy screwing Heather, I happened to be out sleuthing."

"Who kissed you?"

"Are you coming over?"

"I'm on my way, but I can't stay long. Who kissed you? Not Barney?"

I hung up. Jeremy lived a ten-minute drive away. Not nearly enough time to lose ten pounds. Enough time, however, to change into my slenderizing jeans if I worked fast. I threw the ice cream carton back into the freezer, wiped my mouth, and took off my pants. Pulling my slenderizing jeans up over my thighs and butt was a challenge. I had to inch them slowly and tuck in flesh as I went. I allowed myself a moment to rest before tackling the fly. Anyone who'd packed a dorm room's worth of stuff into a duffle bag could appreciate the difficulty. I was halfway there when Jeremy knocked on the door. Too late to extricate myself, I sucked in my gut and tugged for all I was worth, toppling from the effort. I steadied myself, fastened the button, and flew to let him in.

He looked adorable as usual, although tired, which could mean he'd suffered a regret-filled night last night *or* he'd been making passionate love to Heather into the wee hours. "Thanks for coming over. You want tea or coffee?"

He sat on the sofa. "Nothing, thanks. Aren't you going to sit down?"

I had remained standing—not because I wanted to, but because my knees wouldn't bend. The jeans encased me like a body cast.

"Just out of curiosity, what does Heather look like?" The question was a stall. I realized that sitting down could create a lethal tourniquet and I didn't want to die an accidental death due to denim constriction.

He met my gaze with a reproachful look. "I came over to discuss the *case*, not Heather. And to find out which of the suspects you've been making out with."

"Is she fat or thin, answer me that."

He sighed. "She's average. Are you going to sit down, Sophie?"

I'd been struggling with the same question and in the intervening moments had come up with a plan. I leaned my upper body against the arm of the sofa and launched my torso and legs across its length. Gymnastics was never my forte, but I did surprisingly well. My legs slapped board-like across Jeremy's lap. He looked more stunned than hurt.

The maneuver worked. I was in place, stretched out flat with my head and shoulders at a slight angle. He rested his arms across my legs, there being no other place to put them other than in the air or behind his head. I quickly steered us onto other things.

"Evan Lancet planted a tiny kiss on my lips after dinner, that's all." I thought it best to downplay the incident. On reflection, I wasn't ready to get involved with a grandfather. And I wasn't sure I'd make a good mother to Tricia. "We're friends. I spent yesterday with Barney and today with Evan and Tricia. I need help thinking through what they told me."

"Okay, I'm listening. Tell me the key points."

"Key points" was Jeremy's less-than-subtle way of telling me not to be long-winded.

"The key points are that Tricia thinks Ariel had a thing for older men and when Ariel first called the clinic for an appointment, she didn't go through the normal intake procedure. She asked for Barney."

Jeremy leaned over my legs to reach the coffee table where there was a sharpened pencil set out for the crossword puzzle as well as the Sunday paper and Saturday's unopened mail. He took a junk mail envelope and began to jot notes on the back.

I waited, not wanting to rush him when he was taking down my words. "Tell me when you're ready for me to continue."

"You can keep going, Sophie. I'll let you know if you get too far out ahead of me." There was a smug tinge to his smile.

"Barney told me he never fooled around after marrying Gayle, although—this part is in confidence—things recently haven't been good between them, and he cheated on his first wife and had an affair with a psychology intern at the clinic before meeting Gayle. The intern would have been in her mid-twenties when he was pushing fifty."

"Older guy, younger girl. Got it."

"This could be a pattern. He was very self-justifying. He almost had me convinced what he'd done was okay."

"Barney wears his flaws openly, I know. He can hide in plain sight. Go on."

"Tricia thinks Barney was seeing Ariel, but maybe that was before Ariel even met Evan and before Barney married Gayle. Not that this leads anywhere in terms of Ariel's murder or Penny's. They're random things I'm trying to make sense of."

"What does Evan say?"

"He's moving on with his life. He didn't talk about it with me."

"No, he kissed you instead. Is he interested in you, Sophie?"

The question was gratifying. "No, Jeremy, Evan is a friend. We *like* each other. There's nothing for you to get into a tizzy over."

He looked amused. "I'm not in a tizzy."

"Good."

"But I don't go around kissing 'friends' on the lips."

"I guess you and Evan are different from each other. For one thing, Evan actually married the two women he proposed to."

Jeremy tapped the pencil against my leg. He knew when to change topics. "Evan told the police he saw Barney for therapy after Ariel died. Did Barney see other patients?"

"Actually, Evan is the only one I know of."

"That's odd, isn't it?"

"Yes. On the other hand, Barney originally wanted Marnie and me to handle all contact with the Lancet family. He only took over after I told him I couldn't because I knew them personally. That's when he involved himself. And we've been short-staffed with Carrie out."

"Did he say anything to you about the session?"

"Yes, but I can't tell you."

"All right, any other sleuthing tidbits?" He was gazing at me with a fond expression I knew quite well. His hands were resting on my thighs and, to truth to tell, I was arrayed in a somewhat seductive pose, my legs lapped over his thighs, knees slightly cresting. The fact that I'd imprisoned myself in impenetrable jeans, of course, eliminated any actual hanky panky from taking place, but he didn't know that. The idea seemed to be floating in the air between us.

I shifted my weight against his crotch, pretending to stretch. I wanted him to go home in a state of arousal, stirred into realizing that even an entire weekend alone with Heather couldn't keep him from lusting after me. I drove the point home by rocking back and forth and putting pressure on him under the guise of a sudden cramp in my leg.

"That's better," I said, flexing my foot. "Leg cramps are so intense. So, what do you think about what I learned?"

He was glassy eyed. I gave him a moment to collect his thoughts. There was a pause before he spoke. "Either Barney lost his knife, and someone else picked it up, or Barney had some kind of involvement with Ariel. But I don't see a motive for murder. What could she have done that would lead him to kill her? He's not a violent guy."

Jeremy's arousal had faded, but that was okay. The memory of frustrated lust would serve as well. "Jeremy, does the term *serial killer* ring a bell?"

"Yeah, but Barney? And why all of a sudden?"

"Okay, then who do you think killed her?"

"If I tell you what I know, you can't repeat a word. I'm serious, Sophie."

I gave him a withering look. I was trained to keep confidences.

"The police are building a case against Howard Barrow in Penny Harrison's death. They think Ariel's murder was a copycat of Penny's. Different perp. Unrelated. The method was in the news and easy to copy."

Hmm. On the one hand, it was depressing to know there were several murderers running around the neighborhood. On the other hand, I was relieved to know a serial killer wasn't out trolling for young women.

"Your friend Evan has the best motive in Ariel's death," Jeremy continued. "And I'm not saying that because he kissed you. There were problems in his marriage. Divorce was obviously an option, although he would have taken a financial hit. He may have thought Ariel was cheating on him."

"Why would he think that? Was there proof?"

"No. But he could have been suspicious. Men have been known to kill in the heat of jealousy, even when the jealousy is unfounded. Think of Othello."

"Othello is fiction, Jeremy."

He moved his hand down my legs and began massaging my feet. He knew how to domesticate me. I settled back to listen. "Ariel accompanied Evan to a business dinner the night she was killed. She hadn't wanted to attend. In fact, Evan told the police she begged him to cancel and stay home with her. He regrets not giving into her, or so he says."

"You learned this from Detective White?"

"Yes, Reggie brought me up to speed. Ariel went to the restroom during dinner and came back saying she was ill and needed to go home. She urged Evan to stay at the dinner. He thought she had called someone from her cellphone while she was in the bathroom—which it turned out she had. He was enraged that she was abandoning him so she could meet up with another man or her group of friends."

"Don't you think the fact that he admitted that is in his favor? He didn't make up a phony story."

"Yes, but he could have acted impulsively. He walked her home. He could have gone around to the back garden with her on the pretext of checking the outdoor lighting or something. The spot is secluded. He knew his daughter and granddaughter would be out for the evening. It wouldn't have been difficult for him to twist Ariel's scarf around her neck, especially if she was sitting down and he was standing. Quick efficiency is the Lancet trademark. The whole thing would have added less than five minutes to his time away from the dinner. Then he called her cellphone later that night to round out his story."

"You really think he killed her?" The idea roiled my stomach, although my stomach was encased so tightly there was little room to roil.

"It's possible, Sophie. Ariel's friends from Silver Spring all alibi each other. Evan had motive and opportunity. The role of prime suspect is his to lose. The problem is how to make sense of Barney. The only hard evidence the police have is his Swiss Army knife."

"I saw him fiddling with it the day Penny's murder was reported in the paper, but the Monday after Ariel died, he didn't have it on him. That's a small window of time in which it disappeared. But how it ended up in the Lancet yard is beyond me. Barney is adamant he's never been there." Something was teasing my brain, something had coincided with the missing knife, but I had a pressing problem I couldn't ignore—I had to pee, badly. My bladder was about to burst.

"Actually, I have a theory about Barney's knife," Jeremy said.

I didn't know how long it would take me to pull down my slenderizing jeans, and I needed to lose ten pounds before pulling them back up. If I changed into a bathrobe, Jeremy would assume I was trying to seduce him, and I wasn't about to give him the satisfaction of thinking I desired him, unless and until, he re-proposed marriage, set a date for the wedding, and showed up at the fricking altar.

I maneuvered off the couch without injury, although not without pain. "Thanks for coming over."

Jeremy looked confused. "Don't you want to hear my theory?"

"Some other time."

"What happened, Sophie? Did I say something?"

"You said you couldn't stay long, remember?"

I didn't want to wet my pants, and I couldn't hold out much longer. He followed me to the door. "We can talk tomorrow, Jeremy." I closed the door behind him, turned the lock, and made it to the bathroom in the nick of time.

❧❦❧

Monday, Steve joined me in my office for lunch, brown bag in hand. I opened my bag and took out a yogurt and apple. Ten pounds had to come off. "Thanks again for the hair advice," I said.

He stroked his carefully trimmed beard. "You can repay the favor, darlin'."

"How?"

"Come to the gym with me tomorrow evening, and we're even."

"Come to the gym? Or come and work-out at the gym?" There was a big difference. I was happy to hang out in the health club lobby reading magazines and eye-balling the cute guys he wanted a second opinion on. But if this was an underhanded way of luring me into an ex-ercise routine—

"Barney's also coming."

I dropped a blob of yogurt on my pants. "Barney, in a gym?" The blueberry stood out against the gray corduroy. I hadn't realized when you brought yogurt for lunch, you needed to coordinate with your pants color.

"Sadly, yes. Barney woke up this morning to the stunning realization that he's got a gut the size of Cincinnati." Steve took a bite of his peanut-butter-and-jelly sandwich. He had two sandwiches, both neatly cut in half. I had none. "He acts as if he's been the victim of some kind of cosmic catastrophe, like he went to bed thin and woke up shocked to find a boulder on his belly, as if it were an act of God, like an earthquake shifted a blubber mass onto him and somehow it became grafted in place." Steve pushed what was left of the first sandwich into his mouth while I scraped the bottom of my yogurt container. My apple had a waxy look.

"What made him notice, all of a sudden?" I asked.

"His wife told him looking nine months pregnant wasn't sexy on a man. I have to say, I agree."

"They've been having problems," I conceded.

Steve picked up his second sandwich. I took a bite of apple. The inside was mealy. No crunch.

I tossed it in the trashcan and gave my yogurt container a mournful scrape. "It was nice of you to invite him to your gym."

Steve put down his sandwich and peered at me. "*Invite him*? Sophie?"

"You didn't invite him?"

"Darlin', I told him to hire a trainer to come to his house. He can't show himself like that in a gym. But his wife is home a lot, and he said he'd be too inhibited, so I suggested he find a rehab center that caters to people at his level of fitness. There are places that rehab heart patients and stroke victims. He'd do fine with people relearning how to walk, maybe some low-stress aerobics, but he wasn't interested. He asked outright if he could come with me to my gym to try it out. He left me no wiggle room, none."

"Where do I fit in?"

"I have two guest passes. I'd like to leave him with you."

"Oh." There was a simplicity to the plan I had to admire.

"You can keep him company on a stationary bike or something. Make disparaging remarks about the place. Do what you can to discourage him from deciding to join." Steve polished off the rest of his sandwich and pulled a Twix candy bar out of his bag. He held it up. He'd seen the hunger glowing in my eyes. "Please, darlin'."

I held out my hands, and he tossed me the Twix. The deal was sealed.

eѕeѕ

I owned a pair of running shoes from an ancient attempt to establish an exercise routine and a pair of sweat pants dating back to the same era. I packed them both in a tote bag, threw in my college sweatshirt, a pair of socks, soap, deodorant, and a shower cap for when I showered afterward. Towels were provided.

The sight of Barney and me leaving the clinic together carrying gym bags raised a few sardonic brows, including my own.

"Do you really want to do this?" I asked Barney after Steve had signed us in and left us standing in our workout togs staring at the stationary bikes he'd recommended as a good place to start. The room was whirring with buff bodies in various forms of exertion.

"I have to. I promised Gayle."

We mounted our bikes. I started pedaling. Not as bad

as I'd imagined. I tightened the tension a tad and felt a satisfying pull in my muscles. I doubted there'd be much impact on Barney's gut, but cycling side by side was companionable. "Remember the evening you walked Ariel to her car," I said. "What were you two talking about?"

He looked surprised by the question. "I don't know, small talk, nothing out of the ordinary."

"Do you remember what you said?"

"Nothing having to do with the poor girl's murder, I can tell you that. Why is this of interest, Sophie?"

"Oh, come on, Barney. These things are always of interest. You should know that better than anyone. If the situation was reversed, you would want to know every fricking detail I could remember."

"Yeah, you're right."

"The interns said you stood by her car chatting. What did she say?"

"She told me she liked coming to the clinic. She liked working with Marnie. She wanted to know about her."

"About Marnie?"

"Yeah, she wanted to know if I assigned her to Marnie because Marnie was young and I thought they'd be a good match. I said yes, in part. And then she wanted to know if Marnie was gay. She made me promise our conversation was confidential. She didn't want Marnie to know she was asking about her."

"What did you say?"

"I told her I thought it likely. I didn't want to out and out say yes."

"You didn't tell her to talk to Marnie about it during therapy if it was on her mind?"

"No, Sophie. Ariel didn't want to ask her in therapy and make a big thing out of it. She wanted to know. She was curious. Don't you ever get curious about people?"

"Yes, of course." That wasn't the point. His response had been unprofessional. At the same time, I believed him, and what he said raised a new concern: why had Ariel wanted to know if Marnie was a lesbian?

"Did Ariel say anything that suggested Marnie had been seductive to her?"

I was Marnie's supervisor. I needed to know if she'd behaved in an inappropriate way with a patient. I regretted not having the interns tape their therapy sessions. We should have pushed Barney to get the equipment.

"No, she didn't say anything like that, Sophie. She just wanted to know."

His words reassured me, but I was troubled that Marnie may have broadcast her sexuality in a way that made Ariel uncomfortable.

I pedaled some more and felt a jolt of fear remembering Marnie's hooded figure in the parking lot. She'd been so reactive to Ned's offer to accompany Ariel to her car. She distrusted Ned around women—I understood that—but maybe she was attracted to Ariel and her sense of threat with Ned stemmed from competition. She hadn't minded Barney accompanying Ariel.

Barney dismounted his bike. We'd clocked in about eight minutes of low-stress aerobics. Since we were workout partners, I got off my bike as well. "That was a good start," I said. Steve would be thrilled to get a message at the desk that we'd left.

"You ready to call it a day?"

"I am if you are, Barney. Want to get dinner?"

"I'll keep you company. Gayle's cooking tonight, but if I arrive home too early, she'll get suspicious that I didn't exercise enough. The truth is I'm grateful she's back in the house, but these days I have to earn my supper."

◈◈◈

I called Jeremy as soon as I got home. I remembered he had a theory he'd wanted to discuss before I ousted him from my apartment. There was no answer on his cellphone. I left a message and tried his landline.

"Hey, Sophie."

"Ned? What are you doing answering Jeremy's phone?" He wasn't supposed to be taking over his life.

"He has caller ID. I knew it was you or I wouldn't have picked up. Jeremy's not home."

I searched my thoughts for something to say. "Mallory was excited about the quarter you gave her when we ran into you in Georgetown Sunday."

"I learned magic tricks as a kid. So how are you doing?"

I flipped back in my mind to when Barney and I left the clinic with our gym bags. I was pretty sure Ned hadn't been among the hecklers. He probably didn't know about our foray to the gym.

"I'm fine. How are you doing?"

"I'm okay. I think Jeremy's still at work. The man's a total workaholic."

"He has a demanding job."

"What is he, an assistant DA?"

"Yes."

"I'm telling you, Sophie, his girlfriend's a piece of work."

"You mean Heather?" I tossed off her name with casual indifference.

"Oh, man, she calls him all the time. I'd go nuts if anyone called me that much. She can't leave him alone for a minute."

Perhaps Heather was a tad insecure?

"I don't think her calls annoy Jeremy the way they

would annoy you." I waited, praying for the worst.

"I've heard him on the phone with her. Trust me, he's annoyed."

I stifled my glee. "Have you met her?"

"Are you kidding? She won't come here, and not because of me. I'm out a lot. I usually have someone to stay with on the weekends. She doesn't like the hassle of going to the train station and getting on the train. She'd rather let him do the traveling. He's whipped. You can't believe the way he gives in to her."

"Really?"

"Jeremy's a great guy, but choosing a skank like Heather? He can't tell his ass from his elbow."

"I have to go, Ned." I hung up. He had brightened my day.

CHAPTER 19

In the middle of the night, I woke up and couldn't get back to sleep. I kept remembering happy times with Jeremy. Taking Ambien past two a.m. was out of the question because I would sleep too late in the morning. Consequently, I arrived at the clinic on time but so sleep-deprived and bleary-eyed that Ned could have strolled in naked for our supervision, and I would have still struggled to stay awake.

Marnie arrived first. Seeing her, I couldn't imagine her with a furtive attraction to Ariel that distorted her judgment. Marnie was Marnie.

"How are you doing, Sophie?" She eyed me with concern. I must have looked even worse than I felt.

"I'm okay. I didn't sleep well."

Ned strolled in and took a seat. "Tom, my depressed patient, got laid. I thought you'd both want to know." He grinned, looking pleased with himself.

"Congratulations," Marnie said.

I bowed my head in acknowledgement of the feat.

"He met her on an on-line dating site. They went out three nights in a row and on the fourth night—" He snapped his fingers.

"Condoms and whatnot? You talked to him about safe sex?" Marnie asked.

"Yeah, yeah, he's on top of it. We're going to terminate after another session or two."

Ending Tom's treatment seemed like a non-sequitur. "Why?"

Ned looked at me with surprise. "He's not depressed anymore."

"Oh." He had a point. Many patients came in seeking symptom relief and left when they felt better. Nevertheless, Tom had deficits. "Don't you think he's going to need help sustaining a relationship or figuring out if the woman he met is right for him?"

Ned conked his forehead with the heel of his hand and laughed. "Oh, yeah, I forgot about that."

"You are so trifling." Marnie shook her head, cornrows clacking. "It's all about the chase."

"Yeah, well." Ned flashed me a grin. "Can I talk about Ashley, the social anxiety disorder?"

"Let's stick with Tom for another moment. Was it Tom's idea to stop therapy after a few more sessions?"

"Not really. We haven't discussed it."

"So he expects to keep coming?"

"Right."

"Okay, good. There's no reason for you to introduce the idea at this point. We can move onto Ashley. How's she doing?"

"She feels a lot better on Paxil. For a while there, she was meeting guys on Match.com and J Date. But now all she does is moon over a married co-worker. I'm ready to throw her out the window. Any suggestions?"

"Keep your window closed," Marnie said.

"How have you been working with her?" I asked.

"Truthfully? I tune her out and hope she'll be run over before our next session. She drones on about this

dude in her office until I'm ready to blow my brains out."
He looked at Marnie. "I think she needs a female therapist."

"She's your problem, dude, not mine."

"Okay. Then I'm ready to terminate with her. I'll
hang onto Tom, though."

I wasn't sure if he was kidding. "You don't get to
bargain one patient for another. Let's decide about Ashley based on Ashley. She sounds stuck, like she's going
around in circles."

"You could put it that way."

"Then your job is to help her become unstuck. Ask
what she wants to get out of treatment. What are her
goals? Try and get a discussion going."

"I'll try." He didn't sound optimistic. "All she wants
to do is talk about this guy."

"If she's too obsessed to engage, then discuss her in-
ability to focus on anything other than him. Tell her how
distancing that is. She's building her emotional life
around a fantasy."

"She won't concede he's a fantasy. He works in a
cubicle near her, and she hears him on the phone with his
wife. She thinks he wants out of the marriage."

"Then ask her to pretend for a minute that he doesn't
exist. Hypothetically, if he were out of the picture, what
would she think about? How would she spend her time?
Who would be important in her life?" Ned was actually
taking notes. "If she can't spend even a few minutes talking about anything other than him, point that out. Her obsession is serving a purpose that has nothing to do with
who this man is. Try to start a discussion about what
other purpose there might be."

"What if none of this stuff works?"

"Then ask if she finds the therapy useful. If she says
yes, ask how. What does she get from the sessions? If all

she wants is an opportunity to talk about her crush, that's not a good use of your time or hers. But ask about her history and family relationships. That might break up the rigidity of her focus. If she's truly unwilling to talk about anything else, you can suggest taking a break from treatment."

Ned stopped taking notes and grinned as if I were a teacher who'd just handed him a pass to skip class. "Why don't you tape record the session?" I added, uneasy he might end Ashley's treatment without a genuine effort to engage her in a more productive way.

He sat forward. "You want me to start recording our sessions?"

"Yes, with Tom too. Use the same protocol of informed consent you use with Child and Family patients. Delores can find you a recorder."

He bit his lower lip. "Why?"

"Not just you, Marnie too." I glanced at her, and she nodded okay.

"Why?" Ned repeated. He looked affronted by the request.

"Because I need more information to know what I'm doing. It's not a criticism of you, Ned." I was a tad irritable—sleep deprivation did that to me—but why couldn't he comply? With the murders preying on my mind and all the uncertainty with Jeremy, I felt like I was groping my way in a dimly lit cave with no idea what lay ahead. I could barely make out what was immediately in front of me.

All I was asking was for Ned to do *his* job so I could do *mine*.

ᴄᴏᴄᴏ

In the afternoon, I had a fifteen minute break and decided to call Jeremy. "Is this a good time to tell me your theory about the murders?"

"Yes, let me close my door." He came back on the phone. "My theory's based on the assumption that Howard Barrow killed Penny and that her murder and Ariel's murder are unrelated. I know that's open for debate."

"I'm not debating, I'm listening."

"The evidence points to Ariel being killed by someone she knew. Evan is the most likely suspect. The problem is fitting Barney into the scenario."

I peeled a Clementine. No more cookies at work. "So you don't think Barney killed her?"

"No. But Ariel called Barney's direct line when she was looking for a therapist and you seem to think his ethics are malleable."

I separated out a section of the orange and popped it into my mouth. "Go on."

"I think Evan might have initiated the contact with Barney. He could have called him to talk about problems his wife was having as a preliminary to her getting help, a man-to-man thing. Don't family members sometimes call ahead to describe the problem before the patient makes an appointment?"

"Yes, sometimes. But it's equally likely that Evan suggested to Ariel that she call the head guy at the clinic because that's how he operates. Why mess around with underlings? Go to the top."

"That's possible, Sophie, but I'm trying to tell you my theory. For the moment, let's assume Evan called Barney."

"Okay."

"How do you think Barney would have responded if Evan Lancet called him about problems his wife was having?"

I didn't have to think about the answer. "Barney would be flattered."

"I agree. Now, suppose Evan asked Barney to tell him if Ariel was betraying him. Maybe he also asked Barney to tell him what Ariel did with her group of friends. In other words, Evan may have turned Barney into an informant."

I was shocked by the suggestion. "Not even Barney would go that far, Jeremy. He would have been breaking privacy laws and breaching professional ethics."

"Honey, people break laws and breach ethics all the time. Otherwise, I wouldn't have a job."

Honey—the unexpected endearment melted my bones. I didn't agree with Jeremy's theory, but my voice softened. "But where would Evan get the idea that Barney would violate his professional ethics that way?"

"From Barney's reputation maybe."

What Jeremy was saying took a moment to sink in and, during the "sinking in," I realized Jeremy hadn't actually called *me* honey. That was the way his family in South Carolina talked. His speech had taken on that familiar southern dip, and the reason was obvious—he had spent last weekend dipping into his southern honey and was anticipating more southern comfort to come.

"You know what, Jeremy? What you just said is a stunning insult—not just to Barney, but to The Hartley Clinic and, by extension, to Carrie, Steve, and me. You're implying that Evan chose our clinic for his wife because we have a reputation for trampling on patient's rights." My pulse was racing with rage. I felt stupid thinking the endearment was meant for me.

"Sophie, no, that's not what I'm saying. I didn't mean to imply *anything* like that. Maybe Evan even tried a few other places before he had a hit."

I glanced at the clock. My next patient was coming

in a few minutes. I needed to compose myself. And I realized my reaction had been a tad overwrought. The honey/Heather thing was fraying my nerves, but Jeremy hadn't introduced Heather into this conversation. I was the one who had her on the brain. I spoke in a calm voice to reestablish my sanity in Jeremy's eyes. "Okay, that makes sense."

"You know Evan personally, Sophie. Does he have enough charm to make the idea of keeping him informed seem less egregious than it is?"

"Honey, Evan could charm the pants off a virgin." If Jeremy could honey me, I could honey him right back. And if Evan could charm the pants off a virgin, let Jeremy ponder what he could do to me. I gave Jeremy a moment to absorb my comment before resuming the substance of our conversation. "I'm sure Barney would have been flattered to have Evan turn to him and, yes, Barney had access to Ariel's chart. But—" I paused to stress the importance of the point I was about to make. "—Ariel wasn't having an affair."

We fell silent.

Finally, Jeremy spoke. "Evan put his house in both their names. In their two years, together he earned over five million dollars, jointly held. The bulk of his net worth was protected, but still, he might have regretted his generosity."

"Or, Evan is a generous guy who suggested his wife call the head of the clinic, because that's how he operates, and he had nothing to do with her death."

"That's possible, Sophie, but I'm trying to account for Barney's knife being at their house. If Barney went to the Lancet home at some point to see Evan, you no longer have to posit a relationship with Ariel. Barney could have dropped his knife in the garden. Or maybe he dropped it somewhere else, and Evan picked it up, wearing gloves, and planted it at the crime scene to confound the investigation."

"By the same token, anyone could have swiped and planted it," I said.

"That's true, but who else would have had access to Barney's knife? Anyway, that's my theory, for what it's worth. I need to get back to work, Sophie."

So did I. "Are you running off to Philly again this weekend?" I couldn't help myself. I wanted to know. Fear of getting my hopes up and being dumped again was gaining ground. "You might be in a state of confusion, Jeremy, but I'm in a state of very deep hurt."

"I'll figure this out soon, I promise, Sophie. I'm sorry for what I'm doing to you. I don't know my weekend plans yet. Heather might come here."

That was an unwelcome surprise. I'd been pinning my hopes on Ned's description of Heather's narcissism and how unwilling she'd been to share the burden of traveling. Her coming here felt like a sucker punch.

"Look, Sophie, about Evan, I don't know if there was any follow-up to your kiss—and I don't have to know—but he *is* a murder suspect. Keep that in mind. Please. You need to be careful around him. I mean it."

I liked having Jeremy worry about my welfare, but his worrying had a paradoxical effect. The more he worried, the less vulnerable I felt.

When I got home after work, there was a phone message from Evan. He sounded very polite, almost formal. "Sophie, this is Evan Lancet calling to invite you out to dinner Saturday night. It would be just the two of us, as Tricia and Mallory will be away for the evening. Please call and let me know if you'd like to come." He left the same home phone number as Tricia's. That was good. He wasn't trying to take me out on the sly.

He wasn't exactly a grieving widower, but I saw no

reason not to go. The conversation with Jeremy left me feeling demoralized. His trips to Philadelphia were hard enough, but I hated the thought of Heather in his apartment sharing his bed, sleeping where I used to sleep. I didn't want to stay home alone Saturday night while they cavorted together. Why not be a comfort to Evan, and vice versa, let him comfort me during a difficult time. A man who didn't call me honey while sleeping with someone else was a refreshing change. And, in light of Jeremy's theory, I had questions for him about Ariel and Barney.

Tricia answered when I called back. "Hi, it's Sophie. Is your dad there? I'm returning his call. He asked me out for dinner Saturday night." I was blathering, but I felt compelled to tell her up front. I needed to make sure she knew, because I wasn't going out with him if it burdened my friendship with her.

"I'll get him."

She sounded pleased. No tension. I could go ahead and accept.

CHAPTER 20

Steve and I arrived a few minutes early for the Friday staff meeting. His eyes were gleaming. Something was up. Other staff members dribbled in.

I looked at him. "What?"

He shook his head. "You go first, darlin'. You look different. Has your dry spell come to an end?"

"The drought continues, but I have a date Saturday night," I whispered in his ear. "Evan Lancet."

"Oh, my, my. He's not exactly in his first blush of youth, but you can't fault a man for devoting a couple of decades to amassing a fortune. Assuming he's not incarcerated for murdering his wife, could this turn into something?"

"I don't know. Life is a lot weirder than I ever imagined it to be."

"You need to brace yourself for my news."

"Don't tell me—you're in love with a woman?"

"Not a woman, darlin', a dog."

His words left me transfixed. I was unable to speak.

"I'm not fucking a dog, Sophie, I'm adopting a dog."

I hadn't imagined a carnal relationship, but dogs needed to be walked and fed regularly. "You're tying yourself down to a pet?"

"Joey and Tommy are breaking up. They couldn't agree on Hercule's custody so they asked if I'd take him and let them both visit. He's an adorable mutt with an inscrutable grin. Next to him, Mona Lisa looks like a commonplace slut. He's all nuance, Sophie. He savors every witty morsel I throw his way."

"I'm excited for you, Steve, but a dog is a big responsibility."

"That's why I'd like you to be Hercule's godmother. You can be in charge of his moral education."

"I'm honored. I'd love to."

The social worker seated on my other side tapped my arm and passed me a pile of agendas. I took one and handed them on to Steve. The meeting was about to begin. When it was over, Barney asked Steve and me to come to his office for a few minutes. Barney sat behind his desk and motioned us to sit in the chairs facing him.

"I've got some good news. The Hartley Clinic CFO gave me the go-ahead to hire a part time psychologist. I'd like Marnie to step into the position when her internship ends."

Steve and I exchanged a look of disbelief. I was too flabbergasted to respond, so Steve stepped into the breach. "I thought the clinic had a policy not to hire people who train here. Wasn't that the issue a few years ago when you wanted to hire one of the psychiatry residents?"

"Oh, boy, you know what? You're right. We did run into a problem. I'd forgotten about that." Barney smoothed the strands of hair on the top of his head. He appeared thoughtful. "What do you think about men shaving their heads?" He looked from Steve to me and back to Steve. "Is total baldness sexy?"

"You don't want to shave your head, Barney," Steve said, responding to Barney's change of subject.

I was still in shock over his desire to hire Marnie. I liked Marnie a lot. She was a really good intern, but putting aside the policy problem, why did he want to wait until Marnie's internship ended in June when we had money to hire someone now who was fully qualified? It made no sense.

"What are my choices, buy a rug? Use Rogaine and sprout a few weeds? It's a hell of a dilemma."

I had to screen out half of what Barney was saying in order to have a coherent conversation with him. "What made you decide on Marnie?" I asked. Even after her internship ended, she would still need to be supervised, which required additional staff time, and we had a backlog of patients waiting to be seen. "Why not hire a licensed psychologist who could start right away? How did this even come up, Barney?"

He rested his hands on his stomach. "You know me, Sophie. I like chatting with all our students, not just the psychiatric residents. I asked Marnie about her post-internship plans. Ideally, she'd like to work two or three days a week at a clinic like ours while writing her dissertation. I thought—wait a minute: if she's looking for a clinic *like ours*, why not work at *our* clinic? I had just gotten the go-ahead from the CFO. Marnie's a lovely girl. I don't have to tell you that, Sophie. You're the one who's always singing her praises."

Steve had eased out of his seat. His tolerance for Barney had never been high. "I have a patient, so I'll vote however Sophie votes, if we actually get a vote, but, Barney, in terms of the bald look, if you're asking my advice—hold onto your fringe. Bald and muscular is sexy. The muscularity gives baldness its punch. Without muscularity, you're just bald. And long narrow faces look better with a little padding above the ears. I have to run."

He was out the door.

Barney gave me a woeful look. "Steve can be tough."

"You asked for his advice, Barney." I glanced at the clock. I had four minutes before I needed to be in my office. "Can we get back to Marnie? In addition to needing someone who can start working now, how do you think Ned will feel if Marnie is offered a job and he wasn't even allowed to apply?"

"I hadn't thought about that."

Why Barney didn't anticipate the ramifications was beyond me. "You'd be showing unbelievable favoritism that would sour Marnie's relationship with Ned and the other trainees."

"You're right, Sophie. This whole murder investigation has taken a toll. I'm not operating at a hundred percent. Back to the drawing board. I'll have to advertise the position and see who we can get."

⳥⳧

Barney's blunder replayed in my mind throughout the day. He had decided on Marnie without so much as interviewing one qualified psychologist. Stupid ideas were a defining characteristic of Barney, so in a way, there was nothing suspicious about this particular one. The staff usually nixed them in time and shared them for entertainment. But why had he chosen Marnie? Was he in closer contact with her than I had realized?

I puzzled over their relationship as I cleared off my desk at the end of the day. Maybe Barney had an ulterior motive when he arranged for Marnie to be Ariel's therapist. He excused her from our weekly staff meeting, so she could make time to meet with Ariel, which was unprecedented. Maybe Jeremy was right, after all, and Barney had purposely assigned Ariel to a student who would be easy for him to debrief. He could have checked Marnie and Ned's schedules ahead of time and known I would assign Ariel to Marnie because Ned had no openings and Marnie had just freed up a slot. Ned wasn't anywhere near as compliant with authority as Marnie was. Most students would be flattered to have one-on-one attention from the head of the clinic, and Marnie was an impressionable intern. She seemed to look up to Barney. It would have been easy for him to get information from her about Ariel's therapy to give Evan. Within the agency, Marnie was free to discuss Ariel's treatment. She would have found nothing wrong with telling the head of the agency whatever he wanted to know. And we all had access to patient files.

I left my office and walked down the hallway, remembering how Marnie had jumped to defend Barney when Ned criticized him. She dismissed what Ned said as if he'd been making it up. Yet Ned had been right, in the sense that Barney and Ariel had been having a personal conversation. If Barney was telling the truth, he'd been discussing Marnie's sexuality with Ariel. They would have given off a funny vibe if they glanced over at Ned and Marnie while they were discussing her.

The door to Barney's office was shut, but he never locked it. I knocked gently. When there was no response, I peeked inside. No one was there. The coat rack in the corner was empty, meaning Barney had left for the day. I slipped inside and closed the door behind me. As a former philanderer, Barney had experience hiding relationships. He could have shifted into his illicit affair mode with Marnie, even though their secret connection wasn't sexual. Or was it?

Marnie talked openly about being a lesbian, but I had yet to meet her partner. What better cover was there for Barney than to hide an affair in plain sight?

His desk was a mess of papers, mostly scraps of to-do lists relating to personal errands. I wasn't sure what I was looking for. But if Barney had preyed on Marnie's inexperience to pump her for information about Ariel, then he had to be in cahoots with Evan. And if that was true, then Evan could have planted Barney's knife, and they both knew more than they were saying.

Evan may even have killed his wife.

I shook away the thought. Maybe Barney had been up to his old lecherous tricks with Marnie. But that didn't make sense either, not with Marnie. She wasn't like that. She was an openly gay woman, comfortable in her own skin. She had a girlfriend and believed in fidelity. Or was she completely different than I believed her to be?

My hands shook as I opened the upper drawer in Barney's desk. Although I thought of myself as a snoopy person, the truth was I'd never actually done any snooping before. There were two bags of chocolate chip cookies in the drawer, one of which was open. Barney would never keep track of how many cookies he had, so I slipped one in my mouth to calm my nerves. Then I opened the lower drawer.

There was a book on treating baldness and one on weight loss. Beneath the books was a stack of catalogues, familiar ones like LL Bean and Williams Sonoma and unfamiliar ones filled with orthopedic shoes and under-garments such as girdles for men. They were addressed to Barney's home, which meant he'd brought them to work to peruse at his leisure. I shut the drawer. Good old Barney.

I was a little surprised not to find *anything* work related in his desk, but the ever-efficient Delores organized Barney's administrative tasks for him and kept a file cabinet in the main office where she had her desk. Barney's computer didn't get much use as far as I could tell. He never sent me emails. Delores communicated that way, but not Barney. Anyway, trying to hack into his computer was out of the question.

I listened at the door before leaving. I didn't want to be seen exiting Barney's office after he'd left for the day. There were no sounds in the hallway. I went out quickly, shut the door behind me, and felt weak with relief.

Although I hadn't actually discovered anything of consequence to the investigation, seeing Barney's stash of books and catalogues made me realize just how much Barney wanted to be admired. In that context, his desire to hire Marnie made rational sense. She didn't have Ned's cynicism. She looked up to Barney. She imbued him with credibility based on his position.

I had no doubt that, if hired, Marnie's admiration would wane as she gained experience, but I understood Barney's desire for a devoted underling. Gayle was less enamored of him at home. And any seasoned psychologist he hired from outside would quickly develop a jaundiced view of him.

The parking lot was dark when I left the clinic. I got out my clicker.

"Hey, Sophie, wait up." Ned startled me out of my thoughts.

With a few graceful strides, he caught up with me. I felt a twinge of guilt that he'd been slighted by Barney, even if he didn't know it. Marnie was the favored child.

"Heather's coming to stay with Jeremy this weekend. I thought you'd want to know. She actually agreed to make the trip. I'll crash somewhere else and let the lovebirds get naked together."

Exactly the image I wanted lodged in my brain. *Thank you, Ned.* "Have a good weekend." I hastened my steps.

He kept pace and touched my arm. "After my internship ends, will you hang out with me? I won't be your student forever."

Both interns were thinking ahead to the future, but whereas Marnie was trying to nail down a job, Ned was trying to nail me. I was being primed for seduction. I had no doubt that "hanging out" to Ned meant having sex. The way he posed the question was sneaky, because I didn't want to be rude and say no, I won't hang out with you, but agreeing was like saying yes to a test drive with a car salesman. Once I stepped into the car, sooner or later he was going to make a sale.

"Of course, we can hang out together after your internship." What else could I say?

"Cool. And will you write me a recommendation? I'm probably going to apply for jobs in this area." That was a reasonable request.

"I'd be happy to." I always wrote recommendations for the interns with whom I worked. "What about your dissertation? Have you picked a topic?"

"Oh, yeah, the research is done. I just have to write it up."

"That's great."

"Any chance you could give me a hand with the writing, you know, check over what I do, help me organize the material? I'd pay you with backrubs. I'm a great masseuse."

I could but imagine. Great back rubs and, knowing Ned, front rubs, too. He was offering me foreplay if I helped him write his dissertation. If I wrote him a really good recommendation, I could only guess what that would get me in return.

"You're so uptight with me, Sophie," he said with a smile. "Come on. I'll walk you to your car."

♋♋

I felt off-kilter driving home. I couldn't decide if I was reading something into Ned's pursuit of a friendship with me because of my own horniness. I hoped he didn't have me pegged as so needy that he could manipulate me into helping him by a show of attention. Being lonely and confused wasn't easy. If Barney was vulnerable to being admired by an intern, so was I.

I trusted Marnie's judgment that Ned was a player. If we ever got together sexually after he left the clinic, our connection would last only as long as he wanted, probably a week or maybe a weekend was his limit. On the other hand, if Jeremy unloaded me for good, I would be devastated, and no-strings sex could be a rewarding diversion. An intense weekend might be reparative, unless Ned made it contingent on me helping with his dissertation. Even I wasn't that needy. One dissertation per lifetime was my limit.

I parked in the building garage and rode the elevator up to my apartment. Maybe because Ned left me so unsettled, I began to feel unsettled again about Barney wanting to hire Marnie.

I needed to talk to someone I trusted. I tried Carrie, but she didn't answer. Her days were filled with physical therapy, doctor's appointments, taking care of her children, and rest.

I tried Jeremy's office number—I wasn't going to risk having him answer with Heather at his side.

"Jeremy, you're still at work?" I felt better already.

"I'm on my way out. Let me call you back from my cell phone."

"No. Don't—" Damn him. Why couldn't he spend two minutes talking to me without being in transit to her? I got out a carton of mint chocolate chip ice cream. I had no dinner plans for the evening.

When the phone rang, I answered on the first ring.

There were street sounds in the background. He was walking to the Metro.

"You hung up while I was talking."

"I'm sorry. What were you saying?"

"I was saying—*don't fricking hang up.*"

"Sorry, Sophie. What's up?"

What was up? I'd forgotten. The ice cream had begun to soothe my jangled nerves. "I have a date with Evan Lancet tomorrow night. I thought you'd want to know." That was filler, not what I'd called to say. Oh yes. I remembered. "Your theory about Barney may be right."

"Why do you say that?"

I explained about Barney wanting to offer Marnie a part time position and launched into the various scenarios I'd worked up to explain their relationship. He listened without interruption. Finally, I interrupted myself. "Aren't you at Judiciary Square yet?"

The Metro station wasn't far from his office. He should have entered by now, going underground.

"I'm walking to Metro Center. It's easier to keep talking that way."

"Oh." That was gratifying. I took precedence over him racing home to Heather. I soon found out why—he had a lecture he wanted to deliver.

"Listen, Sophie, you just told me that Barney is closer than you thought to the intern he assigned to Ariel Lancet, which means Evan Lancet could have used Barney to spy on his wife, which, you must realize, increases the likelihood Evan killed her. *Killed her*, Sophie. How can you go out with him tomorrow night? What are you *thinking*? Don't those things connect up *anywhere* in your brain?"

Ranting was so unlike Jeremy. He was usually more comfortable maintaining a bemused air while I did the ranting. So was he, perhaps, a tad jealous?

"There's no need to get overwrought, Jeremy. In the first place, Evan's not going to kill me. He'd never risk a second corpse so soon." The ice cream had melted to a delectable consistency. I snuck a quick spoonful.

"This isn't a joke, Sophie. He could have *killed* his wife."

"I know, I know, but theorizing aside, I don't believe it."

"You never used to be this stubborn or stupid."

I took his words as a compliment. After all, he was on the phone worrying about me instead of hurrying home to Heather. "For cripes sake, Jeremy, if it turns out Evan had anything to do with Ariel's death, I'm not going to become one of those jailhouse lovers. But he hasn't even been charged with a crime." Eating ice cream had the same effect on me as getting a foot rub. Possibly the same effect as heroin had on users. Nothing seemed worth getting too upset about.

"He hasn't been charged because there's so little physical evidence. God, Sophie. Aren't you worried about your safety?"

"Sure, especially when I drive myself home late at night and have to park in the garage alone." It was a subtle dig, but not too subtle for him to understand. "With Evan picking me up and dropping me off, I feel safer than I usually do these days. Anyway, how many future dates would Evan get if two women in a row dined out with him and didn't live long enough to digest their food? You're the one sleeping with a sociopath, Jeremy, not me."

"Heather's not a sociopath, and her husband is alive, Sophie, whereas Evan's wife, as you well know, is *not* alive." He had a point, but I ignored it.

"In other words, Evan's a widower, and Heather's an adulterer."

"Couldn't you have found someone to date who wasn't a murder suspect?"

"Frankly, it's not that easy."

He expended a martyred sigh. "Will you at least charge your cellphone before you go out and keep it on, *please*?"

"Okay."

"And will you call me when you get home to let me know you're okay?"

"Sure, if you can promise me that Heather won't be beside you in bed when I call, because I can't talk under those conditions."

He was quiet.

So there it was. He would spend Saturday evening canoodling with Heather, and I would venture out, armed with my cellphone, to take my chances with Evan.

I finished the carton of ice cream and called my mom. "Hi."

One word was all she needed to sniff my unhappiness. I could hear the anxiety in her voice. "Sweetheart, is everything okay?"

The Jeremy fiasco had sent her into red alert. She couldn't detach from my situation. I loved talking to her, but I hated making her miserable because I was miserable. Friends were so much easier when things went wrong. My troubles didn't affect their mood.

"Everything's fine, Mom, I called to say hello." I had a long probationary period ahead before her concern settled down. I didn't dare tell her about Evan. "What's going on over there?"

"Nothing much."

"I thought maybe I'd come visit this weekend." I had a sudden urge to flee DC. I didn't want to be in the same city as Heather. And Jeremy had raised my anxiety about Evan. Leaving town would provide an easy excuse to break our date. "I could drive up tomorrow morning and spend the night. Come back Sunday." They still lived in the house I'd grown up in on the Jersey shore, about a three-and-a-half-hour ride.

"Sophie, sweetheart, we'd love to see you. Can you come next weekend instead? We have plans tomorrow night, something we can't cancel."

"Oh. What are you doing?" My parents were never too busy to see me. Tears flooded my eyes. I covered the mouthpiece so she wouldn't hear me sniffle.

"You remember the Williamses?"

Of course, I remembered the Williamses. They were our next-door neighbors from the time I was three. My mother was stalling. I could feel her discomfort. "Yes, I remember them. Why?"

"Well, their daughter's getting married." There it was. No wonder she was being cagey.

"Pass along my congratulations," I said. "I'll call you on Sunday." That was our usual time for talking.

"Okay, sweetie."

She blew me a kiss, and I blew one right back at her, sad kisses, her mood now as low as my own.

CHAPTER 21

I slept late Saturday and awakened to cramps and my period. Outside the sky was gray, a cold March day, snow flurries forecast, maybe even snow. But that was fine. Gray and miserable suited my mood. I followed my morning routine, drank coffee, ate breakfast, and read the newspaper, but I couldn't shake a sense of dread. I wasn't sure what was causing my unease, the upcoming date with Evan or Heather being in DC. Or maybe having a killer loose at close quarters was making me a tad jumpy.

I felt like I was swimming alone in choppy waters—I could feel the movement of sharks beneath the waves.

When the phone rang, I checked caller ID. The number was Ned's cell phone. I picked up warily.

"Hey, Sophie, I'm glad I reached you at home."

"What's up?"

"I was wondering. Can I hang out at your place for a few hours today? Where I stayed last night is kind of skanky."

Company was the last thing I needed. And Ned was still an intern.

"We could watch a movie, or I'll work on my dissertation if you're busy. I won't be in your way."

I let out a sigh. He needed a place to park himself while Heather was in town. "When do you want to come over?"

"In an hour maybe, around one. I'm going to stop by Jeremy's first to get a change of clothes. And I've got somewhere to spend the night, don't worry."

"You can come over, but how about picking something up for us to eat? I'll reimburse you for my share." He was the one living rent-free. He could afford to buy his own lunch and spare me having to run to the store.

"Okay."

With company due over, I had no choice but to shower and tidy the apartment.

His physical presence was overpowering in the confined space. I had to keep maneuvering so as not to brush against him. He set his backpack on the floor and handed me a bag of Chinese carryout. "I got it at the restaurant down the street." He gave me the bill

Food was a welcome distraction. I paid my half and walked to the kitchen. "Sit down at the dining table. I'll set stuff out." I preferred having him contained in one place.

"I met Jeremy's lovebird," he said, digging into a shrimp dish he drenched in soy sauce from a plastic packet.

I was eating Kung Pao Chicken, but menstrual cramps suddenly twisted my gut. "What's she like?"

"I gotta tell you, she's hot. Not what I expected from Jeremy." In other words: Heather was hot, I was not. "You know what's spooky, though?" he asked.

"No. What's spooky?"

"She's an Ariel Lancet look-alike, tall, thin, with blonde hair. I wish Marnie could see her. She looks like Ariel's twin sister or something."

I nodded. "That *is* spooky."

My appetite was gone, but I ate anyway because I didn't want Ned to notice and ask why I wasn't eating. Terrible thoughts seeped through my mind. For one thing, Jeremy had lied. He told me Heather was "average" when, in fact, she was thin. But putting that aside, Ariel Lancet, Penny Harrison, and Heather all shared the same body type. Jeremy had been in an animated conversation with Penny Harrison at the fundraiser over the summer. I could picture them together in my mind. And the night of her murder, he dumped me.

I hadn't laid out the timeline in that way before, but it made me wonder. Was Jeremy implicated in Penny's killing? He'd come to the Palisades neighborhood to see me, or so he'd said. When he arrived at the clinic, he was out of breath and terribly distressed—presumably because he was breaking off our engagement, but maybe he had killed Penny before coming to see me.

As far as I knew, Jeremy hadn't known Ariel, but he wasn't with me the night she was killed. And now there was Heather, a third woman who fit the profile. Heather was still alive—for now.

Ned was shoveling down food. "You're being quiet, Sophie."

I helped myself to a little of his shrimp dish. "I'm tired. I wasn't expecting company today."

"Maybe we can watch a movie when we're done."

"Good idea." A movie would allow me to retreat and calm my fevered brain. My thinking was off, the way Barney's had been, weaving paranoid fantasies that made no sense. The thought of Jeremy being involved was crazy. Monday I would corner Jack Cassidy and ask him to prescribe anti-anxiety medication. My nervous system was running amok.

"Let's see what's on," I suggested after clearing away our dishes. "I have On Demand."

"Any chance you could look through my dissertation stuff first?" Ned pointed to his backpack in the living room. "Help me organize it?"

"Not today. I don't feel up to it."

"How about next weekend?"

Cripes almighty! I had enough to worry about without his fricking dissertation. I'd barely muddled through my own. "I *don't* know."

He smiled and handed me the remote. "Hey, relax, okay."

I clicked on the TV but waited for him to sit down first, so I could plant myself out of range of his feet, or hands, or any other body part of his that might encroach. He took the chair, so I plopped down on the couch and scrolled through the listings. *Groundhog Day* was starting—a classic I was happy to watch again. Ned had never seen it. He had a treat in store. I stretched out on the couch, pressing a pillow against my stomach to ease the pain. One hour to go before I could take more Advil.

"You have cramps?"

He was supposed to be watching the fricking screen, not watching me. Whether I had cramps or not was none of his business. We weren't lovers. We weren't even friends. I was so caught up in my pique, I didn't register him moving toward me until he was perched on the edge of the couch beside my legs. I froze as his powerful hands spread over my lower back, fingers kneading deep into my muscles. "Don't be so skittish, Sophie. This'll help you feel better."

I didn't know what to do first—scream or whimper with pleasure? How in hell had he ended up with the heels of his hands pressed halfway down my ass? I felt completely porous, like he'd breached a seawall and was flooding into me through his hands, violating the boundary I'd put in place, violating *me*. I was outraged. He was my student. But my cramps were melting away. I felt like I was seeping into the fabric of the couch.

"You've got the wildest hair," he said, moving my mop off my back as his hands began to massage higher, not the direction I had feared, but his fingers still posed a problem. They were dipping around my sides at breast level.

I bolted upright and twisted around. "Thanks, Ned. That's enough."

He withdrew his hands. I curled up at the end of the couch to watch the rest of *Groundhog Day*, and Ned returned to his chair. Afterward, we segued into a *Law and Order* rerun, during which Evan called. I was too lazy to answer in another room, so I held a whispered conversation confirming our plans for the evening.

"Who was that?" Ned asked as soon as I hung up.

"*Excuse me*?"

"Don't tell me you have a new boyfriend already?"

"Are you always this fricking intrusive?"

He grinned. "Pretty much."

"None of this is your business. Watch the show."

"That's okay. I have to meet some people soon anyway. Thanks for letting me hang out."

I walked him to the door, relieved to be alone.

∽∾∽∾

The fact that Evan hadn't known me when I was slender took the pressure out of getting dressed to go out with him. He didn't have to readjust to me being pudgy each time he saw me. To him, I was a pudgy person, period. He had asked out a pudgy woman, and he expected to see a pudgy woman when he picked me up. That made choosing clothes easier, although it failed to address whether he'd killed his wife and if he was still homicidally inclined.

The issue was too vexing to ignore, but I couldn't figure out a constructive way to deal with it. Turning down a good meal, somehow, didn't seem like the answer, especially when he was taking me to a place noted for its desserts. And Jeremy's fears for my safety had a bogus ring. If he were really worried, why didn't he blow Heather off for the evening so I could check in with him? And speaking of Heather, what did it mean that she so closely resembled Ariel? The coincidence preyed on my mind.

The new outfit I'd bought with Steve was hanging in my closet ready to be worn again. I clipped my hair behind my neck with Steve's cloisonné barrette then added a dab of powder to my nose, lip gloss to my lips, and I was ready for an evening out with a man who wasn't Jeremy. The thought made my stomach flip over. I had a sudden urge to rummage through my past. Evan wasn't due for another fifteen minutes.

I turned on my computer and stared at pictures of Jeremy, smiling, with his arm slung affectionately around my shoulders. Who was Jeremy—*who the hell was he*? I thought about Jack Cassidy's comment about Barney being a blob, and a blob not having a dark side, but Jeremy was no blob. He had undercurrents, maybe even a dangerous undertow.

Had there been something between him and Penny Harrison? He'd waited several weeks after Heather got back in touch with him before dumping me, anguishing weeks that coincided with Penny's murder. Was there a connection? Jeremy had been obsessed with Heather since childhood. I didn't doubt he loved me, but Heather owned a piece of his mind. He was battling an obsession.

He couldn't control his thoughts and desire for her. He must have hated feeling so controlled. He'd admitted how much Heather's call upset him. She had the power to turn his life inside out on a whim. Penny, Ariel and Heather all had the same body type. Had Jeremy displaced his obsession with Heather onto Penny? What if, in a spasm of rage, he destroyed Penny to end the torment in his mind? Had Penny been killed as a surrogate?

I stood up and paced. I had drifted into the twilight zone. Jeremy wasn't a murderer. My brain was malfunctioning. The idea of Jeremy as a killer was laughable. Jeremy was Jeremy. I was the nutcase. Except—the killings really had happened. Two young women were dead. And even though Howard Barrow was now being held for Penny's murder, Alan was unconvinced. Maybe Howard was innocent. But if so, that meant Penny's killer was still in our midst—and Ariel's murderer as well.

Looking at old pictures filled me with foreboding. I closed the computer. Evan was due any minute. I didn't want to go. I wanted to run away and hide. I should have fled to my parents' house. Who cared if Jill Williams was getting married and my parents would be at the wedding? I would have been safe in my childhood bed with the pale-yellow comforter pulled up to my chin, watching old movies and eating ice cream.

My cramps were excruciating. I popped a third Advil, more than the recommended dosage, but I couldn't very well greet Evan doubled over in pain. I'd never been this nervous before a date.

The phone rang. Evan. "I'm a few minutes early, but I wanted to let you know I'm here. I pulled into the driveway in front of your building. Take your time, Sophie. Come down when you're ready." God, he was courteous.

"I'll be down in a minute." I cast a frantic glance

around the apartment. What was I forgetting? I had a coat, purse, keys, and my cellphone. I turned out the lights and locked the door. Then I stood in the hallway and took a deep breath.

∽∾∽∾

One drawback to being a mental health professional was the pressure to present as being mentally intact. I usually had a handle on my neuroses in public, but my delusional thinking was new and troublesome. I didn't really believe Jeremy was homicidally inclined, but I couldn't discount the possibility. And that went for Evan as well.

He opened the passenger door for me. "You look lovely."

Talk about delusional. I eyed him like he was smoking crack and mumbled thanks. The car was a luxury sedan. He drove well. Classical music filled the air.

"Are you comfortable, Sophie? Not too warm?"

"The temperature's just right. I like the music."

He handed me an empty CD container. Mozart.

"I don't know much about classical music," I admitted.

"That's okay, as long as you don't mind listening."

"No, it's beautiful." I settled back against the plush leather. Evan seemed absorbed in the music. There wasn't any need to keep a conversation going, which was a relief, appearing to be of sound mind was easier when I didn't have to speak. We drove into Bethesda and then out of Bethesda. Hmm. "Where's the restaurant?"

He'd told me the place had great desserts, which covered the essentials, but I was curious how far away we were going.

"It's a bit off the beaten track. A few more blocks. I

suppose I'm trying to avoid running into people I know. I'm red meat for newsmongers." That made sense. I didn't particularly want my name in the paper as dating a recently widowed murder suspect. We left the car with the parking valet. Inside we were seated at a quiet table in an alcove, very private, out of view. "It's nice to be here with you, Sophie. Thank you for coming."

I smiled in response. We ordered drinks, a vodka martini for him, a white Russian for me, and then perused our menus, selecting fried calamari and an antipasto platter to start us off, followed by entrées, veal scaloppini for him and pasta with shrimp and scallops in red sauce for me. I demurred to him to select our wine, although I hinted for something not too dry. I didn't want to have to empty a packet of sugar into my glass when he wasn't looking. Our drinks soon appeared along with a basket of rolls and bread sticks. Evan offered a toast: "Here's to enjoying the good times and surviving the bad. Let's hope for better times ahead."

"Speaking of which, how are you doing?" I asked.

"Surprisingly well. This might sound like over-indulgent hogwash to you, but I've been reviewing my life in a way that's new for me. I feel like I'm getting a fresh start."

Hogwash? Introspective assessment was as natural to me as sipping my morning coffee. I lapsed into therapy mode. "What have you discovered?"

"I've tried to take a step back and see a panoramic view of my life. Evaluate where I've been and where I want to be. I'm fifty-eight, Sophie."

The white Russian helped muffle the impact, but fifty-eight years was still fifty-eight fricking years. He was older than my father. I drained my glass.

"Jeanine and I had a good marriage. We were two halves of a whole. We balanced each other. I needed her softening touch. After she died, I hardened. I held myself together by setting goals and working my ass off to attain them. I took care of Tricia the best I knew how, with help. We always had housekeepers. But I drove her into a disastrous marriage—I see that now. I expected her to adapt to my way of doing things the way her mother adapted. Ah. Our appetizers. Do you like lemon?" I gave a nod, and he squirted lemon juice on the calamari. "Here. Help yourself. I must be boring you to tears. I don't know why, but I find it easy to open up to you."

"I'm not bored."

"You're sweet to say so. I guess my point is I owe Tricia a second chance. I'm determined to do everything in my power to see she gets one. She and I have had some very frank discussions. She's as stubborn as I am, and that's not going to change. I was trying to make her into someone she could never be, and I'm afraid I did the same thing to Ariel, much to my regret. We should never have married. I don't know what came over me to pursue her the way I did."

"You were cut off from your family."

"Yes, but I chose such a young girl. I felt driven to mold her like Henry Higgins molded Eliza Doolittle, lifting her up from the gutter and transforming her into a lady. Not an admirable ambition. I'm not proud of my desires. I remember imagining all the wonderful things Ariel and I would do together, but they were my fantasies, not hers, and I ended up with another rebellious adolescent on my hands. I made the same mistakes all over again."

I reached for another calamari glad to see his interest lay in the antipasto platter. "Do you miss Ariel?"

"No. Does that sound callous?"

"A little."

"I wish she were off somewhere living her life the

way she was meant to live it, working just enough to get by, hanging out with her friends, laughing at nonsense. After Tricia and Mallory moved in, I could see that I'd married a child. She disrupted the house."

"You could have gotten a divorce."

"I would have, eventually. It was only a matter of time, although the truth is I'm not quick to admit my mistakes. I can be stubborn that way."

Three calamari remained on the serving dish. I restrained myself and plucked an olive from the antipasto platter. I didn't want Evan to reach for some calamari and find they had all disappeared when I was the only other person present.

"I don't mean to sound cold-hearted about Ariel. I feel terrible about what happened to her and terrible I wasn't there to protect her. But we were in a state of constant tension. I don't miss that."

I was right to be prudent—he nabbed a calamari with his fork. I tried pimento on a piece of bread. Not bad. Our wine appeared. A steward uncorked the bottle and poured a few dollops for Evan. After a moment of suspense, he pronounced it a go and my glass was filled.

"It's very odd, Sophie. Ariel's death seems more like a tragedy I read about in the newspaper than a profound personal loss. I find my detachment somewhat strange. There was a time when I couldn't get Ariel out of my mind. And yet my grief is nothing like what I suffered when Jeanine died. I'm surprised by my reaction."

"What do you mean?" I reached for another pimento.

"I've never been particularly introspective. I don't like naval gazing. But it took me aback to realize I'd lived two years with a young woman I hardly knew, someone I'd more or less manufactured in my mind. I wasn't celibate during my unmarried years, but Ariel was the first woman since Jeanine whom I wanted to marry.

She evoked something in me. There was a sexual component, of course, but also a need to nurture her into adulthood. Instead, I ended up reliving Tricia's adolescence with my wife. I'm talking too much. Tell me about yourself, Sophie."

I preferred to stay in listening mode. After all, what was there to say? He knew my former fiancé had dumped me. I didn't want to mention my delusions—if that's what they were—that Jeremy was killing every woman in sight. He might suspect me of needing to turn Jeremy into a psychopathic killer in my mind in order to come to terms with his leaving me. "There's not much to tell."

"How old are you, Sophie, twenty-seven? Twenty-eight?"

"Thirty."

Evan raised his wine glass, sipped slowly, and placed it back on the table. His eyes met mine. "I'm not sure how to say this, Sophie, but I want to be straight with you. You're a good friend to our family. I find myself attracted to you. I'm not looking for another wife—not at the moment, at any rate. And I suspect when I am, I'll cast my net among an older group."

My respiration sped up. I had no idea where he was heading. I swallowed, transfixed. There had to be a "but" coming. My last serious relational talk was when Jeremy broke my heart. But how could Evan reject me before our entrées even arrived? Ah, he couldn't. The entrées were on their way. Evan and I broke eye contact as one waiter cleared away our appetizers and another set down our dinner plates.

We tasted our food and nodded, signaling pleasure, and then he continued. "What I was saying is—" Our eyes locked again. "—I think we can be a comfort to each other during this time in our lives. Whether that includes sexual intimacy or not is up to you."

I stopped breathing. We were discussing sleeping together in advance of any experimental groping. Jeremy and I had our clothes off before we actually acknowledged what we were doing the first time.

"Either way, I like spending time with you, Sophie. I can't talk about my personal life with many people."

I stared at him. "I don't know what to say, Evan."

The words croaked out of my mouth. Water helped. I liked that he liked me. It was the part about sexual intimacy that was causing the frog in my throat. I looked at my food and added salt and pepper.

"You don't need to say anything, Sophie dear. I just want you to know where I stand."

That was a relief, but at the same time, I wanted him to know I appreciated his sentiments. I liked him, too, and, yes, I wanted to bring him comfort and happiness and, perhaps, sexual fulfillment. He was very attractive. And his numerous years of non-celibacy suggested a wealth of experience. And yet sleeping with Tricia's dad would be weird and sleeping with Mallory's grandfather weirder still.

"I like spending time with you, too, Evan."

I wanted to offer more in return. My desire to please him was uncomfortably strong, as if I were beholden in some way. Or maybe I was reacting to his wealth and prestige or to his age. I ate a few forkfuls of pasta and washed them down with wine. I couldn't think of anything to add.

"How's your pasta, Sophie?"

"It's great. How about your veal?"

"Pretty good. A little overcooked."

Our conversation was sinking. I was going to ask about his work, but frankly, the upscale construction he was spearheading was pricing me out of the housing market—his windfall meant I'd probably have to leave the city if I wanted to own my own home. And what about the poor renters who would soon have no place they could afford to live?

"Is there any news about the murder investigation?" That was the safest topic I could come up with.

"The police haven't been communicating of late. Dr. Hisselman appears to be their only lead, and he's a dead end. The man's cunning astounds me. That he would pose as a disinterested doctor, wanting to know how I'd been affected by Ariel's death. I revealed intimate details of my life to him. I should have been asking the questions, not the other way around." He tilted his wine glass and watched the liquid seesaw. "His pocketknife was found in our garden. I had no idea he'd ever been there. I can't make sense of his connection to Ariel. It makes me painfully aware how little I really knew her."

"Had you and Ariel discussed her going into therapy?"

"I was the one who suggested she get help. She was making herself miserable and making everyone around her miserable. I know having Tricia and Mallory move in was difficult, but her reaction seemed pathological to me. I regretted not getting Tricia help when she was young. I didn't want to make the same mistake again."

"How did Ariel end up coming to our clinic? There are so many therapists in DC, why choose us?"

"You know, I'm not sure. I got several names from an associate of mine, but Ariel wanted to choose a place on her own. She had an exaggerated sense of my power and control. I have a hunch one of her old friends had gone to your clinic at some point and recommended it."

"Do you know why she asked for Dr. Hisselman by name?"

"Did she do that? I didn't know."

"Maybe not by name. She may have asked for the

man in charge. But most people simply call the main number and ask for an appointment."

A smile softened his face. "I don't know why, but that touches me. She might have actually followed one of my suggestions. I used to tell her not to waste her time, to ask for the person in charge. I knew the higher she went, the more likely she'd be treated with kid gloves. She had a habit of getting into set-tos with low-level employees. She was easily frustrated, not much patience. I suppose I enjoyed spoiling her—she was such a beautiful creature. Looking back, I realize I was entranced."

"It sounds as if, at some point, you stopped wanting to spoil her."

"Her demands became tiresome. I bear responsibility. I helped create her sense of entitlement." He picked up the wine bottle and pointed it toward my empty glass. I covered the glass with my hand. I was a little tipsy already. Evan refilled his glass. "How about dessert?" he asked. We had finished our meals.

Our waiter must have been watching. He immediately signaled the busboy to clear our dishes and presented us with dessert menus. I selected the hazelnut torte topped with a scoop of hazelnut ice cream cloaked in chocolate sauce. Evan ordered fresh berries in heavy cream. His eyes held mine as soon as the waiter withdrew.

"Tricia and Mallory are out of town. They've gone to New York to see a Broadway show."

I gulped. He was telling me we had his mansion to ourselves for the night. I needed to decide if I wanted to go to his place and we hadn't even discussed safe sex, sexually transmitted diseases, or whether he had a penchant for killing young women. "A night in New York sounds like fun."

"They were both excited. Ah, here come our desserts."

I gasped in admiration. After several yummy bites, I moved the plate toward Evan. "You have to try it."

Barney would have had a public orgasm. Evan took a nibble and returned the plate to me.

"That's very good. Try some of mine. The berries are fresh." He gathered a spoonful and tipped it into my mouth.

"They're wonderful."

He lifted a napkin and dabbed my lips. We smiled at each other. I took another bite of my dessert combining ice cream, torte, and dripping dark chocolate.

"I'd like to make love to you, Sophie."

No kidding. I felt like he already was.

"Will you come home with me tonight?"

If we could have pulled a curtain and had sex while eating dessert, I'd have succumbed in a heartbeat. But without the aphrodisiac chocolate hazelnut combo, and leaving aside the thorny question of homicide, there were two problems. I had my period, which was a messy way to start a relationship. And Jeremy's face kept appearing in my mind's eye. The good Jeremy, the one I thought I knew. Actually, there were three problems. My father's face had also started to intrude. It was unnerving to know he was younger than Evan.

On the other hand, having Evan attend to my physical desires could be fun. And I didn't want to say no to him. Everything around me was leaning toward yes, the force of his expectation bending me into compliance. I hated to disappoint him.

"You're awfully quiet, Sophie. I didn't mean to put you on the spot. You know I'll drop you off at your home if you'd like."

"I know."

"You don't need to decide right now. And it doesn't have to be tonight."

"I'd rather not tonight."

There it was. Done.

☙☙

We drove home in what I hoped was companionable silence. I felt as if I'd reneged on something, like quashing a business deal after protracted negotiations. But I owed him nothing, certainly not sex. And I owed myself time to think about what I was doing. A low hum vibrated against my leg from inside my purse. I reached down and retrieved my phone. Jeremy was checking up on me. I switched the phone off, sending him to voice mail. Leaving the issue of Heather aside, I wasn't going to chat with him from Evan's car.

"I'd love to hear your Mozart CD again," I told Evan.

"Good." He turned it on. "I appreciate you not taking that call. Ariel never came unplugged. It used to drive me crazy."

I let the music carry me the rest of the way home, listening with my eyes closed. The car shifted as we entered the circular drive in front of my building. I faced him, my head resting comfortably against the seatback. "Thank you. I had a lovely time."

"Me too, Sophie, dear." He planted a kiss on my lips. And then he planted another one, lingering a little longer, and another, diving deeper with his tongue. I was a little woozy. Making out felt nice—not too intimate, but luscious and dreamy. He pulled away slowly. "I guess I should let you go." His voice was reluctant as he stroked the side of my face.

I didn't want to move. I wanted to keep smooching

the way we were. But I didn't want to take things any further and, sometimes, if you didn't move decisively in one direction, you drifted off in the other, so I forced myself to open the car door.

"You're right. I should get going. Thank you, Evan."

"My pleasure, Sophie. We'll do it again."

CHAPTER 22

I'd been delivered home, safe and sound. I let myself into the front lobby, quiet now, no one at the desk, and rode the elevator up to my floor. Inside my apartment, I hung up my clothes and put on a nightie and bathrobe. Coming home after a date was so much more relaxing than setting out on one.

I plopped down on the sofa and took stock. I had an invitation to become Evan's lover, although I wasn't sure how long the offer would remain in effect. His startling directness was no doubt related to his mansion being vacant this weekend.

I tried Jeremy's cellphone. He had called me, so calling him was returning his call to me, and he would want to know I'd come home in one piece. No answer. His phone relegated me to voice mail, which was annoying.

I put down the phone. Although it was true that Jeremy's rejection had coincided with the murders, now that my date with Evan was over and I was in a less psychotic frame of mind, I sensed a fault in my logic. Correlation did not imply causation. There was such a thing as coincidence.

I hesitated to call Jeremy's landline. The lovebirds

could easily be in bed. I checked voice mail to see if he'd left me a message. He had. "Call me, Sophie. I need to talk to you." He sounded pressured, filled with suppressed excitement. I hit replay. "Call me, Sophie. I need to talk to you." I hit replay again. What was the urgency about? Concern over Evan? Did he know something from the DA's office I didn't know? Had my decision to come straight home saved my life? I tried his home number and went to voice mail.

What was so important that he had to tell me, and then he couldn't be reached when I tried to call back? I was too keyed up to think about sleep. My mind was awhirl, playing back the day's events—Evan's proposition, Ned's wandering backrub. Even if I never found love, or got married, or had children, or owned my own home, maybe I could still enjoy sex and good food.

Speaking of which—I cruised to the kitchen. I needed something to sop up my restless energy. Reading took too much concentration after Jeremy's urgent sounding message. If he'd spent the evening locked in Heather's arms, why was he calling me? I opened the door to the freezer. There was an untouched carton of mint chocolate chip ice cream. I stared at it trying to decide what to do. The hazelnut dessert had been substantial, but dinner with Evan seemed a long time ago.

And yet, it hadn't been.

I shut the freezer door and loaded up the coffee maker, thinking ahead to the morning. I needed to hold out until breakfast, then I could eat again. But sleep was out of the question. I returned to the sofa and clicked the remote. *Saturday Night Live* was coming on, but the older I got, the less funny I found it. I scrolled for a movie. There was nothing I wanted to watch. Evan's invitation kept echoing in my mind. If I had said yes to him, I'd have been in his bed at that very moment—and hopefully still breathing. Imagining Evan as my lover was strange, strange too to remember Ned's hands traveling up my sides, his fingers flirting with my breasts. What in the name of holy crap had he been thinking? Had he actually believed I'd forget who I was and make love to him?

I turned off the lights. My cramps had settled down. I climbed into bed, but my mind wouldn't stop percolating. Ned's advances that afternoon had been totally out of line. There was a predatory quality to his sexuality. He was like an animal watching, waiting to spring. He'd been purposely stirring me up, trying to tempt me into a danger zone. Evan's affection for me felt real, affection linked to desire. Evan wanted the closeness of a physical relationship.

Ned was different. I didn't experience him as wanting me. His intention seemed to be to arouse me to want him. But why, what was he after? His interest felt like a game, as if he was toying with me.

I put on my slippers and robe, padded into the bathroom and opened the medicine cabinet. I was trying to be careful with the Ambien and only take one when necessary. I dropped the container into the pocket of my robe so I wouldn't have to get out of bed for a pill if my mind didn't wind down. I doubted Jeremy would call again this late. The sooner I fell asleep, the sooner I'd wake up and find out what was going on.

I wandered to the kitchen for a glass of water and was hit by the realization: *Ned wanted me to break the rules.* That was his goal. He'd been dangling his sexuality to lure me over the line. I returned to my bedroom and put the water glass on the nightstand. The phone rang. I flopped across the bed on my stomach as I grabbed the receiver, hoping it was Jeremy.

"Sophie, I'm glad I reached you." It *was* Jeremy. "I'm sorry to call so late, but I wanted to tell you how much I love you. I don't love Heather. I'm an idiot. I'm so sorry for all I've put you through."

His words floated through me. They warmed my body and loosened the tightness and tension inside. I felt light headed. My breathing slowed. Jeremy loved me. He was choosing me over Heather. We were going to spend our lives together, after all. Tears of relief ran down my cheeks. "Where is Heather now?"

"She's at her home. It's over between us."

"Where are you?"

"I'm driving back to DC. Do you think you can forgive me, Sophie?"

I was confused. Something was off. Heather had come to DC for the weekend? Jeremy wasn't supposed to be in Philly. Why was he lying about the details, unless Ned was the one who'd been lying? If Heather hadn't come to DC, then Ned didn't know what she looked like. He could have made up that she looked like Ariel to heighten my distrust of Jeremy. But why would he want me to distrust Jeremy?

"I thought Heather was in DC this weekend."

"She was."

So Ned hadn't lied. "Then where are you driving from?"

"From her place. I drove her home. We're done. I'm not going to see her again."

I shifted onto my side and propped up on an elbow. "You drove all the way to Philly and back in one night?"

For all I knew, he was lying. And if he had driven Heather home, was it to make sure she arrived safely, or had he done away with her at a safe distance from his residence? Evil questions were popping into my mind. I wasn't as trusting as I used to be.

"I know, it's crazy," he said. "But I didn't want to prolong things with Heather, and I wanted to start trying to patch things up with you—if you still want me, Sophie."

Colliding thoughts made it impossible to respond. Could I ever trust him again? Did I want him to come over tonight? Heather was history. She'd blown into our lives, wreaked havoc, and blown away. Now we had to rebuild. Unless I wanted to cut my losses, which I didn't want to do. I wanted Jeremy.

I rolled back on my stomach. "What made you decide?"

"I hated to keep hurting you, Sophie, and I realized how stupid I was to risk losing you. I don't love Heather."

He put me through a carload of crap because of his stupid infatuation. "I almost went home with Evan tonight."

"But you didn't, right?"

"No. But I almost did. And I don't like the fact that you came rushing back because you knew I was out with him, like I'm your property, and you needed to protect what was yours." My analogy was off-base. He had never treated me like property, but taking a swipe at him gave me the same satisfaction as thwacking him with a pillow. He needed to absorb some of the impact of my hurt.

"Sophie, honey, come on, that's ridiculous. I was jealous at the thought of you being with Evan because I love you, not because I feel like I own you."

I no longer minded being called honey. "What about Heather? How did you finally discover you don't love her after all, after spending the better part of your life believing you did?"

"I didn't spend the better part of my life—I wasn't actively in love with her all those years. I didn't think about her. But I admit I was stuck in an adolescent mindset. I'm not proud of it."

"Pre-adolescent."

He laughed. "Okay, pre-adolescent. I was hypnotized by the idea that we were meant for each other. I'm ashamed of the whole thing. I feel like an idiot for buying into the fantasy. I wish she'd stayed married to her husband and saved us all a lot of trouble."

"I want to hear about your break-up. Was the idea yours or hers?" I bunched a pillow under my chin.

"Mine. I made the decision. I don't love her. I was living out a fantasy that had nothing to do with who I am or who she is as a person."

"Speaking of who she is as a person, tell me three things about her you don't like."

Silence.

"Do you know how annoying it is when I ask a question and you don't say anything?"

"Do you really think telling you negative things about Heather will help?"

"Jeremy, for a smart person, you have the social IQ of a nematode. Of course, it will fricking help. You said you're never going to see her again, so she'll never know. She won't care. But I, personally, would like to hear three things you don't like about Heather, and you shouldn't have to think that hard. I can name three things about you that annoy the holy crap out of me off the top of my head." I pounded and fluffed the pillow to get more comfortable.

"You can?"

"Yes, I can, but I'm not getting sidetracked. In fact, the way you sidetrack me is one of them. I want to hear about Heather, now."

"Okay, her driving. Most people signal, not Heather. She feints left and turns right like she's trying to outwit the other drivers and keep them guessing what she's going to do."

"And you actually got into a car with her?"

"You don't know the hazards I faced."

This was more like it. "Good. What else?"

"She's passive."

Passive? Was he saying Heather was a sexual dud? My heart soared. They'd been having lackluster sex? "Passive in what way, exactly?" I stifled my chortling with the pillow.

"Passive probably isn't the right word. She's indecisive."

"Oh."

"She can't make the simplest decision, which drove me out of my mind if you want to know the truth. And the third thing is she gets lost in inessential details of no possible interest, details completely irrelevant to whatever she's trying to say, which I can rarely figure out, because the point of her story gets lost while she spends ten minutes struggling to remember the name of someone totally tangential and another five minutes debating with herself whether it was on a Wednesday or Thursday that she ran into the person who had no relevance to whatever she was saying in the first place. God, Sophie, I made a huge mistake."

This was heartening…well, more than heartening, but I wasn't quite ready to move off of Heather. "Is she beautiful?"

"Yes, and very sought after. I was stupid."

"Willowy?"

"I guess."

"Sexually—what didn't you like about her?"

"Sophie, please."

"I want to know at least one thing that turned you off sexually."

"I don't feel right talking about that."

"You don't have to feel right about it, but you better

fricking do it anyway, because I won't feel right making love to you *ever again,* Jeremy, if you can't come up with one sexually negative thing about Heather, and it has to be true, so don't make up something to appease me. I need to know that you were turned off by her in some way, or my mind's going to put me through all kinds of creepy comparisons. It won't be good for me, or you, if I'm thinking about your hot times with Heather when we're in bed together."

The threat of a sexual slowdown compelled his attention. He accepted the wisdom of my words. "Okay. I don't like the way she kisses."

Heather was an icky kisser. That was good to know.

"I don't want to kiss anyone but you, Sophie, ever again." He was definitely getting the hang of this.

I pointed my toes, flexed, and pointed. "See, that wasn't so hard."

"Can I come over?"

"You better come over. Where are you? How soon can you be here?"

Suddenly, there was a sound in the hallway. My apartment door was opening. Jeremy had never given back my keys. I smiled as I tracked the soft tread of his footsteps. He must have called from right outside, hoping I'd say yes.

"You know where to find me." I hung up the phone and waited for him to come into the bedroom. I was too lazy to roll onto my back. I wanted him to stretch out behind me and kiss down the back of my neck the way I craved with soft, slow kisses. I closed my eyes in anticipation so I could feel his touch before I turned to face him and take him back into my life.

CHAPTER 23

He crept into the room the way he did when he worked late and came to my place after I'd gone to bed. I felt the mattress depress as his body lowered beside me, and I took a deep breath in pleasurable anticipation of his touch. His hand caressed my neck, brushing aside my hair, gently working around to my throat. I waited in suspense for his fingers to begin to drift down over my breasts. But his hand stayed on my throat, fingers pressing my windpipe.

I gasped for breath. He was blocking my air. I was losing my life, losing everything. I couldn't fight back, not face down on the bed. The betrayal made me sick with despair.

Suddenly, the pressure released, and I breathed.

I heard whimpering and then realized I was making the sound. I was scared to turn and look at his face. I couldn't bear the horrifying knowledge of who he was and what he'd done. He wouldn't let me live anyway. I pulled my knees to my chest and rocked. Poor Heather was probably dead already.

"Stop sniveling."

It wasn't Jeremy's voice. I turned my head. Ned's

face loomed above me. I could just make out his features in the dark room, a lock of hair falling across his forehead, an icy glint in his eyes. I was going to die. And yet I had a moment of relief, knowing Jeremy wasn't a killer. Jeremy loved me.

The phone rang. Ned answered with a gloved hand and hung up, breaking the connection without saying a word.

"What are you going to do to me?"

"Get up. Let's go into the living room. There might be something good to watch on TV."

Ned sounded…normal? My body was shaking out of control. I couldn't make sense of what was happening. He seemed cut off from the fact that he'd broken into my apartment and practically choked the life out of me. Had he dissociated? Gone into a killing trance and now, somehow, miraculously snapped out of it before I died? Was he the killer who murdered Penny and Ariel?

The living room sounded good. The last place I wanted to be with Ned was in my bedroom. Maybe he'd only been pretending to choke me. Sneaking in and pretending he was going to kill me could have been his perverse idea of a joke. He was perverse. He probably took pleasure in seeing me cower. I had been terrified. I still was. He got off on manipulating my emotions.

Ned gripped my arm as we walked to the living room. I had the sensation of being in a dream and wanting to scream, the urge stuck in my throat, no sound coming out. "Sit on the couch, Sophie."

I did what he said. He was bigger and stronger and he'd already demonstrated he could snuff out my life. He sat close enough to restrain me if I tried to get up. I couldn't stop shivering, even in my nightgown and robe. Some form of molestation seemed inevitable, whether he out-and-out raped me or not.

All I knew was I didn't want to die.

He clicked on the TV, lowered the volume, and scrolled down the listings. "Was that Jeremy on the phone before?" he asked.

I had a hard time finding my voice.

"Was it?"

"Yes."

"Where is he?"

"He's driving back from dropping Heather off." I couldn't think of any reason to lie. What did it matter where Jeremy was?

"Yeah, but did he say where on the drive? Was he getting off the turnpike? How far away is he?"

"I don't know."

Ned checked his watch, frowning. He must have made copies of my keys from the set Jeremy had. He might have been worried that Jeremy would barge in any minute. But would that dissuade him from raping me or force him to act quickly?

I jumped at the sound of the phone.

Ned's hand darted out and grabbed the portable off the coffee table. He held it beyond my reach and checked caller ID. A sickening smile creased his face. "It's your boyfriend." The ringing stopped, and my machine picked up.

"Sophie, please pick up," Jeremy said. "I should be there in about an hour and a half. Let me know if you're going to bed, and I'll let myself in. I can't wait to see you."

I was drenched with dread. In an hour and a half, Ned would be gone, and Jeremy would discover my lifeless body.

"Oh, hey, *Notorious* is on Turner Movie Classics. We missed the beginning." Ned clicked on the movie.

"Get comfortable, Sophie. You might as well enjoy the film."

"What's going to happen?"

"You really want to know?" He ran his hand up my legs. I grabbed his wrist and tried to thrust it away, but he was much too strong for me. His hand pressed down and lingered a moment between my legs before climbing up my body to my throat. He tickled my throat and smiled. "Watch the movie. It'll help pass the time."

The screen was a blur through my tears. "Why are you doing this?"

"Shush. We'll talk after the movie. There'll be time."

Watch a movie and wait to be killed. Ingrid Bergman's predicament was somewhat comparable, but she had Cary Grant looking out for her and Alfred Hitchcock yelling cut between scenes. I had Jeremy tooling along I-95 South with no idea I was in trouble. My murder would shatter my parents. Jeremy would blame himself—Ned had copied keys he neglected to return. The closer *Notorious* came to the end, the closer I came to mine.

CHAPTER 24

Cary Grant drove away with Ingrid Bergman and Ned turned off the TV. "See, Sophie, plenty of time left. Jeremy won't be here for another forty-five minutes. So what do you want to know? I'll tell you about Penny or Ariel if you want. Penny is as good a place to start as any."

"Why are we waiting for Jeremy?"

"Let's save him for later. Shall I start with Penny Harrison? You must realize by now that I killed her."

Letting him talk seemed the best way to spend my final hour. With a homicidal sociopath, the options weren't great. "Why did you do it?"

"Whoa. I don't want you getting psychoanalytic on me."

"Then don't tell me why, tell me *how* you killed her."

"That's a better question. I left the clinic in my car around six and spotted Penny crossing the street a block away."

"You knew her?"

"Only slightly. I'd spent the night at her house a few times with one of her roommates, so we'd met. I'd also met her boyfriend, Howard. He liked to get laid before heading home to his wife and kid."

"What did you do?"

"I drove around the corner, parked, and walked back so we would bump into each other."

"Why did you want to bump into her?"

He flashed a grin. "She was hot. I wanted to fuck her ass to hell and back. I thought maybe she'd let me, too, but she was hurrying home. She told me Howard was waiting for her. So I asked if her roommate was around, the one I'd slept with. She said both roommates were out, she had the place to herself. She was making conversation. But think about what she told me, Sophie—her boyfriend was waiting for her, alone, and she was with me. We were walking by the recreation center. It was dark. There was no one else around."

He shifted his weight on the couch. "I was itching to kill her. I hadn't killed anyone since moving to DC— that's a long dry spell. And the fact that Howard was waiting at her house was a bonus I couldn't resist. He was in the neighborhood with no alibi, he was bound to be blamed—one less stuck-up bitch in the world and one more arrogant prick wasting away in jail." Ned rested his hand on my trembling knees. "I needed the rush, Sophie. The internship is a crushing bore. I was dying inside."

I breathed deeply, trying to go into a trance so I could pretend to be somewhere else.

"I told Penny there was something on the grounds of the recreation center she had to see, something she wouldn't believe and it would only take a second. She followed me. We went to a deserted area hidden by trees. I pointed up and told her to look. She did. The oldest trick in the book—she stood there and looked up. I was wearing gloves. Penny had a scarf wrapped around her neck. I moved behind her, twisted her scarf and 'Bye, Bye Miss American Pie.'"

I felt too sick to speak.

"In case you're interested, my virgin run was killing my father's girlfriend. I was young and too inexperienced to fully enjoy it. Now I'm learning to hone the pleasure points. My dad is rotting away in prison for her murder, by the way." Ned smiled and checked his watch again.

"What are you *waiting* for?" The question screamed out of me, propelled by panic.

Ned smacked my cheek, sharp and quick, and put a finger to his lips. "Keep your voice down or this will get ugly."

My cheek stung. I didn't want ugly. "I won't do that again."

"Good. So where was I? Penny, and then there was Ariel."

"Tell me about her." I was shaking up to my teeth.

"Man, Ariel was another fox. I mean where do these sexy bitches come from? That was another amazing night. The stars aligned just like tonight. Everyone played to my hand."

My throat was shutting down.

"I was at a Georgetown bar, minding my own business, looking around to see if there was anyone in the place worth picking up. The bar had a big glass window that looked onto the street. I glanced out and saw Ariel standing on the sidewalk all alone. I paid for my drink and headed outside to talk to her, but her husband appeared. He grabbed her arm and dragged her away. I followed." Ned gave my knees a squeeze.

I didn't want his attention on me. "Evan said he walked Ariel home and left her in front of their house."

"I know. My luck was amazing. She stared after him like she couldn't believe what a gigantic asshole he was.

She didn't even see me until I was right beside her. I pointed to a house down the street with lots of lights on and told her they were having a great party, acting like I'd stumbled out of the house. She laughed. That's what a dumb stoner she was. She thought 'Hey, man, they're having a great party' was a punch line. But she was hot. And she recognized me from the clinic, from seeing me with Hisselman when we walked out together. I liked that she remembered me."

"Then why did you kill her?"

"Hey, come on, silly question. I was on a roll after Penny. And the whole psychology thing's been a big disappointment. If I didn't really want the degree, I'd have dropped out a long time ago. Anyway, the opportunity was perfect. I told Ariel I'd scored some weed, and she took me around to the back of the house away from prying eyes."

"Did you have weed on you?" None was found at the crime scene.

"No. When we got to the garden, I told her I wanted to go inside and fuck her brains out. Sometimes the direct approach works, but not with Ariel. All she could do was complain about Evan. She bored the living shit out of me. But you taught me how to listen, Sophie. I give you credit for making Ariel's death so simple."

He removed his hand from my knees, and I held my breath, praying his hand wouldn't settle down on a more personal spot, but he leaned back and clasped his hands behind his head, the picture of relaxation. He had me in his power. Restraint was unnecessary. I seized up in a spasm of grief. He gave me a warning look, and I muffled my sobs in a wad of tissues.

"Everything came together like a brain rush. I'd been carrying Dr. Hisselman's Swiss Army knife around in my pocket and this was an opportunity to plant his ass at a murder scene." Ned flashed a naughty boy smile. "Ariel was tipsy. She sat on the bench droning on about her husband. I was wearing gloves. She had a scarf wrapped around her neck. Killing her was almost too easy." He made a twisting motion with his hands.

I rocked my shivering body, trying to deflect the horror from penetrating to my inner core.

"I left Hisselman's knife at the scene and almost fell down laughing. The dumb fuck still doesn't have a clue how it got there."

"How did you get his knife?"

"Remember I told you he called me in to talk about my *Simpsons* lunch box? The knife was on his desk. I took out a handkerchief and pretended to blow my nose, then I rested the handkerchief over the knife and tucked them both into my pocket. I distracted him by commenting that you appeared to be gaining weight. He couldn't resist the topic." Ned reached his hand out and gave my thigh a condescending pat.

I wanted to bite his wrist. Ned couldn't just molest and kill me? He had to comment on my fricking weight? I was worried enough about becoming a corpse, and he needed to humiliate me into worrying about being a pudgy corpse. The urge to fight back surged in my veins, but how? I wasn't strong enough, agile enough, or anything enough, to escape him. I was at his mercy, dead meat.

I had a flash of insight—the twist in Ned's smile when he said his dad was rotting away in prison, the kick he got at Howard Barrow being blamed for Penny's death, his glee at turning Barney into a murder suspect, his derision of Evan Lancet—killing women wasn't Ned's only pleasure. He enjoyed screwing with the men in their lives. The realization deepened my despair. My murder was going to be pinned on Jeremy.

I couldn't let that happen.

I imagined reaching out and scratching Ned to get his skin under my fingernails before I died, but he was so ruthless he'd probably cut off my fingers. Why couldn't anyone see what was going on? No one suspected him. Even if Jeremy figured things out eventually, his insight would come from inside a prison cell. Everything was so obvious now. Ned had access to my keys. And he knew Barney—he'd had access to Barney's knife. And he knew sleight of hand. He'd been the gorilla hiding in plain sight. I'd watched him pluck quarters from Ella and Ian's ears. He did magic tricks. He swiped things. He was a master of misdirection.

"Did you intend to leave Barney's pocketknife at a crime scene when you took it?" I wanted to keep him talking. I needed time to think.

"No, Sophie. I'm not an obsessive planner. I thought you knew that about me. I like to improvise. But I knew I'd find a good use for the knife. That's why I carried it around with me wrapped in a handkerchief. I always keep a bag of tricks. Some things are pure serendipity. I couldn't have known Jeremy would call with an update on his arrival time. He did that on his own. My genius is in how I pull all the moving parts together."

His hand dug into his pants pocket and pulled out a set of my keys. I was shaking so hard, I could have been sitting in a vat of ice. He held the keys in front of my face. "I had these made as soon as I moved into Jeremy's place. I had no idea when I'd use them, but I knew they'd come in handy. I have keys to three other women's apartments, but I've been seen out with them. The police might investigate me if they were killed. You're different. We have a professional relationship. I've come over several times, so there's no need to hide my fingerprints. You've helped me out and been a good friend to me.

Why would I break into your home? The answer's obvious: I wouldn't."

"Why did you?" I asked between chattering teeth.

He put my keys back in his pocket. He could discard them anywhere in the city. They'd never be found. "Why? Because your boyfriend made it so easy I couldn't resist. He kept your keys in a desk drawer. I took them, had them copied, and added them to my bag of tricks."

"Why use them? Why are you doing this?"

"You don't understand me, do you? The hoopla over Penny and Ariel is dying down. I need a buzz."

"You would take my life for a passing thrill?"

"Come on, Sophie. You know it's more complicated than mere thrill seeking. I took an Abnormal Psych Class. I have my own unique nature/nurture mix and my own take on life. I'm no cookie-cutter sociopath. Anyway, killing you won't be a *passing* thrill. I promise you that I'll look back on tonight and chuckle over your death for years to come. The thrill will live on. I won't forget you."

I wanted to butt his stomach with my head and bore a hole through his gut.

He reached into a pocket and pulled out a plastic bag. I was scared to look. "This will amuse you, Sophie. Jeremy fucked Heather this morning and ditched her this evening. I guess he wanted one for the road." He dangled the bag in front of my face. There was a used condom inside. "I stopped by Jeremy's apartment. The lovebirds were out, and I was lucky enough to find this little souvenir. So, yeah, you were asking why—these two items are why—Jeremy's sperm and your keys. I couldn't let a treasure trove like that go to waste. And you were becoming difficult to deal with, Sophie. I didn't like that bullshit about wanting me to record my therapy sessions. You wouldn't even help write my dissertation." He glanced at his watch, stood, and held his hand out to pull me up.

"What have you got to eat? I'm getting hungry, and you need a snack."

"Why do I need a snack?"

"So the medical examiner will know when you last ate. You got any ice cream?"

My legs were weak, but he propelled me forward. I didn't protest. Eating ice cream was better than the alternatives. I didn't doubt his ability to improvise a less appealing Plan B. I pulled the carton of mint chocolate chip from the freezer and leaned against the counter to steady myself while I took off the lid. Something pressed against my stomach—the Ambien container in my bathrobe pocket.

If I swallowed a few Ambien, I would pass out and not have to experience Ned's hands at my throat. Everything would be over. I was helpless to save Jeremy, anyway. There was no way I could take revenge. I was too short and too weak. All I had was big hair. I didn't even have long fingernails. Any attempt I made would be laughably feeble, and I didn't want to add to Ned's amusement. My best hope was a quick painless death. I felt emboldened. "Jeremy will tell the police you had access to my keys. They'll ask where you were tonight."

"No need to worry about me, Sophie. I have an alibi. I'm spending the night with Gina. She's a good lay, although a little needy for my taste. That's why I got tired of living with her and decided to find another home base. She didn't like me staying out all night. But we're cool. We had sex tonight and went to sleep together. She passed out. She had a lot to drink. She won't know I've been out."

Part of my brain was registering that Marnie had been right. There was no landlady. Ned had been living off Gina. But mostly I was realizing Ned was creating a scenario in which I had a late-night snack while waiting up for Jeremy. Of course, I'd be dead when Jeremy arrived, but my body would still be warm. The police would think we quarreled, and Jeremy killed me. His message on my answering machine expressed frustration I wasn't picking up the phone. The medical examiner would tell the police I was alive when Jeremy called. They'd misinterpret my not answering to mean I was angry with Jeremy. Even if I'd been in the bathroom and missed the call, I could have called back, but I didn't. My tear-swollen eyelids would fit right in.

Everything fit perfectly into Ned's scheme.

Swallowing a fistful of pills was my one chance to save Jeremy. Why would Jeremy kill me if I was already passed out? That didn't make sense. He was coming over because he loved me, his message made clear he was eager to see me and, presumably, Heather would testify that they'd broken up and Jeremy was coming back to me.

Ned's scenario only worked if the police believed I was awake and argumentative when Jeremy arrived. Taking the pills would protect Jeremy—and I would die an easier death.

But Ned would try to stop me.

I'd have to sneak them into my mouth when he looked away. Even if he caught me, I could swallow fast and get them into my system—provided I had enough saliva. My mouth was unbelievably dry. I took two ice cream bowls down from the shelf then took spoons from the cutlery drawer and pulled open the small drawer where I kept the ice cream scoop.

Ned's hand clamped down on mine.

There were knives in the drawer, although the last thing I wanted to pick up was a knife he could turn against me.

"Put your hands in your pockets, *now*," he ordered.

I did as he said. My right hand closed around the

Ambien container. I pried off the lid while he placed paper towels over the garbage in the trashcan. He put the knives on top, and moved the can out of reach. "Okay, you can take your hands out of your pockets. What do you have around here that I can pee into?"

He wasn't the only one with a full bladder. "Can't we take turns using the bathroom? I don't usually pee in the kitchen. There's nothing here to use."

"That's okay. I'll find something—for me, not for you. You have to exercise control. Keep going with the ice cream."

I didn't like the idea of being an incontinent corpse on top of everything else, but I focused on my plan and took out the ice cream scoop. A garlic press had been pushed to the back of the drawer. A new plan popped into my mind, but it meant I had to act quickly. I left the drawer slightly ajar.

"If the ice cream's too hard, put it in the microwave. And here, pour some of this on top." Ned handed me the bottle of Kahlua I bought after drinking white Russians with Steve.

I unscrewed the top with shaking hands. I was breathing rapidly. If I didn't calm down, I'd be gasping for breath. The ice cream was soft enough to scoop. Ned opened the fridge and took out an orange juice container. He poured the contents down the sink and unzipped his fly. He was going to urinate into the container.

I had one chance only and very little time. Ned needed to pay attention when he peed, so he didn't risk splashing his DNA on my floor. I had to decide what to do. The instant he looked away, I could drop a bunch of pills in my ice cream and swallow them that way. Or—my heart pounded against my ribcage—I could try to escape. But if Ned caught me, I'd lose the chance to vindicate Jeremy. And my death would not be painless.

Ned was standing behind me, but my body obscured his view of the ice cream bowls. I switched the scoop to my left hand. The Ambien was in my right bathrobe pocket. I prayed that Ned's bladder held a lot of urine. I needed every second.

The sound of his urine splashing the inside of the carton was like a starter gun going off. I grabbed a fistful of Ambien pills and dropped them into the garlic press inside the drawer. If Ned peered over my shoulder, I was dead, but he was peeing in a steady stream. I removed the garlic press, squeezed powdery bits of Ambien onto his ice cream, then dropped the garlic press into my bathrobe pocket, so it didn't clang going back into the drawer. His flow was slowing. I switched the scoop to my right hand and added more ice cream to his dish to cover the pills.

I listened as he set the orange juice carton on the counter and zipped up his fly. He leaned over my shoulder. A few pill shavings showed on the mint green ice cream. I quickly grabbed the Kahlua bottle and dowsed his bowl.

"Whoa, that's too much of that stuff." He took the bottle out of my hand. "You take that one."

My knees buckled.

He propped me up.

Eating his ice cream meant certain death. I'd never regain consciousness. He would kill me while I was passed out. I would never see Jeremy again or my parents or anyone I loved. "I hate Kahlua."

"So why'd you buy the stuff?"

"Jeremy likes it, not me. I can pour some of yours in the sink."

He tried a spoonful. "Wow, that's good. Never mind. Carry them to the table. We'll eat there." He held my arm as I picked up the bowls. I glanced back at the orange juice container. "Don't worry, Sophie. I'll empty it in the toilet before I leave, and I'll drop the container in a dumpster near Gina's house."

We sat at the table. I savored each spoonful of ice cream, holding the creamy flavor in my mouth and swallowing slowly. I had no idea how intense the Ambien's effect on Ned would be, but the pills should at least slow him down. Hopefully, they'd throw off his reflexes enough to give me a fighting chance. He wolfed down his ice cream, shoveling in spoonful after spoonful.

"You were a good supervisor, Sophie, before you went all hard-assed on me. I think you ought to know that."

"Are you really going to work as a therapist?"

He smiled. "I'll give it a shot. I like messing with people's heads." He scraped the bottom of his bowl, all gone. The pills hadn't kicked in. If I swallowed half a pill, I'd have been woozy. He'd eaten a handful. I swirled ice cream around in my mouth. Maybe he would wait for me to finish.

He checked his watch. Killing me was next on his agenda.

"What is this thing you have about murdering women and screwing over the men in their lives?" I asked. "I'm curious. What's the pay-off?"

He pushed back from the table. "The pay-off, Sophie, is messing up their perfectly constructed lives. They don't get to have it their way anymore. I get to have it my way." He laughed. "I'm afraid, Sophie, the time has come."

"Was your father a hard-ass?" I was shivering again, body and soul, everything in me jumping with fear.

"You want to give me a free therapy session before you die?" He checked his watch again. "Jeremy should be getting on the Beltway around now. I've got to finish you, wash my dishes, flush the urine, put the knives back, strip off your clothes, do enough to let the cops know you've been messed with and leave Jeremy's sperm at the scene." He sounded like a harried bureaucrat reviewing a to-do list, hoping to get out of the office by five. I wanted to twist his head off.

"Okay, Sophie, you've got three minutes to cure me. The answer is yes, my dad was a rigid prick who bailed on my mother and set up house with his tall, slender girlfriend, the one who met an untimely end. My mother was not a fun person to grow up with, Sophie. Some people shouldn't be parents, know what I mean?" He had eaten a handful of sleeping pills coated in alcohol and his eyes still hadn't glazed over.

"Why do you want to ruin Howard's life and Jeremy's and Evan Lancet's? They didn't do what your dad did."

"Don't be so literal minded, Sophie. They're all arrogant pricks. Howard's a big shot who gets laid on the side, Evan owns half the world and still needs to control his wife, Jeremy gets off on prosecuting people while he's got two women begging for his attention, and Hisselman, the dumb fuck, gets to do whatever he wants. I'm smarter than the whole group of them put together."

He stood abruptly and yanked me up. "Come on, move. Put those dishes in the sink. Wash and dry the one I used." He dragged the garbage can back and replaced the knives in the drawer. He pushed the drawer shut and leaned against the counter, watching me dry his ice cream dish.

"That Kahlua is strong stuff." His words slurred together.

I froze. I didn't know whether to move away from him and risk sudden death if he came after me or wait till the pills really knocked him out. "Can I use the bathroom?"

He didn't respond. He was staring at me. He looked stunned. I inched backward toward the front door.

"Stand *still*."

I stopped, caught up in a deadly game of "Simon Says." I shouldn't have stopped. He lunged. I ran for the door. He staggered after me. The door was locked, and the chain was on. I'd run the wrong way. I should have headed for the bathroom.

He fell against me. My fingers shook. I couldn't undo the chain. His weight had me pinned. He was going to finish me off in seconds. He could barely stand, and still, his hand was at my throat pressing my windpipe. Just my luck—he'd kill me and seconds later collapse in a heap.

The garlic press—

I pulled it from my pocket. He was cutting off my supply of air. I opened the press on his hand and squeezed with all my strength. He yelped. I wanted his skin and bone to come through the little holes and grind into powder like the pills. I wanted him to die in agony and rot in hell. I was squeezing so hard I went down with him when his legs gave way.

He was out.

I backed away on my rear end, gasping for breath. From the distance of a few feet, I stared at his body. Was he alive? I couldn't tell. Killing him was creepy, but I liked the idea of him being dead. I didn't want him waking up and lunging at me again. Even now, he could be faking, biding his time for an opportunity to spring. I was scared to take my eyes off him. The moment my back was turned, he could be on top of me. My throat still hurt. My neck was sore, and my fingers ached where I'd grasped the garlic press.

He moaned.

Shit. The creep was alive. I scrambled to my feet and scanned the room. The phone—I punched in nine-one-

one cursing each unanswered ring. He could choke me to death before they picked up.

Finally. I yelled my address into the phone and pleaded with the dispatcher to send the police.

"Do you need an ambulance?"

"I need the fricking *police.*"

Ned was the one who needed an ambulance. But I only thought about him needing help after I'd slammed down the phone. Grudgingly I redialed nine-one-one. "Okay, you were right. You better send an ambulance too."

"Who is this?" The voice was unfamiliar, a different dispatcher.

"Sophie Myerson. I called in a minute ago." I repeated my address.

"You spoke to Rochelle. Hold on."

"Sit tight," Rochelle said. "The police are on the way."

"There's a guy here knocked out on Ambien. He needs an ambulance."

Suddenly, Ned's legs twitched. I gave a start, dropped the phone, and backed away. He could overtake me in a panther's leap. I'd be dead before the police arrived. I kept him in sight as I grabbed a broom from the closet. I had a vision of flailing ineffectually while he pulled the broom from my hands and broke it in two—up against a psychopathic serial killer, and I had a fricking *broom.* The bristles weren't even straight.

But I could use the broom to brace against the bathroom door if I barricaded myself inside, except—no, not a good idea. There was a problem: the bathroom was around the corner: Ned would be out of sight. I'd have no idea if he were awake. He could silently stalk the apartment while I quivered in fear. And if I were hiding in the bathroom, the police would have to batter down the apartment door which, unfortunately, opened in, not out. They'd have to break through the chain and the lock and then push against Ned's weight. Plus, the bathroom lock was flimsy. I wasn't even sure it worked. I never used it. If Ned woke up, he could hurl himself against the door, and we'd be in the bathroom together. I couldn't count on the broom to protect me.

I needed to keep him in sight. But I didn't want to watch helplessly if he came at me. If he attacked, I wanted to fight. A knife was out of the question. I needed something he couldn't turn against me. There was a frying pan Jeremy used to make eggs and French toast. I sidled toward the kitchen. I could bonk Ned on the head with it to keep him out a while longer. But even that felt risky. I didn't want to get that close to him. What if he grabbed my arm, twisted the pan from my hands, and pulled me down on top of him? He was ten times stronger than me. I'd be dead in seconds. He wouldn't be in a mood to mess around.

I had a better idea: *boiling water.*

There was a teakettle on the stove, but the pour spout was problematic, and I never liked handling the thing—a pan of boiling water would work better. I could fling it at his face. *That* would disable him. And he couldn't throw it back.

Good. I had a plan. I knelt down and pulled open a drawer, keeping my eyes on Ned while I felt for a pot. He was still on the floor, propped up against the door, eyes shut. I didn't want to think about his eyes blinking open. What would I do if he stood up? Panic clogged my throat.

I had the pot. I swiveled my head away from Ned so I could thrust it in the sink and turn on the tap. He hadn't moved—so far, so good. But how much water should I boil? I didn't know. Defending myself against a killer was turning out to be every bit as complicated as cooking. Too much water and it might take too long to boil, too little and it might not be enough to slow him down. I didn't have an instinct for these things. I counted to ten slowly and turned off the tap. Okay.

Done.

I lifted the pan to the stove. I was going to need an oven mitt for when the handle got hot, which meant having to root around in another drawer. And I still had to drag Ned away from the door to let the police in— hopefully sometime in this fricking century.

What was keeping them?

Either the city was hopping with crime, or someone was running a special on doughnuts.

Doughnuts.

Dough—I felt like Homer Simpson. Doughnuts went with coffee, and my coffee machine was fully loaded. I didn't have to mess with oven mitts or the wrong amount of water. I flicked the switch on the automatic coffee-maker. In a few minutes, I'd be armed and ready. The carafe was easy to grip. If he came at me, I'd hurl steaming coffee in his face.

Where was the phone? I wanted to call Jeremy.

Finally—sirens blared in the distance. They were drawing close. And the scent of coffee was calming me down. Ned's body lay sprawled against the door. The sirens stopped. The police were at the building. Soon they were banging on the door.

"Open up. Police."

I leaned over Ned and undid the chain and bolt, but I couldn't bring myself to touch him. "You have to push hard," I directed through the door, stepping back out of the way.

My phone rang. I ran to answer. It was Jeremy. "I'm five minutes away." The police were inside kneeling over Ned. There was no need for Jeremy to be involved.

"Go home. I'll call you later. Trust me. I have to go."

I hung up. Ambulance workers had arrived. I approached the two uniformed cops. "He tried to kill me. Look, he's wearing gloves. And he has my boyfriend's semen in his pocket."

They exchanged a look. I wasn't explaining well, but I was overwrought. Ned was being loaded onto a stretcher. I didn't want them to treat him like a drug overdose when he was a homicidal maniac. There was evidence to collect.

"He broke in to *kill* me. Look in his pocket. There's a condom with my boyfriend's semen. He was going to plant it here to frame him. Listen, call Reginald White. He's a homicide detective. I have his number. This man killed Penny Harrison and Ariel Lancet."

That got their attention.

"He has keys to my apartment in his pocket. He *broke in.* Can you page Detective White? This is a *serial killer.*"

"Okay, calm down. We'll make sure the police take charge of his stuff at the hospital."

One cop went with the ambulance. The other stayed with me and called Detective White. When she got off the phone, she wrinkled her nose. The orange juice container had a pungent smell. More evidence.

"He peed into that container so he could keep me in sight." Normal visitors didn't urinate into cartons they left on the kitchen counter. They didn't wear gloves indoors or carry other men's semen in their pockets. "You have to lock this man up for life. His name is Ned Olmason, and he's killed a lot of people."

CHAPTER 25

I drifted in and out of sleep. If I started to pull awake, I reminded myself that I didn't have to get up. I could sleep as late as I wanted, but this time I inhaled the scent of coffee, freshly brewed.

The previous night, I'd called Jeremy to come over after Detective White arrived. With the two of them listening, I recounted all that had happened with Ned. Around three in the morning, Detective White left, and I fell into bed. Jeremy crawled in beside me, but I was asleep within seconds.

The coffee smelled wonderful. I looked at the clock—*two-thirty*? I slept until two-thirty in the afternoon, amazing. The adrenaline that had coursed through me the night before had drained from my system. Putting on my bathrobe took effort. I poked my head out the bedroom door. Jeremy looked up from reading the newspaper in the dining area.

"Sophie, you're awake."

"Almost awake." I detoured to the bathroom then ambled out to join him. He poured me a cup of coffee and set a plate of muffins on the table. He'd been to the bakery. A bag shaped like a loaf of olive bread sat on the counter promising more good things to come. But first I reached for a poppy seed muffin.

Jeremy refilled his coffee cup. "I still can't take in what happened, Sophie. If you hadn't out-witted Ned, you would be dead, and my life wouldn't be worth living. The thought makes me sick."

I leaned back in my chair and rested my feet in his lap. He began to massage the ridge just beneath my toes. Hmm. I wanted to bask in the sense of safety, not relive the horror, not yet. "These muffins are yummy."

"Word of Ned's arrest is out. Your phone's been ringing non-stop. I turned off the ringer in your bedroom and let the machine pick up. You have over twenty messages from reporters, admirers, former suspects freed from the cloud of suspicion—"

The phone rang again. We both listened. "Sophie, its Tricia. Mallory and I just got back from New York. You're our hero. My dad has his life back. I'm glad you're okay. Call me."

Jeremy pointed to the answering machine. "Evan Lancet also left a message wanting to thank you in person. He called you 'Sophie dear.'"

"I'll listen to it later. Did my parents call?"

"No, I don't think they heard about this in New Jersey."

"Good."

"Carrie called and said she's grateful you're okay, stunned about Ned, and relieved Howard and Barney have been cleared, as is Alan. She wants you to call when you feel up to it. They can't believe what you went through. Carrie's the only one I answered and talked to. I wasn't sure if you wanted the others to know I was here."

"That's fine, who else?"

"Steve—he said you made him and Hercule proud, whoever that is. I didn't know Steve was seeing someone.

And Barney called to say his wife finally understands he was an innocent victim and not a psychopathic killer, and she's going to stay home more. He was blubbering into the phone."

"Do I have to call the reporters back?" I wanted to eat muffins, drink coffee, get a foot rub, and feel safe.

"No. The cops can deal with the media. You don't have to talk to them."

"Will the police tell the reporters *everything*?" There was the little matter of Jeremy's transported sperm. I noted a flicker of panic in his eyes.

"God, I hope not, Sophie."

"I hope not, too." The thought made me a tad uneasy as well. "Detective White didn't ask you last night, Jeremy, but I would like to know how a glob of your semen got ejected into a condom on the same day you broke up with Heather and told me you loved me?"

A flush crept up his neck. He deserved to be mortified. Either he made love to Heather when he was getting ready to dump her—cad-like behavior—or they decided to indulge in one for the road, but if that was so, it called into question his claim that he didn't like the way she kissed. Had he only said that to mollify me?

I waited. He had the twitchy look of a squirrel with a pile of nuts and nowhere safe to hide them. Not a bracing sight. If he lied about Heather's kisses, he might have also lied about breaking up with her. Maybe, she dumped him, and he raced back to me on the rebound. If that was true, I wasn't the love of his life—I was the booby prize. I polished off the remains of the poppy seed muffin and reached for one with nuts and little cranberry pieces.

"Do you want me to repeat the question, Jeremy?"

"I'm thinking how to explain."

"Okay, here's an easier question. Why did you leave a used condom where Ned could find it?"

"Ned told me he'd be away all weekend. I thought I'd have time to clean up."

"Why leave it on the bed?"

"Because I was agitated, Sophie. From the moment, Heather arrived I knew I had made a huge mistake. I didn't want her there. I should have told her not to come. I wanted you. I wanted to be with you. I love you, Sophie. I don't love her."

He was beginning to make sense. "Keep talking."

"I don't know how to explain."

"Start with Friday night. Tell me what you did."

"We watched a movie then went to bed. I was tired. I didn't want to fool around. I was preoccupied with how to tell her I wanted to end things once and for all. I was desperate to put her on a train back to Philly the next morning."

"Did you tell her?"

"Not that night, no. She wanted to have sex, and she was persistent, frantic almost. I think she felt me slipping away. She wouldn't leave me alone."

"So you had sex Friday night?"

"Sort of. It didn't work out. I couldn't get into it."

A smile twitched at the corners of my mouth. "You were impotent with her?"

"Thanks, Sophie, yes, I was having trouble finding the word."

"So what happened?"

"We went to sleep, more or less. Neither of us slept well. I made breakfast the next morning. Ned was still out. He told me he would stay away all weekend to give us privacy—I didn't give him a second thought. After breakfast, I told Heather I didn't love her. I said I had given things a try, and we weren't meant to be."

I raised a skeptical brow. "And then you hopped back in the sack?"

"No. But Heather wouldn't accept what I was saying. She kept fussing about my 'problem' the night before."

"Your impotence?"

"*Yes, Sophie*, my im*po*tence." His southern accent slurred the middle syllable. "She kept reassuring me it was a fluke, and I shouldn't run away from her because of one little setback. She was relentless. I couldn't get through to her. She thought I was backing off in reaction to the previous night, when the truth is I'd lost all desire for her. I didn't love her. I just wanted out."

"Then why in God's name did you go back to bed with her, Jeremy?"

"I know, Sophie, but she was hell bent on curing my 'affliction.' I felt like the easiest way out was to show her my sexual performance wasn't the issue, so she would accept that I wasn't running away from a sexual problem. I was running away from *her*."

"And *somehow* you managed to perform."

"Only by going far away from her in my mind. Afterward, I told her we were through. She cried, but she finally agreed there was no sense staying the rest of the weekend. In the midst of all that drama, I forgot about the condom. My sole focus was on getting her out and having things be over between us. Driving her home seemed the most humane and efficient way. Ned must have come in after we left. Maybe he saw my car was gone and figured the coast was clear."

Two muffins were enough. I was full. His explanation also satisfied me. I moved over to sit on his lap.

"You saved so many lives, Sophie. Ned was a killing machine." Jeremy's eyes teared up, this time for a good reason. "I love you, Sophie, and I am so, so sorry."

I didn't say I loved him back. He already knew I loved him. But I told him what he needed to hear. "I accept your apology, Jeremy. You're forgiven."

"Thank you." He whispered the words and buried his head in my breasts. I wept. He did too. Finally, he raised his head. "Can I ask you a question, Sophie?"

He was, perhaps, a tad curious what had happened with Evan? "Sure, go ahead."

"The thing I find most amazing, Sophie, and what I don't understand—when did you learn how to use a garlic press? I didn't think you even knew what it was."

I let out a sigh. There was so much Jeremy didn't know about me. But we had a life time ahead for him to discover my hidden depths, and he was only beginning to scratch the surface.

About the Author

Laura Munder graduated from Wellesley College in 1971 and received a PhD in Clinical Psychology from George Washington University in 1976. Her forty-year career as a psychotherapist in Washington, DC, colors her new mystery *Impulse to Murder*.

9 781626 948693